Jernigan's Final Battle

Merry Christmas
12/25/17

Ken Mallender

Ken Gallender

www.jerniganswar.com

Thanks go to Betty Dunaway Gallender whose devotion and collaboration help make this and subsequent books possible.

Special thanks go to Marie Downs for her extensive help in editing and making this book possible. Marie has been an invaluable contributor in this creation and her encouragement has been appreciated.

Thanks also go to my good friend Bill Downs for insights into directions the storyline took.

ISBN-13: 978-1976478598

ISBN-10: 1976478596

Library of Congress Control Number: 2017915170
CreateSpace Independent Publishing Platform
North Charleston, South Carolina

BIOGRAPHY

Ken Gallender has always been able to spin a yarn. As all good Southerners do, Ken likes to "visit" with people putting them at their ease with his warm personality and subtle wit. Ken lives in Gulfport, MS, with his wife, dog, and two grand cats. He is an avid outdoorsman having spent countless days on his Grandfather's farm in the Louisiana Delta, walking turn rows, hunting and fishing. His great love for his family and country has guided his entire life. Ken's motto has always been "Family Comes First, Take Care of Family." His greatest fear is having his country descend into chaos at the hands of witless voters and corrupt politicians willing to take advantage of them.

CHAPTER 1

Dix's breath fogged as he exhaled in the cold Ozark Mountain air. Standing on a rock outcropping, he peered down the length of the valley. He squinted as he sighted down Fox's arm. "I see it now."

A wisp of vapor rose from what appeared to be a rock perched on the side of the mountain. Fox pointed farther up the valley. "Do you see that big pine tree on that hill up there?"

"I see it. What about it?"

"That ain't no pine tree; no pine tree that tall can be that perfect and picturesque. The top would be blown out or some of the big limbs would be dead and broken."

"I see what you mean; that's an antenna array. I can see the satellite dish in the top disguised to look like an eagle's nest. I'm going to radio Colonel Miller and tell him what we found. We've already lost three groups who've come up here to check this out. I want to get in a report before they find and kill us. For all we know, they already know we're here and have people on their way to intercept us."

"Tell me again, Dix. Why we're not back home hunting, gathering and watching our children grow. Rachel was none too happy when you decided to come traipsing up here. My wife Bonnie is fit to be tied. Who's going to feed and care for them if we don't come back?"

"Fox, all I agreed to do was come up here and look around. I don't have any plans to start fighting again."

"You didn't have any plans to get remarried, settle down and start raising kids either. How'd that plan work out? Shouldn't we have some kind of transportation other than our two feet?"

"Fox, I can't help it if the engine blew in the Jeep. At least, we made it almost all the way here before we got stranded. We radioed Cooney, and he's got Porter coming from Louisiana with a string of mules. Porter came over to help get Cooney moved over to his ranch in Texas. He's agreed to come up, help us look around and bring us back."

"Are you sure we can't find a running vehicle and

drive back or a river we can get on and float back?"

"Fox, how come you've become so civilized? Has having a wife and a baby settled you down?"

"I guess it has. I had given up all hope of ever having a life after the collapse hit. I sort of turned into an animal; the only thing I wanted to do was clean out the roaches that destroyed my family."

"I was the same way, and I thought we had killed them all, but then we discovered this nest hiding in these old mines up here in the Ozarks."

"Who do you figure they are, Dix?"

"Hell, we know who they are! They aren't members of the New Constitution Army, or they would have been in touch with us. They're remnants of the communist American government and their willing accomplices from the media. If our men hadn't disappeared when Colonel Miller sent a squad up here to investigate, we'd have never known of their existence."

Fox nodded. "I had heard rumors of a huge underground shelter somewhere up here that was set up and stocked in case of a catastrophe."

"I heard about it too. There was a cable TV show that explored conspiracy theories. When they finished the show, a person felt silly for even considering such a thing. Turns out most of the theories were correct. Looks like this one is real too."

"What's your plan, Dix? How are we going to keep from disappearing like all the others?"

"There are only two of us here, and we aren't going to start anything. We are going to keep quiet. If I see we need help, I'll call Colonel Miller, and we'll get our old team up here."

As Fox turned to head into the woods, he slipped on a loose piece of rock. Dix, jumping to his rescue, fell and slid down hill with him. The distinctive pop of rifle rounds passing inches above them answered the question of if they had been discovered. They stayed low and crawled on their bellies up the side of the ridge until they were well into the cover of the forest.

Fox turned to see a look on Dix's face that he knew so well. "I guess this means we are finished looking around, and we're ready to get shot at some more."

"I guess so, Fox. Let's high tail it back the way we

came and find us a hole to hide in."

They were double-timing it up the ridge toward the road where they left their gear when they were stopped dead in their tracks by a deep voice from in the shadows of the woods. "Fox White, what in God's name are you doing up here? You're going to get yourself killed."

Both Dix and Fox had their rifles aimed in the direction of the voice. Dix was aiming the old Springfield 1903, and Fox was pointing his trusty old 30-30 deer rifle.

Fox grinned. "I'd recognize that voice anywhere. Jonas, I figured you'd make it if anybody could."

Jonas seemed to appear from nowhere as he slipped from his cover and met them on the trail. "Y'all had better follow me now; they'll be here in five minutes. I heard the shooting; they don't usually miss. I already stole your gear so we can pick it up back down the trail."

Dix grinned. "If we old farts hadn't almost fallen off the side of the mountain, they wouldn't have. Old Fox here took a tumble, and I came after him just as they squeezed off their shots."

They followed Jonas down the side of the mountain and retrieved their packs. Jonas stopped, took some pieces of jerky and hung them every so often on a fishing line with #10 fish hooks attached. Fox gave him a puzzled look.

"Don't look surprised; listen."

In the distance, they heard dogs barking and baying. Jonas pointed. "They'll try to run us to ground and close in for the kill. We'll wait on the next ridge until the dogs get into these baited hooks; we'll be able to shoot from up there." As they passed, Jonas raised some of the lines to catch their pursuers about chest high.

Fox looked at Dix. "We could have used him down in Vicksburg."

Dix and Fox were breathing hard as they followed Jonas up the opposite ridge. They stopped just short of the top, and Jonas pointed to hiding places for Fox and Dix. "I'll start with the ones that are bringing up the rear. Fox, you aim for the front ones, and you with the Springfield start in the middle. I don't want to make a terrible mess by all three of us shooting the same man."

As they separated, Fox said, "Jonas, this is Dix Jernigan."

Jonas cocked an eyebrow. "I heard of you; I thought you were dead."

Dix grinned. "Came close a time or two."

They waited on the side of the ridge where rocks and bushes provided excellent cover and concealment. A short time later, they heard the men with the dogs. Then they heard the dogs yelping as they became entangled and impaled on the sharp hooks. Not long afterwards, several of the men who were also snared started cussing.

Jonas whispered. "There are usually about a dozen; let's give them time to gather. That's the only trail so don't shoot until I do. If anyone comes in from behind us, follow me into the cave behind me and move quickly. I'll blow the entrance, and we'll head out the back door."

Silently, they watched as the other men caught up. Four took up a post to cover the others while they untangled themselves from the fish hooks. Jonas motioned for Fox to take the two on the right and for

11

Dix to take the two on the left. Jonas flicked the safety on his ancient Remington deer rifle and aimed at the chest of the last man he could see. He squeezed the trigger, and the rifle bounced.

CHAPTER 2

Porter looked over his animals in the paddock behind his grandfather's barn. Old Dollar and Ruth came over and poked their noses over the worn wooden rail looking for a treat. He didn't disappoint them. Reaching into his coat pocket, he brought out one of the Chinese MRE cookies and broke it in half. He passed each animal a piece and watched as the pieces disappeared through their green, grass stained lips. Cooney, leaning on a walking staff made from a length of bamboo, came limping down the trail. A knife blade was affixed to the top of the cane with rawhide and reinforced with epoxy resin. "Porter, it looks as if our trip back is going to be delayed. Dix and Fox are stranded in northern Arkansas. You'll need to take your stock north to retrieve them."

"I thought the war was over; I haven't run into any bad guys in almost a year. What's going on that's got them up there?"

"Colonel Miller has them investigating the disappearance of several squads he sent up there and haven't heard from since. Dix radioed in and stated that they lost their Jeep. I'm sending you and Morgan as soon as Morgan gets his affairs in order. Most of our families are moving over into Mississippi. Dix has moved to an old plantation south of Natchez. Morgan, Butch and some of the others are in the area and are helping work and guard the plantation."

"Grandpa, I have some lady folks back home who say they can't wait for me to get back. I'll tell you one thing; I am looking forward to getting back myself."

"Porter, I can't say I blame them; you've grown into quite a man. I still don't think that it was a great idea your coming all this way and leaving them alone."

"They can shoot almost as well as I can, Grandpa. I wouldn't want to be caught within rifle range of any of them. Little Ally can shoot the .22, you gave me, from the hip about as well as she can by aiming."

"Porter, do you think they are capable of killing somebody if they have to?"

"Sandy has killed a half dozen or so; Katy's killed three, and little Ally at least two. We had three separate attacks in the first year we were back on the ranch. Indian Joe's ranch was hit, and he called me on his radio. While I went to help, members of the same group hit our ranch. That was a busy day, but we only lost Indian Joe's wife and one of his daughters was wounded."

"How did the girls make out?"

"Katy and Ally were out moving the cows when the raiders caught Sandy home alone. She was in the barn when they arrived. They didn't see her so she slipped into the tack room and retrieved, from where we had them stashed, one of the Chinese AK-47's and a magazine pouch. She was wearing her pistol like we all do. She dropped the first one that came through the barn door and then lit out the back. Katy and Ally heard the shooting so all three stayed hidden and shot from cover. I didn't take long to wipe out the intruders at Indian Joe's, and when I returned to our place, I polished off the stragglers and the wounded. The other two attacks came from some lone wolf packs of people looking for easy pickings; I added all of them to the bone pile down by the river. Besides, we have some puppies from Indian Joe's Australian Heelers that don't miss anything around the place. They make an excellent early warning system."

"Dang, son, you've been through more in your life than most men."

"Not really, Grandpa. Everyone alive has gone through difficult times, or they'd be dead."

Porter reached into a canvas sack and dusted the mules with some D.E. powder to help kill the flies, ticks and every other bug that find mules and horses delicious. As he rubbed his hands across the mules' rear ends, he dislodged the engorged ticks. The chickens, milling around the barn, quickly realized that the ticks were a treat so they ate them as they hit the ground.

When a half-grown Catahoula Cur came running round the corner of the barn, Cooney caught him.

"Give him a dusting while I hold him; he's a puppy off Dix's dogs, and he'll be joining us on our trip to the ranch. I've been trying to think of something to dip him in."

"We can dust him with the D.E. powder until we can find or make some sort of dip."

Porter looked up at the water line high on the barn wall. "What did you do when the river blew out the levee last spring?"

"I did what the Indians did for thousands of years. We have three Indian mounds within a mile of here. When I realized what was happening, I moved all the animals, tractors and vehicles there out of harm's way. I took my old boat from down in the swamp and floated my houseboat out and up alongside the biggest mound. Then I spent the next two months guarding my animals and smoking meat. I had just about quit limping on my broken leg, but I managed to aggravate the damn thing when I was moving everything."

"I'm surprised that Mr. Dix and Mr. Fox tried to drive to Arkansas. In the last three years, most of the roads have been blocked by fallen trees and washed-out bridges. The roads are deteriorating real fast with no maintenance."

"They started their journey in a Jeep pulling a trailer with fuel, food and supplies. They managed to make it all the way there, but the motor finally quit. That's where you come in, Porter."

"Is Jonesville abandoned? I bet the flood ran almost everybody out."

"Jonesville is a ghost town now. The flood trashed nearly everything in the Louisiana Delta. Most folks have moved into the Jena hills or across the river into Mississippi. A few folks have built houses on some of the Indian mounds. Some old houses that were built high enough to stay above the floodwaters have people living in them."

"Was there enough room for everyone to relocate?"

"Sure, Porter. There's more than enough room. With all the people killed from the initial collapse, the war, and the plague, people have had their pick of houses and farms."

"What's going on with the plague? Is it still around or has it run its course?"

"From what we hear, it has burned itself out. The flood took Doc's virus factory and, along with it, all his specimens and samples. Just like the plagues in the dark ages, this one made its run and disappeared."

"It's going to take a while, but I'm sure we'll slowly

build everything back. All it's going to take is living and rebuilding."

"Do you think that we'll have huge cities, roads and such again?"

"Hell, Porter, as far back as the history of man goes, it's been an endless string of cities, catastrophes, wars, and pestilence. This won't be any different. There are more than enough of us to repopulate the world. Several hundred years from now we should be back to normal. Most of the world is back in the Middle Ages for all intents and purposes. We probably have another hundred and fifty years of junk we can salvage. After that, man will have recovered enough to make new materials."

At that moment, they both turned to the noise coming down the driveway of the farm. A large vehicle painted an olive drab turned and headed toward them. A trail of wood smoke wafted from a smokestack on the back of the strange looking contraption. Porter reached for his rifle, but Cooney cautioned, "It's, ok; it's Morgan in his Army Duk."

"I saw one of those once. There was a company up

in the Northwest that took people on tours through the woods and across a lake. Mama refused to let us take the tour because it was an Army vehicle."

"Yeah, I remember how your mother used to carry on about the evil military. Your dad managed to find a gal that was just like his mother. I think the only reason he put up with all that crap was because she was drop dead gorgeous. That's the only reason I put up with his mother. Good looking gals seemed to do that to men sometimes."

"Why did you and grandma split up, Grandpa, if you don't mind my asking?"

"No, it's ok, son. I worked all the time and made a lot of money. Your Grandma decided that she enjoyed the big city life so she spent more and more time away. She bought a townhouse in the city and took your father with her. I couldn't manage a construction company and live in the city. She informed me that she wasn't going to live in what she thought was the country. So she lived in the big city, and that was that."

"I understand. I have two strong willed ladies and another one well on her way. At least mine don't have the lure of a big city calling them."

The Army Duk idled up to the fence where Morgan killed the engine and slid back the window. "What do you think of this for the trip up to retrieve the Major?"

Cooney grinned. "That's one hell of a machine; you've made a few modifications since the last time I saw it."

Morgan disappeared from the window and opened a hatch. A set of steps folded down almost to the ground. Morgan, holding on to a rope rail, gingerly stepped down and hopped to the ground. "I built an aluminum body on top and turned it into a motor home of sorts. I knew where there was an old abandoned Bluebird Wanderlodge motor home so I salvaged the windows and other items out of it."

Porter walked around admiring the rig. "Where did you find this thing?"

Morgan grinned. "There was an old oilman that lived west of Natchez. He bought it and was going to turn it into a float for the Christmas and Mardi Gras parades. The only thing original about it is the body. He replaced the engine, transmission, transfer case and axles from a one ton Ford truck. I can run it down the highway just like a normal vehicle now. It has an engine powered hydraulic pump that powers a hydraulic motor that runs the big prop in the back."

Cooney asked, "What happened to the old man?"

"I have no idea; he, like so many others, disappeared. Several years ago, an old man that lived up the road saw him leaving in his motor home pulling a trailer and a Jeep. No one has seen or heard from him since."

Cooney slapped the side of the Duk. "It looks as if he spent a small fortune on it."

"He must have because there's a lot of custom work on that new drive train."

Porter looked up at the smokestack. "What are you cooking?"

"Wood gas."

"Wood gas? What the devil is wood gas?"

"When we were setting up the new library, I found an article in a magazine that showed a layout of how to run a gasoline powered engine using gas created by burning wood to heat other wood. I know you have sat around a fire and watched the flames. The flames you are looking at are coming from the gas that is being emitted by the wood as it gets hot enough to burn. This wood gas generator uses that gas to run the engine."

"So, you're telling me that as long as we can find wood to burn, we won't run out of fuel? How's it in the water?"

"I haven't tried it in the Mississippi, but it has more than enough power to run up and down the Black River."

Cooney piped up, "Morgan, is this the only wood gas generator you've made?"

"No, sir, I have a tractor, a generator and a pickup truck running on it, and I've made several for other folks around the country. It makes a very good bartering tool."

"I imagine so. When you get back, I want to see if you can get a couple going for me and Porter to carry back to Texas."

"No problem, Mr. Cooney; I mean Captain."

Porter asked, "What's your rank now, Morgan?"

"Major Jernigan made me a Lieutenant with all the pay and privileges that go with it."

"I haven't heard about the pay."

"There isn't any, but Major Jernigan gets a kick out of pretending they're paying me more."

Porter climbed up the steps and peered back over his shoulder at Morgan. "It looks like a combination fort and motor home. Tell me about it."

"Since I'm a single man, I put in two bunks. The water storage is just like a motor home so we have plenty of drinking and washing water. It doesn't have a bathroom, so we'll have to hit the woods, but we can take hot showers on the fantail I installed. The wood gas generator heats the water. I used rolling tool chests as kitchen cabinets and hung commercial steel overhead cabinets as well. There are a couple of school lockers that I have set up for gun storage, and all we have to do is open the back door to cook on the top of the wood gas generator."

"What about spare parts? I would hate to get all the way up there and be stranded; it would be a long walk back."

"I've thought about that. I have an extra alternator, water pump, thermostat, belts, hoses, etc. Unless we throw a rod in the motor, we should be able to take care of most repairs, and besides there are plenty of abandoned old Ford trucks if we need to scavenge parts. I have extra tires and wheels on top; plus the tires are foam filled. We can be ready to go in a week or so."

Porter climbed back down the ladder followed by Morgan. As they walked over to Cooney, Porter nodded toward the mules. "As much as I hate to leave the mules, I think this will get us up there quicker, and I really miss sleeping on a mattress. Can you look after them while I'm gone?"

"You know I will."

Porter turned back to Morgan. "When do you want to leave?"

"If you'll load up your things, we'll head back to my shop. You can help me finish getting it ready to roll.

We'll need some firewood cut, split and stowed on board. I have two electric winches to mount on the front and rear. After that, I'll need some help setting up our radios and a solar panel in case we need to charge the batteries without firing up the engine. Other than that; all we'll need is food, medicine, and tools. We are going to have to go heavy because we may or may not be able to find what we need on the trip."

Porter pulled a duffel that contained his clothes and toothbrush from inside the barn and handed it to Morgan. Next, he handed him his AK-47 rifle and three packs of loaded thirty round magazines. Lastly, he handed Morgan his .308 deer rifle and five boxes of ammo. His final item was his backpack with everything he would need in case they had to walk home. His warmest jacket was tied across the top of the backpack, and a sleeping bag was rolled up on the bottom.

Morgan disappeared up the ladder and busily readied the Duk for departure. The column of smoke grew more pronounced as he added wood to the fire and to the gas generator compartment.

Porter turned to his grandfather. "Grandpa, it looks as if I'm off again. We'll radio you our progress, and

I'll try to get back soon; meanwhile, get yourself packed. I don't have to tell you that we can't carry back any grand pianos using mule power."

Cooney laughed and gave Porter a mighty hug. "Be careful, son; I'll see you soon."

They left the farm and traveled to the boat launch on the Little River. Morgan nosed the Duk down the ramp, and as soon as they felt it floating, he put the transmission in neutral and flipped a switch on the dash. The switch activated the electromagnetic clutch on the front of the engine mounted hydraulic pump. A gentle whine behind them indicated that the propeller in the back had come to life. Morgan pulled out a throttle knob on the dash, and the engine settled into a high idle. On the firewall next to the driver's seat was a lever. It was mounted to a cable that allowed him to turn left by pulling it back or to go right by pushing it forward. The cable was attached to the rudder that was on the stern of the Duk. Porter thought as he relaxed in the passenger seat *this is too good to be true; I hope we don't wind up coming home on foot.*

CHAPTER 3

Several of the men had sprayed the woods with their M4 carbines. After the shooting stopped, Dix, Fox, and Jonas sat hidden and waited. No more gunfire came from the jumble of the dead and dying men. A crimson circle high on Jonas's shoulder expanded as they sat waiting. After a long ten minutes, Jonas reached in his coat pocket and retrieved a dark green handkerchief, folded it double a couple of times and winced as he shoved it under his shirt and up to the bullet wound. He repositioned the suspender strap on his left side so that the strap held it in place. He looked over at them and whispered, "I've had worse." Knowingly, they nodded back at him because each of them carried their own battle scars.

Dix looked back at Jonas. "This is your battleground; what do you want us to do?"

"Let's ease on down. We'll go one at a time. The other two will cover and make sure they're all dead."

Fox winked. "Me first; I want to see these bastards up close."

Fox crouched low and eased in the direction of the carnage. The breeze coming up the side of the mountain brought the smell of fresh blood, spilled bowels, and burnt gunpowder--all smells familiar to the men. One by one they eased forward until they were among the dead and dying. One man lay gasping for air; each rasp brought forth pink froth from his nose and mouth. Jonas produced a long blade from under his coat and with one motion silenced the man.

Another man had no obvious wounds, but lay motionless. Dix stepped on the man's rifle, and Fox plunged the tip of his knife about a quarter of an inch into the muscle on the man's neck. His eyes sprang open, and he started to beg. "Please don't..........." A crack to his skull from Fox's rifle barrel knocked him out.

Dix said, "Don't kill him yet; he's got some talking to do. They trussed him up, gagged and blindfolded him. They quickly gathered all of the weapons and ammo they could carry and hid the rest. Dix noted that the dead were all well dressed and wearing good boots. He and Fox found two pair that fit and discarded their well-worn ones. A long time had passed since they had replaced the boots they were wearing.

Jonas pointed up the mountain. "We'll have company soon so grab a couple of those radios and follow me. We're going underground."

Their captive wore a tactical vest that had a handle high on the back. Swat teams used that type so that their members could be dragged away in the event they were incapacitated. Jonas, Dix and Fox took turns dragging him down the side of the mountain. They reached a deep ravine that was mostly huge slabs of rock and slowly made their way down into it. They continued until they reached a precipice where a beautiful mountain stream gurgled away below them. Six feet below their feet was a narrow ledge, and the stream was a good thirty feet further down.

Jonas pointed up the mountain in the direction from which they had come.

"I think I hear some movement back there. Unless they have dogs, they'll lose our trail where we reached the rocks. Just below here is an opening to a cave. We can collapse the opening if they happen to find it, and I have several backdoors where we can slip out. So far they haven't found me in here yet." Deftly, he grabbed onto a rock outcropping, swung his legs around and gently slid to the ledge.

"Pass our guest over the side, and I'll catch his legs. If he starts kicking, I'll just have to let him plunge to his death."

Dix felt the man, who had been playing possum, stiffen as he and Fox lowered him over the side. The entrance to the cave was almost invisible. The rock ledge overhead created a roof over the opening; a small trickle of water ran across the ledge and dripped through a green mat of moss that ran all the way to the stream below.

Just inside the cave they came to a timber holding up the rock ceiling. A strategically placed beam was wedged under it, and a steel cable was wrapped around it. The cable disappeared into the darkness. Jonas pointed into the abyss.

"I have a boat winch back there. A couple of turns on the handle will yank this post out, and the whole thing comes down. I also have some IED's further back that will do the job if that doesn't do the trick."

Jonas came out with a small, but powerful, flashlight and pointed into the cave. "Follow me."

Without question, they followed him into the cave. Their captive grunted as they dragged him across the rocks and debris in the entrance of the cave. The air was noticeably warmer inside the cave.

Jonas spoke without stopping. "It's always warmer in the winter and cooler in the summer inside here."

Dix asked, "How did you find this place?"

"You might say it found me. When I was a boy, I was squirrel hunting up on the ridge. I shot a big old fat squirrel, and he fell down the side of the hill above us. My foot slipped, and I stepped into a hole. I slid all the way to my crotch. When I pulled myself out, I realized that I had almost burst through into a cavern. I came back with a flashlight and a rope and started exploring."

They stopped well back in the cave but were close enough to observe the entrance. A steel cable ran up to a large rock with a boat winch securely strapped to it. "Sit and rest, guys. We'll know soon enough if they found out our secret. Keep your voices down, because the sound of a voice can travel a long way below ground, and make sure our guest stays quiet too."

Fox pulled out his knife and let the cold blade touch the neck of their captive. The man jumped, and Fox let out a low chuckle. "Ok, partner, if you so much as break wind, I'll open you up from ear to ear."

From somewhere deep within the cave, they heard the sound of men talking and cursing. Although they could see one another from the light reflecting in from the entrance, they were invisible to someone looking in the cave from the outside.

Jonas made a motion with his head in the direction of the sound. "Those voices are coming from a hole somewhere up the mountain."

Fox whispered, "How many caves are up here?"

"The Ozarks have thousands of caves, and many of them are undiscovered and not mapped. I never told anyone about this one. My Maw wouldn't have let me come back if she knew, so I turned this into my private fort."

They sat quietly in the darkness until all sound from

the outside faded. Jonas flipped on the flashlight beam and rose. "Follow me, and bring our guest."

The tunnel fell away as they snaked their way into the bowels of the mountain. After a couple of twist and turns, they came to a cavern with a small stream running down one side. A large shelf stuck out from the wall with the stream running beneath it. An aluminum ladder leaning against it allowed access.

Jonas pointed toward the top and said, "Wait here."

He scrambled up to the shelf and a moment later the area was flooded by lights. Fox looked down at his red-faced captive. A goose egg size lump at his hairline was a testimony to the rap he had received from the barrel of Fox's rifle.

Fox poked him in the ribs. "Don't worry; you can relax here in the bat poop while we decide what to do with you."

Dix watched as Jonas climbed down the ladder with some cookies and candy bars. "Where did you come up with those items? We ran out of those goodies over a year ago."

"I have a private stash that I keep for emergencies."

Fox broke into one of the chocolate bars and took a bite. "I thought I'd never taste milk chocolate again. Do you have any tobacco?"

Dix shook his head. "I thought you were about broke from smoking and chewing."

"Nope, I never got over the urge. I traded some .22 bullets for some seed not long ago. I was planning on growing me a row or two of it this year. I don't have to worry about dying from tobacco; just following you around will probably do the trick."

They all laughed as they snacked on the goodies.

Dix motioned to their captive. "Make sure he doesn't have anything he can fight with."

They rolled him around and made sure that his pockets were empty and that he didn't have hold out knives or pistols. They double wrapped his ankles together with duct tape and cut his hands free. They pulled him into a sitting position and cut the tape holding his elbows. He pulled the gag from his mouth and the blindfold from his eyes. He squinted back at them in silence.

Dix pointed to Fox who had his knife at the ready. "If you so much as think about trying anything, Fox will gut you like a fish. Do you understand?"

The man answered, "Yes, Sir."

"Crawl over there and get your face cleaned up in the stream and drink your fill. We've got some visiting to do so I want you refreshed."

The man crawled on his belly over to the water where he washed and drank. He wiggled back to where they were sitting. "Are you going to kill me?"

"I haven't decided yet. How old are you, boy, thirty-five?"

"I'm thirty-two."

"Tell us about yourself. How is it you ended up trailing me and old Fox here through the mountains with dogs?"

"Well, sir, we received notification that we were being infiltrated and that enemy forces had been engaged. We were assigned to recover any bodies and hunt for survivors."

"I think I already figured that part out; let's go back a little further. What is your name, son, and where were you born?"

"My name's Jason Edwards, and I'm from New Jersey."

"The state or city?"

"The city."

"Ok, where is your family?"

"I don't have a family; I was raised in foster care until I was old enough to join the army."

"How long were you in the army?"

"Fourteen years."

"Son, have you been in this outfit long?"

"I was in the army for seven years before my commander asked if I would be interested in transferring to a special unit outside of the regular army but under the command of the People's Party. He, or rather she, said that I had what it took to take my career to the next level."

"I'm curious, son. Tell me about this officer. How long was she your commanding officer and what is her name?"

"She has been my commanding officer for the past four years, and her name is Major Candice Olsen. She took over when Major Bill Randall was forced to retire."

"You seem to keep getting things mixed up. Is the commander a man or a woman?"

"We treat her as a woman. He started out as a man, and then one day he started dressing like a woman and announced to the company that he was transgender. He changed his name from Charles to Candice. A couple of weeks later Major Bill Randall was charged with a hate crime because he kept referring to Major Olsen as a man and would slip and call him Charles. They allowed Major Randall to retire rather than face a court-martial."

"How did you feel about all that?"

"I try to mind my own business. The chow is good,

and the duty was light until the bottom fell out."

"Is Major Olsen in command?"

"She's the highest ranking military officer; Elliot Planter is the man in charge."

Jonas interrupted, "Elliot Planter is the former head of the EPA. I met him with my folks when he came to a town hall meeting. I was home for a visit. He explained that it was for our benefit that they were closing every business and moving every human from within this fragile and irreplaceable watershed."

Dix nodded. "Continue."

Jonas replied, "They moved everyone out who was within eight or ten miles of that Mountain you discovered with the fancy pine tree. After everyone was out, they went to work tearing down the houses with the exception of some mansions overlooking several of the lakes. The administrators and party officials needed someplace to stay while the, so called, reclamation took place. The only other thing that didn't need reclaiming was the huge grocery and merchandise distribution center that's located in Pine Tree Mountain. It continued to operate up until the collapse."

Dix turned back to his captive. "Have you met Mr. Planter?"

"Oh, yes, he addresses us at least once a month, and he usually leads the first prayer of the day several times a week."

"Is he a religious sort of guy?"

"Oh, yes, we all have to pray five times a day wherever we are."

"What religion do you guys practice?"

"We follow the new world religion; it's a combination of all the great religions of the world. Our god is Gya, and we are Gyans."

"I'm just curious, is Christianity included?"

"No, its teachings were deemed to be too offensive."

"What about Judaism?"

"I don't know what that is."

"Of course, you wouldn't know. That's ok, son, this isn't a test."

Dix turned to Jonas. "Jason is obviously in pain and

needs some rest. In all of your supplies, do you have anything you can give him that will let him get a little sleep?"

Jonas looked at the man. "How about a little bourbon and cola?"

Jason gave him a grin. "That would be good, sir."

Jonas went back to his loft and came back with a glass full of liquid and a bag of chips. "Here you go; just relax."

They watched as the man eagerly downed his drink and munched on his chips. A few moments later his chin was resting on his chest. Fox asked, "What did you give him, and do you have some for me? I haven't gotten a good night's sleep since I met Dix."

"He might not wake up; I put a Xanax and an Ambien in his drink. I've got a chain around a rock where we can lock him up. When I first got here, I held a few prisoners here for a few days."

They dragged him into a side cavern and secured a chain around his neck, covered him with an old blanket and left him snoring; the only light came from a candle sitting on a rock nearby. They returned to the cavern with the stream and climbed the ladder up to the ledge where Jonas had his camp.

Fox spoke up, "I guess it's time you guys were formally introduced. Dix, this is Jonas Hank, and Jonas, this is Major Dix Jernigan."

Dix and Jonas shook hands, and Dix looked around. "Fox, how did you come to know Jonas?"

"Remember when we were hanging out in your Catamaran out in the Gulf, and I told you about the guy that went in and cleaned out the camp full of Jihadists?" He pointed at Jonas. "This is him."

Dix grinned. "We can sure use a good man like you."

"What do you mean use a good man like me?"

Fox interrupted, "Don't say a word! He'll have you talked into a lifetime hitch in the Constitution Army."

"I'm a Major in the Constitution Army; Fox here is a Lieutenant. There isn't any pay, uniforms or anything else. We provide our own gear which is usually stuff we've stolen from people who try to kill us.

We are motivated, in large, by blind vengeance and the desire to rid the Earth of anyone who can hurt our new families. Changing the subject, do you have a first aid kit? The blood is starting to soak through your shirt again."

Jonas glanced at his shirt. "I've got one in that industrial, black plastic trunk at the foot of my bunk."

Fox dug out the kit while Dix positioned Jonas in the light where he could inspect the wound. He winced at the sight of Jonas's shoulder and back. "The hole in your shoulder looks like the bullet just punched a hole. It's going to be sore as hell for the next few days."

Jonas asked Dix, "Have you ever stitched up a hole?"

Fox pulled a suture kit from the first aid kit. "I have. Where did you get this kit? It looks like the ones the field medics had in the army."

"I got it from the same place I get all my other supplies. I get it from our friends in Pine Tree Mountain. There's also some Novocaine in the kit. I would appreciate it if you would deaden the area before you go much further."

43

Fox pulled out a syringe and drew some of the clear liquid into the syringe reservoir. He soon had administered the Novocaine, packed the wound with antibiotic cream and sewed the holes closed. Placing a bandage over the stitches finished the procedure.

Jonas looked at Fox's dirty fingernails. "Did you wash your hands before you worked on me?"

"No, I didn't wash my hands, but I did pour some bourbon over them. While I was at it, I drank a couple of good pulls from the bottle to steady them. What happened to you after we split up in North Africa?"

"I was invited to join the black ops. I spent all those years traveling to hot spots all over the world. The money was good, and I amassed almost enough money to retire. I married a pretty nurse in Germany that I met when I was in the hospital getting patched up about five years ago. She died from the plague. I couldn't get back in time to save her. I was in Iraq guarding a U.N. big wig when the plague hit. When I realized what was taking place, I lit out with a couple of my brothers. We stole an airplane from those idiot U.N. officials and headed toward Europe. We made it into Syria before the plane gave out. To make a long story short, we

44

made it to the Mediterranean and stole an ancient cargo vessel. It had plenty of fuel along with some food and supplies. My black ops brothers got me within sight of the coast of France where they dropped me off in a lifeboat. They were heading for the states; I haven't seen or heard from them since."

Dix and Fox listened to his story as the afternoon turned into evening. Jonas continued, "I spent eight more days trying to get to Frankfurt. The whole world was in total chaos. People were fleeing the plague and mobs; the borders were closed, and people were being shot on sight. I avoided all contact, traveled at night and rested during the day. I found her in our apartment and was with her when she died. I buried her in the courtyard and hung around the complex for the virus to take me out. People all around me were dying, but I never got sick. I either have a natural immunity to it or was exposed to a related virus someplace in my travels. I have been in every imaginable hell hole on the planet, have been sick from every desert and tropical disease that it was possible to catch and survived."

Dix nodded in sympathy. "I assume you came back

here because it was home."

"I left home after high school and joined the army to get the GI bill for college. I never made it back to go to college. I only saw my folks once or twice a year. This place was sort of like Walton's Mountain. My family has been here since shortly after the Revolutionary War. This was a hard country with just a few places to farm. Since the turn of the century, they made their living cutting timber and had a saw mill down the valley from the entrance to Pine Tree Mountain. Mr. Planter forced them to sell out under eminent domain. My parents bought a small place about fifty miles from here; I found their bodies when I got back."

Fox lamented, "Everyone who is alive today has gone through hell and back twice."

Dix nodded in agreement. "How long did it take you to get back?"

"It took two years for me to get out of Europe. I tried to make it back to see if my parents were still around. I made my way into France and down to the Mediterranean looking for a boat. Every vessel that was seaworthy was taken by people trying to get away

46

from the plague. I followed the coast until I found a villa overlooking the sea. With virtually everyone dead, it was mostly a peaceful place. One day I spotted a sailboat drifting offshore. I hopped in a small dingy and rowed out to find that it was abandoned. The captain's log was in French so I'll never know what happened to the owners. It had enough fuel left in its tank for me to crank the engine, so I brought it back and docked at the Marina. I stocked it with food, water and supplies and spent a couple of weeks learning to sail in the Mediterranean. I then proceeded to sail home. Solo sailing a forty foot sailboat through the North Atlantic in the winter was exciting! Anyway, I wound up in Portland, Maine, and finally back here about a year ago." They sat and talked into the evening. They all slept up on the ledge above the river. Jonas was in his bed, and Dix and Fox were asleep on pads inside their sleeping bags. The distinct thud of an explosion was felt through the rock under their feet.

Dix and Fox turned to see Jonas smiling. "Oh, I meant to tell you guys, don't go wandering around down here. I have it booby trapped and mined; that way I sleep better when I'm camping down here."

CHAPTER 4

By working intensely for a couple of days, Porter and
Morgan installed the winches, radios, and antennas.
With every compartment filled with provisions and
tools, one would think they were leaving on a year-long
safari. Porter stood back and admired their work. "I
hope we haven't overloaded it."

Morgan grinned. "We are a long way from
overloading it. I upgraded the wheels, axles, and tires
from military vehicles. The tires are even foam filled, so
they won't go flat unless we actually rip them apart on
something."

"Morgan, why did you do all of this?"

"All I have is time. I build and repair items for
people in exchange for food and things I need. I built
an alcohol still for a corn farmer, and I get ten percent
of the profit or ten percent of the liquor, whichever I
want. I don't have any family, so, like I said, all I have
is time and the ability to make things."

"Hell, Morgan, I know there are dozens of available

women around; I can't believe you haven't paired up with at least one."

"Oh, I have about a dozen that are after me. I just can't forget about my wife; it just doesn't feel right so I don't do it."

"I understand. Sometimes I think I've bitten off a little more than I can chew with my three wives." They both broke out in laughter as they climbed aboard the Duk. Porter asked, "Shouldn't we give your vessel a name?"

"You know that wouldn't be a bad idea. What should we call it?"

"What's your mother's name?"

"That's a great idea; we'll name her the Violet Marie. I've got some black paint that will stand out on the hull."

They proceeded to print her name on each side. Since they were out of champagne to christen her, they just kicked the tires and climbed aboard. The smoke from the fire generating the wood gas rose from the back of the Duk. When Morgan hit the key, the engine cranked straight away. He dropped it into drive and pulled out on the road as Porter unfolded their map and asked, "Do you think we should travel by river or road?"

"We can travel faster by road if we don't have to stop and clear debris or blockages. Although most of the bad guys are dead, that doesn't mean we won't run into some. Law and order is still sporadic, so we're pretty much on our own. Members of the New Constitution Army can't be everywhere all the time. That generally leaves people on their own."

"Let's travel back to Jonesville and see if we can parallel the Ouachita River. If we see it's going to be difficult, we can find a landing or someplace we can drive down the bank into the water. If we follow or run the river, it could take us a third or more of the way to the Ozarks."

"Exactly where are we going?"

"My grandfather is supposed to let us know where to meet Dix and Fox. Our goal is to head toward the Ozarks. When we radio him tonight, he'll outline our mission and direct us. While we are on the way, we'll also be in touch with the Major."

Using the highway, they returned to the old town of Jonesville, Louisiana, where they followed a dirt trail down to the water. The Duk settled into the river, and the current began to pull the bow downstream. Morgan engaged the propeller and powered the Duk down the stream until he could turn it toward the landing on the Little River tributary. The Ouachita, Tensas, and Little Rivers all converged here to form the Black River. The current of the river wasn't bad, and the Duk easily powered its way up the stream and over to the landing. The only person there was a fisherman running his wooden catfish traps. He waved when he recognized Porter; the old man was in his Grandfather's command. Once they reached the landing, Morgan turned the Duk, and as soon as the wheels hit bottom he killed the prop and drove the machine up the ramp, across the parking lot and stopped out on the road.

Porter flipped on the radio. "This is Porter calling Cooney Jones."

Cooney answered, "Where are you guys?"

"We've crossed the river at Jonesville and are

heading north following the Ouachita; I just wanted to do a radio check before we got too far along."

"Porter, I want y'all to head toward Eureka Springs up in the northwest corner of the state. When you are a couple of hundred miles out, I want you guys to stop if you haven't heard from me or Major Jernigan. We've had some really good men disappear up there, and I am getting a little concerned about the Major. Hopefully, we'll hear from him tonight. Be careful when you stop for the night, you don't have Old Dollar standing guard."

"Don't worry, Grandpa; I pretty much sleep with one eye open all the time."

Porter rolled out the map on a piece of plywood that was serving as their kitchen table. Morgan pointed. "Let's head toward Monroe; with a little luck, the roads will still be passable."

The Duk effortlessly pulled up the hill to the main highway. Morgan kept the speed around forty-five miles per hour as they powered down the road toward the little community of Harrisonburg. From Harrisonburg, they meandered up through the country past abandoned farms and overgrown pastures. Morgan slowed as a herd of wild hogs crossed the road in front of them with several large dogs in pursuit.

Porter lamented, "I hate those wild dogs; I've run up on them more than once."

"I've had to kill quite a few around my place. They've become the top predator in the food chain, but I'm sure we'll start seeing big cats before long. One of the guys coming through from Tennessee told me a pride of lions was loose in north Mississippi. He believed that some zoo animals had escaped; he even had the hide of a lion on his pack horse."

Porter observed, "I imagine all sorts of animals that were in zoos and private collections will be running loose. I know I saw a kangaroo and some Emus out in Texas. I came through a wild game ranch out there that had a collection of African and Asian big game. I know for a fact there was a big hole in the fence for them to escape."

"You know, Porter, it ain't going to matter much one way or the other a hundred years from now."

"You're right; it won't be our problem by then."

They took the roads and highways that best followed the river. When they spotted downed timber near the road, they stopped to top off their supply of firewood. Late in the afternoon, they approached a farm that had a column of smoke coming from a stove pipe through the roof. A young boy who appeared to be only eight or nine years old was walking down the road with a .22 rifle across his shoulder. Two fat rabbits were dangling from a rope he had slung over his shoulder. As they approached, he dropped the rabbits and took cover with his rifle. They pulled up within shouting distance and killed the engine.

Porter leaned out the passenger window. "Hey, kid, do you live around here?"

Not leaving his cover he called back, "Yes, Sir, me and my Mama live here; I think you ought to know that me and my Mama are good shots."

"Don't worry, kid. If we were bad guys, you'd already be dead. I'm Porter Jones and this is Hunter Morgan; we're officers in the Constitution Army."

The boy smiled. "My dad was in the Constitution Army; he got killed fighting the Chinese down in

Jonesville."

"Sorry to hear it, son. We were fighting over there with him. Is there a good place for us to camp around here?"

"I'll have to ask my Mama first; if it's ok with her, you can park out here in the yard."

"You go ask her, and we'll wait here."

He grabbed his rabbits and ran up the driveway toward the ancient farm house. A few minutes later a beautiful brunette came riding down the road in an electric golf cart with an AK-47 leveled across the bar in front of the steering wheel. She smiled. "Boys, don't let my looks fool you; I've put my share of people in the ground."

Porter gave her his best grin. "Mam, we aren't looking for any trouble. We're officers in the Constitution Army; I'm Porter Jones and this is Hunter Morgan."

Morgan spoke up, "They just call me Morgan."

She answered, "I'm Frankie Johnson, and my son's name is Jimmy. My husband was killed in the fighting down in Jonesville."

Porter saw that Morgan and Frankie were eying each other as he continued, "As I was saying, we are officers of the Constitution Army and our commanding officer is Captain Cooney Jones."

"My husband served under Captain Jones. How's his broken arm healing?"

"His arm wasn't broken; it was his leg."

She smiled. "I was just checking your story; I wanted to make sure you knew Captain Jones. Come on down. If y'all know how to clean rabbits, you can get a hot meal."

Before Porter could answer, Morgan spoke up, "Yes, Mam, I haven't had a hot meal cooked by a lady in a long, long time."

To add to the meal, Morgan searched around in their larder and came out with some cornmeal, sweet potatoes and some coffee. He also fished out a bottle of honey and, from his distillery venture, a jar of corn squeezings.

"Don't you think you should wait and see if she has a

boyfriend before you give away all our stuff?"

While they watched Frankie and Jimmy return to the farmhouse, Porter asked, "By the way, when did you take up lying? I know for a fact that we had three different women stop by with home cooked meals for you back at your place, and I know all three were willing, ready and able. Where in hell did you find coffee?"

"I've been saving it for a special occasion. None of those ladies who came by to see me were ladies, if you know what I mean, and none of them looked anything like this one. If she had a boyfriend, don't you think he would be around? She's just a poor unfortunate widow woman who needs my, I mean, our help. After all, we are officers in the Army, and it is our duty."

Porter thought *it's about time Morgan got back to living instead of mourning his dead wife. He isn't likely to find a better looking one than Frankie.*

Morgan and Porter quickly cleaned and cut up the rabbits. They rubbed the sweet potatoes with butter and placed them in the hot coals of the wood stove. The corn meal went into a Dutch oven sitting on the stove, and the rabbit was fried in a skillet. A pot of mustard greens completed the menu. The delicious repast and was followed with hot coffee, containing a shot of the moonshine, a dollop of honey and some heavy cream from the milk cow.

As was his custom, Jimmy retired upstairs where he could see or hear any traffic on the road. Their little rat terrier Barney was hot on his heels. For the next hour, the adults sat and talked about their world and what they had been through.

Frankie pointed around the old house. "This is the house that my great grandfather built about a hundred years ago. He bought the land from a timber company. When the family arrived, they found only cut-over timber. Nothing but stumps, left-over tree tops and briars remained. My grandfather, his brothers and sisters helped their parents clear the entire place by hand. The first three years, they plowed around the stumps and used the cut-up tree tops for firewood."

Morgan admired the handcrafted structure. "I can appreciate that all the woodwork and molding is handmade. I see very little that would have come from a lumber yard."

"They all lived in a one room shack that is now the chicken house out back. They took two years to build this house, and when you're outside, you can see that they built it in stages. As they acquired materials, they added on until it became what it is today. The original parcel was four hundred and seventy-five acres with about thirty acres lying across a little lake on the east side of the property where the timber company couldn't easily access. Most of the wood for this house came from that section. My great grandfather had a deal with a man who worked at the saw mill to cut wood on halves. He would carry whole logs to the mill, they would cut them up, and he could have half the wood back."

Porter empathized, "I'm living in someone's old family home as well; these old places were built back in the days before electricity and modern plumbing."

She smiled. "My dad set up a water storage tank on a stand next to the barn with a gutter feeding it and with gravity running the water to the house. A water tank on the back of the wood stove gives us hot water for showers."

Morgan asked, "Is your dad still around?"

"No, he and my mother were killed along with my little sister and her family. They were helping my sister get moved over here to be with us when they were attacked out on the highway between here and Winnsboro. Jimmy and I are all that's left of my husband's and my families."

About that time, Jimmy called down from upstairs. "Mom, they're coming."

Porter reached for his rifle that was an arm's length away. "Who's coming?"

Frankie looked worried. "It would be best if you weren't caught inside the house. Cecil won't be happy and will make our lives a living hell if he finds you here."

Morgan had a disappointed look on his face. "Is Cecil your boyfriend?"

"God, no! I don't have a boyfriend. Cecil has decided that he wants me as one of his women, and I don't want anything to do with him."

Porter asked, "Is he in the Constitution Army?"

She looked back with a frown on her face. "Hell, no!

When the fighting started, he, his two brothers and several cousins disappeared. They hid out in the Jena hills and came back only after everything quieted down. They are just getting by on what they can steal and scavenge. They aren't getting me or any of my belongings! This will be about the tenth time he's come by, and he gets more aggressive each time. He just won't take no for an answer. Y'all need to go before he decides to hurt you and take your RV."

Porter looked at Morgan. "Lead, or backup?"

"I'll back you up; you're a better shot than me."

Without a word, Morgan disappeared through the back door. Porter turned to Frankie and Jimmy. "Jimmy, take Barney and get out in the barn and stay put until one of us adults comes to get you. Frankie, I want you where you can get back inside. If shooting starts, I want you to dive behind that steel wood heater. I'm heading out the front door where you can introduce me to your friend."

Morgan waved from behind an old abandoned tractor out in the edge of an overgrown pasture. This spot gave him good cover for shooting across the yard and down the road.

A four wheel drive pickup rolled into the yard with four burly, unkempt men inside. Dust drifted across the yard as they rolled to a stop and opened the doors. All of them were wearing side arms, and the one in the back came out with a short barreled twelve gauge shotgun.

Porter thought *he's my first target.*

Frankie jostled Porter's elbow. "The one driving is Cecil."

Cecil stepped out wearing a shiny badge on the vest under his open coat. He pointed to the Duk sitting in the driveway. "Frankie, you planning to take a trip?"

"No, Cecil, this belongs to Porter; he's passing through. We don't want any trouble."

"Now, Frankie, you know I'm not going to give you any trouble. As the new sheriff, it's my duty to make sure that all our citizens are safe."

"Cecil, this is Port....."

Porter interrupted her, "Frankie, I'll take it from

here."

"Porter, you're just a kid. Let me handle him."

Porter gave her a cold, stern look. "Frankie, I said I'd handle it." She took a step back.

"Cecil, I'm Lieutenant Porter Jones with the Constitution Army. I didn't realize that a local government had been organized up here and that elections had taken place."

Cecil gave him a smirk. "Shit, boy, I thought the Constitution Army had all been killed off. Are you sure you aren't just playing army?"

Porter grinned. "I assure you this is no game. Who made you sheriff?"

"I made me sheriff; me and my boys."

"How many boys do you have?"

"There are about a dozen of us. What's it matter to you?"

"It really doesn't matter. I just wanted to get some idea of how many I would need to kill."

Frankie stiffened when she heard the safety click on Porter's rifle that he had slung down behind him under his coat.

Cecil looked indignant. "Boy, you think you can kill me and my men? You're under arrest you little smartass, and we'll be impounding your RV thingy out there. Frankie, you and I are going to have a nice long visit after his trial."

Cecil turned to his men. "Snatch his ass up, boys, and tie him in the back of the truck."

As Cecil reached for his pistol, Porter brought his rifle up and fired before it reached eye level. His first round went through the head of the man with the shotgun. His second shot hit Cecil's arm as Cecil was reaching across his chest to pull a pistol from his shoulder holster. The bullet passed through the arm, through the chest and into the ground behind Cecil. Porter was aware of gunfire off to his right, but he didn't stop. He placed rounds in the other two men as they were falling or diving for cover. After making sure they had each been hit, he turned his attention to Cecil, who with his good hand, had managed to get his pistol from the holster. Porter felt the bullet snag his pants leg as Cecil shot at him. Squeezing off two more shots, Porter hit Cecil in the chest and head. The fight was over in less than five seconds. Without a word, Porter walked around to the rear of the truck where he shot the one with the shotgun through the chest two more times. He looked up as Morgan came jogging from his position. Morgan saw Frankie, who was standing on the porch with her hand covering her mouth, sobbing. He ran up on the porch.

She threw her arms around his neck and pointed to Porter. "He's just a kid. I've never seen anything like this."

Porter called out toward the barn. "Jimmy, stay put; your Mama's ok."

Porter turned to Frankie. "Do you want to go sit with Jimmy while Morgan and I clean up the mess?"

"No, Jimmy needs to see this; he can't be a little boy any longer. We talk like we're bad, but I've shielded him from everything until now. I shot a couple of people back at our house in Monroe, but we didn't let him see any of the carnage. It's time."

Porter could feel blood running down his leg, but he

knew it wasn't a bad hit. He bent down and, using his bandana, he quickly tied off the wound. His injuries could wait until the business at hand was finished.

Suddenly, the sound of lug grip tires on pavement caused them to redirect their attention toward the highway.

CHAPTER 5

Fox sat up with his rifle at the ready. He whispered, "What time is it?"

Jonas, who was still grinning, kicked off his cover. "Calm down, boys, it's 4:30 am. I believe our guest managed to pick his lock and has tried to slip out."

While his pistol rested next to his pallet, Dix pulled on his boots. "If you dropped dead, how would we get out of here?"

"You probably wouldn't, but not to worry though, we won't be staying." Jonas put on his boots, pulled out a Colt 1911 pistol and headed down the tunnel with a green headlamp shining. "Stay put, I just want to make sure our guest didn't make good his escape." A few minutes later he was back. "Our little street urchin, turned commando, managed to pick his lock using a little D ring from his vest. He had filed it down on a rock."

Fox gave a disgusted look. "I guess we got to help you drag the corpse out?"

"No, I have already dumped him down one of the bottomless pits in here. All kinds of cave bugs live in here; he won't be around long enough to stink."

Dix couldn't help but notice the look on Fox's face. "Jonas, I know what Fox is thinking; we haven't seen much of anything alive down here."

"Stop worrying. There are cave crickets, beetles, fungus, mold, and bacteria. I see rodents from time to time, and I know there are raccoons and possums that winter around the entrances to the cave. I have never detected any odors, and any food I leave out disappears quickly. Come on. The sun will be up soon, and we need to hit the trail. Only travel during the day around here; those folks at Pine Tree Mountain pretty much own the night with their night vision cameras and scopes."

Jonas spotted Dix pulling a Chinese cookie out of his pack. "Save your cookies. Look in that locker you're sitting on; it's full of breakfast food."

Dix popped the top and flipped on his small flashlight. It was full of granola bars, pop tarts and other types of cereal and pastries. "Where do you get this stuff?"

Jonas peeled back the wrapping of a Pop Tart. "I really love the blueberry ones. I'll come clean. I steal every bit of this from our friends over in Pine Tree Mountain. Many years ago when they were hollowing out the mountain and building the food distribution center, my Uncle Elmer worked on the blasting crew. In one corner of the complex, they unexpectedly punched through into a natural cavern. At the time, it was in a storage area for tools and equipment so all they did was cover it up. My uncle and some of his buddies were old pot heads. They kept the location a secret and used it as a place to go on break, hang out and smoke dope. Eventually, they made a door and hid it by putting some large electrical switch boxes in front of it. That doorway and those switch boxes are there to this day. My uncle explored the cavern following it out to a cave opening on the opposite side of the mountain. He lived with my parents; I found his diary, blueprints and a cave map in his room at their house. Most of the locals know to stay away from The Mountain and warned me to stay away too."

Dix exclaimed, "This is great news! I feel as if we

just received the plans to the Death Star. This means we can get in unobserved."

Fox took a bite from a granola bar. "I think they are too busy looking out; to look in."

Jonas gathered up his gear. "Follow me and don't stray off. We'll be going out a different way. Once we're back to my cabin, you can radio in a report. All the roads are monitored within five miles of here in every direction, so we'll be going through the mountain trails."

Stowing the guns and gear they had salvaged from the dead attackers in airtight, resin storage bins, they headed down the dank, dark passages. They carried only their gear, extra guns and ammo. The lights on the bill of their caps lit the passageway before them.   A mass of cave crickets covered the ceiling just over their heads.

Jonas chuckled. "Don't look them in the eye; they sense fear."

Although intellectually the guys knew the crickets were no danger to them, the look of the massive swarm made the hair on their necks stand on end. The feeling was like encountering a flying roach.

They stopped just shy of the opening to let Jonas turn off his entrance booby trap. Once they passed, he replaced the trigger. They quickly descended a trail that was all but invisible. Careful not to break any limbs or disturb the area, they silently meandered their way down the side of the slope until they were able to cross the stream at its base. A huge tree had fallen across the stream, and with care, they used it as a natural bridge. They saw several large trout hanging out in the shadows under the log where it was suspended over the water. About halfway up the opposite side, Jonas looked back to find Dix and Fox sweating profusely and breathing heavy.

"I take it you guys don't have many mountains where you live."

Fox answered between huffs. "No, and if we did, I wouldn't be climbing them. We still have a few working vehicles and horses."

"If the roads weren't monitored, we'd be riding as well. When we get up on top of this ridge, we can follow it to where I have something for us to ride."

71

Dix, who had finally caught his breath, asked, "Where are we going?"

"We are traveling to my cabin, which is located about twenty-five miles south of here. Once we get there, we can set up your radio so you can contact your headquarters."

"Good, I'm sure they think we've been killed by now."

"I'll take it easy on you guys. I had to spend a couple of months up here before I could begin operating. My knees still want to give up at times. There's something you need to be aware of this is wild country, not unlike the Wild West. A lot of hard people live here. Most of the nice people died. What we have left are no nonsense people. However, I am fortunate that a lady runs a trading post near my cabin. Most of the roads are nearly impassable due to rockslides, downed timber, and washouts. There are trails connecting most of the communities. The trails criss-cross and utilize the roads whenever possible."

They spent another two hours zig-zagging their way to the top of the ridge. This was an area that had not been logged in the last century. Although the big woods were beautiful, they lacked a lot of underbrush which diminished the security of concealment and cover for them. At the top, they paused on the old forestry road long enough for Jonas to get his bearings. "I think we need to go down this road to the south. We came by a different route from the one I usually take because I wanted one that would be easier on you two younguns."

Fox just shook his head. "I would hate to see your normal route. We could have used some harnesses and rope in a few places on the track you just followed."

"Truthfully, I normally use a different route, but since we killed a slew of them yesterday, we couldn't go back that way. They'll still be combing the mountain trying to find you two and hauling out their dead. They'll spend the better part of next week looking for our little New Jersey street urchin who is now feeding the cave worms."

A half a mile down the road, they came to a side road that was little more than a foot path. At the end, covered under a tarp, sat a four-wheel ATV. They dragged the tarp off the vehicle and stowed it behind the rear seat. Jonas climbed in placing his rifle on an overhead rack where it rested within his reach.

"Pile in boys. We are in the nearest thing to a Cadillac that you're gonna find up here on the mountain."

Dix climbed in and groaned as he lifted his aching legs over the side rails. Fox wasn't in much better shape.

"I hope we don't get into any more scrapes for a while. I've got to recuperate from all the running, hiding and escaping."

The electric powered ATV silently glided down the trail back to the road. A light cloud of limestone dust kicked up behind it and drifted off into the woods. Dix admired the vehicle.

"How do you keep it charged?"

"I have a solar panel on top and a bank of solar cells and batteries back at my cabin. I am just about ready to install a small hydro plant as well. I make my living stealing goodies from Pine Tree Mountain and trading them for what I need. You'll see."

They rode along in silence down the forestry roads

until they reached a paved mountain highway. They had to go around some downed timber, but the ride was uneventful. The road wound down into a valley that had a small river running down the middle. There were a few abandoned houses along the river. An old water-powered mill slowly spun as they drove by. A man stood by the road and waved to them as they passed. Jonas threw him a thumbs up.

"That's Bob Cartwright. He was a car salesman before the collapse. He, his wife and kids have managed to resurrect the old mill and now use the water wheel to run an electric generator. Here he has a shop set up as a blacksmith, a woodshop and anything else that needs electricity to run or create. He has salvaged computers and printers. He prints photos for people who managed to save photos and such from their personal computers. Who would have thought that everything that was stored in the cloud would no longer exist?"

Dix said, "I need to make a run back to the Mississippi Gulf Coast. I buried all my family pictures and the computer hard drives in PVC pipe when I buried my family. I need to retrieve them and to place grave markers. If I don't, there will be no record that any of them ever existed on this Earth."

They continued in silence as tears rolled down Dix's cheeks at the thought of how so much was lost; he then thought of the residents of Pine Tree Mountain who were instrumental in what had taken place. The tears stopped as the memories brought to the surface the hate that was always simmering just beneath. Dix looked over at Fox in the back seat. Fox was lost in thought as well.

"Fox, look in the back and hand me one of those M4 rifles and a pack of those full magazines."

He turned to Jonas. "I'm going to need to borrow one of the captured rifles; my AR-15 is hidden in the woods close to our broken down Jeep near Pine Tree Mountain."

Jonas nodded. "Sure, I've got more where those came from. I hope you have your rifle wrapped up well." Looking at the sky, he said, "I think we're going to have some snow."

"We have our extra gear stored in water tight, black resin cases that we hid away from the Jeep. How much further to your cabin?"

"We have another hour or so, but we'll need to stop down the road at Bill's Bar so we can recharge the batteries. The owner, Kitty Carson, has an extensive solar charging station set up. We can trade her some of our supplies for the service. I don't know how married you guys are, but she has about a half dozen working gals if you know what I mean."

Jonas winked. "How married are you two guys?"

Dix shook his head. "I'm about as married as a man can get. Fox, what about you?"

"Hell, no, I ain't getting hoodwinked into hooking up with any more women. I was doing fine until Dix's wife hooked me up with her friend. Before I knew what happened, I had a haircut, my beard was trimmed off, and I was married with a baby."

Dix grinned. "Serves you right. After all the grinning and pointing at me by you and Beagle, you got what was coming to you. But admit it; it was a good thing."

"I suppose you're right, but I miss living in my houseboat."

Jonas looked puzzled. "You lived in a houseboat?"

"I sure did, and I was happy living in it until Dix got it blown to smithereens. I'm giving you some advice Jonas; the best thing you can do is just drop him off somewhere up here."

They all laughed as Bill's Bar came into sight. Bill's was formally a bikers' bar off the beaten path down on the river. The bar was elevated about twelve feet off the ground to keep it safe from the river that would occasionally flood outside of its banks. Underneath were some picnic tables and a line of motorcycles. Several bikes were electric and were plugged into the charging cradle, and a number of them were Harley's and other gasoline bikes.

Jonas pointed. "Those with gas engines have been tuned to run on alcohol. I'm thinking about getting me one when I can no longer find batteries to use in this rig. We'll need to charge for a couple of hours then we'll be good to go. Fill your pockets with some bullets and be sure to wear your pistols. Sometimes this place can get out of hand."

They climbed the wooden creaking steps that led up

to the front porch. At the top of the steps sat an old codger with a full beard and wearing a worn out baseball cap. He was drinking beer from an old mayonnaise jar.

"Hey, Jonas, killed any bad guys lately?"

Jonas winked at Dix. "No, my friend, everything's been quiet. I picked up some old friends so I thought I'd bring them by for a steak and a beer."

"Kitty just got in a load of fresh beer, and I just butchered a big old hog."

"Sounds great, Buck. I think a big thick, pork steak would go good about now."

Buck looked down at the boots on Dix's and Fox's feet. "Those are some mighty fine boots you fellers have on. The only other time I've seen any like that are on those fellows from up there in no man's land. You ain't with those folks are you?"

Without pausing, Dix looked down at his feet. "No, we're from down in South Mississippi. Some guy came through with a wagon full and was peddling them. These cost me a silver dime and four .22 bullets. Fox won his in a poker game. I think the guy was drunk. Fox is a terrible poker player 'cause he has a terrible poker face."

All Fox could do was grin and shake his head in agreement. "It's true. I'm lucky I'm not running around barefoot."

Old Buck grinned a semi-toothless grin. "Don't get drunk and let those gals get a hold of you; those boots will be gone in a heartbeat."

Jonas clapped him on the shoulder. "Don't worry, Buck. I'll watch over 'em."

They pushed open one of the double doors and walked into the dimly lit bar, where they took a moment for their eyes to adjust. Off to the right were several pool tables. Kitty was behind the bar and yelled out when she recognized Jonas.

"Where you been honey? We were about to turn your picture down on the mantel."

"Oh, you know me, I've been out doing some horse trading."

"Whatcha bring me back this time?"

Jonas reached in his pack and handed her a box of chocolate. "I know how much you love chocolate. I'll try and get you some more on my next trip. Could you have your cook rustle up some pork steaks for us?" He reached into his pack and came out with a big bag of coffee and one of sugar. "Will this cover the food, beer and charging for my rig?"

Her eyes widened, "It's more than enough." She looked over Dix and Fox. "Who are your friends?"

Jonas pointed to Fox. "This is Fox White, and this is Dix Jernigan."

At the mention of Dix's name, everyone stopped talking and turned in his direction. Kate's eyebrows tightened. "Did I hear you right? Did you say, Dix Jernigan?"

"You heard me right; this is Dix Jernigan."

"The Dix Jernigan?"

"Yes."

For a long moment, everyone was silent. "We heard he got killed in a big battle down in Texas."

Dix shrugged his shoulders. "I've almost been killed several dozen times."

Fox interrupted. "Don't worry folks; he's going to keep trying until he's successful. I just hope he doesn't take me with him."

Kitty laughed and motioned for a couple of her girls. "What brings you up here in our neck of the woods?"

"I'm a major in the New Constitution Army. I've been sent to see how things are going up here and report back."

"Jonas can bring you up to speed on what's going on up here; meet Hester and Annie Ruth. Everything's on the house for you guys including the ladies. Girls, Jonas is mine; don't forget."

The girls led them to a table in the corner and set them up with beer. Soon three plates with hot pork steak, cornbread and sweet potatoes were set before them. It was quite a meal. Hester showed up a few minutes afterward with some honey flavored rolls for desert. They had just been served their second beer when the sound of motorcycle exhaust came from the parking lot below. From beneath the floor, they could feel the reverberations of the engines as they came to a stop underneath. One cyclist revved up his engine before killing the motor.

Hester looked up at Kitty across the room and muttered under her breath, "That'll be Willie Ray. There's going to be trouble. I'm glad y'all are here."

Fox looked at Dix. "Why did she say y'all? We came up to just look around. I don't like all this 'there's gonna be trouble' talk."

They saw Jonas take his .45 pistol from his holster, cock it and hide it under the table in his lap. Dix and Fox both followed suit with their pistols as well.

Fox whispered to Dix, "I wish you had that twelve gauge shotgun of yours close by."

"I do too, Fox. I do too. Jonas, who is Willie Ray?"

"Willie Ray and his group of jolly men have formed what you might call a vigilante group. There is no law and order, so they have decided to create order by basically running around bossing, taxing and commandeering what they want in the name of law and order."

Dix thought about it a minute. "Actually, Fox and I are the closest thing to law and order around here. We represent the American Government, or what has become of it. We are and have been acting in a capacity similar to the old Texas Rangers. There is no tax structure in place, and everyone is a volunteer. Once the state governments are re-established, a new congress will be formed. There will probably be only one national election for the office of President. So acting under the authority forced on me by the New Constitution Army, Fox and I are the only lawmen that exist. Quite simply, it's my decision on what's right or wrong. It's as simple as that."

Hester had a puzzled look on her face. "I'm not sure that Willie Ray's going to understand all that."

They heard the steps creaking from the weight of the men coming up the stairs.

Without taking his eyes off the door, Dix told Hester, "We'll explain it to him, Hester. You go get behind the bar with Kitty, and you too, Annie Ruth." Dix pointed to the juke box in the corner. "Fox, get over behind that. I don't like this situation, and we don't have much cover."

Still concentrating on the door, Jonas said, "I'll point out Willie Ray. If we kill him first, the others will lose a lot of their nerve."

The door was shoved open by a man wearing chaps, a heavy coat and a wool stocking cap. He was packing a short barrelled shotgun, and he looked more like a lumberjack than a biker.

Jonas nodded. "That's Willie Ray with the shotgun."

The four men with him were dressed much the same, but, by far, Wille Ray was the largest of the group. They walked over to the wood heater in the corner and warmed their hands. Willie Ray bellowed, "Kitty, where's my girl?"

"She's still in bed from where you beat her up last week. Y'all aren't welcome here."

"Kitty, you know we didn't mean for things to get out of hand. She wouldn't give me any credit; everyone knows I'm good for it."

Dix interrupted, "Willie Ray, I think this has gone far enough."

Willie Ray bristled. "Who in the crap are you?"

"I'm Major Dix Jernigan with the New Constitution Army."

"Everyone knows that the famous Dix Jernigan was killed in Texas. You're just a gray-haired old man. How do we know you aren't just saying you're him?"

"I guess you're just going to have to take my word for it. I represent the United States Government, and I'm giving you a chance to back down. I'm the law, or what's left of it."

"I suppose old Jonas here is one of your deputies?"

Jonas spoke up, "That's right,Willie Ray. I just joined the New Constitution Army. We don't have a jail, so we won't be placing you under arrest."

Willie growled, "What the hell does that mean? Do you think you old farts can take us?"

His men all had their hands under their coats. Jonas caught the top edge of the table and flipped it up just as Willie Ray cut loose with his short barreled shotgun. The buckshot didn't penetrate the heavy oak planked table. The full metal jacket bullet from Jonas's .45 had no trouble going through the table and onward until it met Willie Ray's arm at the crook of his elbow. The shotgun rattled across the floor and discharged again in the process. Gunfire erupted from both sides, filling the bar and dance floor with smoke. Dix and Fox fired into the tangle of men who were oblivious to the bullets and splinters dancing around them.

Suddenly, Dix became aware that he was looking up at the ceiling of the bar. An ancient ceiling fan was suspended from the middle of the room; a bear trap was displayed on one of the rafters;and the mount of a trout, caught long ago and stained yellow from tobacco smoke, adorned another. Christmas lights, hung across the ceiling, blinked and reflected in the frilly, shiny garlands that were part of the decorations. After a moment, his head cleared. As he rolled his head sideways, he was looking into the eyes of Willie Ray who was lying on the floor about twenty feet away and was fumbling for his pistol with his good hand. A little stream of blood was running down a crooked floor board which was located underneath his body. Dix felt around and couldn't find his Browning pistol, but he had a pocket pistol in the zippered compartment of his shirt. He labored to get the zipper down, pulled the little Ruger .380 from its pocketed holster, squeezed off one shot and then another at Willie Ray's head. Everything went black as he struggled to pull the trigger a third time.

CHAPTER 6

Porter looked at Morgan and Frankie who were standing on the porch. "Do you know who's in the vehicle we hear coming?"

Frankie quicky nodded her head. "That'll be Cecil's brothers and the other cousins."

At that moment, they heard the radio in Cecil's truck come alive as a high-pitched voice came over the speaker. "Cecil, did y'all stop at Frankie's?"

Porter reached in, retrieved the radio off the dash and keyed the mic. "Yeah, we're visiting with her now."

The voice came back with a laugh. "Do you think she's gonna take them drawers off for you this time?"

Porter switched the magazine in his rifle to a fresh one and keyed the mic. "I think today's the day, and you fellas are in luck. Three of her girl cousins have come to live with her, and they're about half drunk. See ya when you get here."

He and Morgan grabbed the dead by their collars

and dragged them out of sight as the truck neared.

Porter turned to Frankie. "Get behind that stove."

He yelled to Jimmie, "Stay in the barn. Do you hear me?"

Jimmie yelled back, "Yes, Sir."

Morgan jogged back to his previous position behind the old tractor. Porter flipped the selector switch on his AK-47 to full auto. When the truck pulled in the driveway, he held his fire. The truck came roaring up with dust and dirt flying. Porter knew that an ambush was the last thing they were expecting. Just as they stopped, but before they opened the doors, he and Morgan opened fire on the cab of the truck. The three men inside were trapped in a fog of bullets, glass, plastic and metal as two AK-47's on full auto chewed through the truck and its occupants.

After the firing stopped, Frankie came to the door. "Is it over?"

Morgan shouted over his shoulder as he and Porter replaced the spent magazines. "Stay behind the stove until we call you or head out the back door and stay with Jimmy."

As was his custom, Porter popped each one through the head to make sure that the threat was indeed silenced. He turned toward Morgan. "Tell Frankie it's clear."

Morgan crossed the porch and found Frankie still cowering behind the stove. "It's, ok, Hon. It's over. If you want Jimmie to see, go get him. Porter and I have some housekeeping to tend to." She nodded ok and hugged his neck for a long minute.

Porter dragged the bodies out of the truck and onto the ground as Morgan confiscated all the gear and guns the men had possessed. He went through their pockets to salvage the useful items and piled everything up on the porch. They loaded all the bodies in the back of the bullet riddled truck, and with a water hose, washed the blood off the grass and sidewalks. The little dog Barney arrived first, and with every hair on his back raised, he sniffed at the blood seeping from the dead bodies. Frankie and Jimmy came around to the porch.

Jimmy standing on his tiptoes tried to peer into the truck. "Is that them?"

Morgan put his arm around the boy's shoulder. "That's them, or what's left of 'em."

"Can I see?"

Frankie nodded. "Let him see. He's the man of the house right now."

Frankie stayed on the porch as Morgan carried the boy out to the truck and around to the tailgate where he could see the bodies sprawled in the back. Morgan set him down. "Do you know why they are dead?"

"I sure do, Mr. Morgan. They were going to do bad things to me and my momma. That skinny one tried to show me his weiner the last time he was here."

"They won't be hurting anyone else again. Your Daddy was a hero. He fought to keep the world safe from bad people like these. You remember that."

"I won't forget."

Frankie walked over to the truck and spit into the back. "I'm glad they're dead; they had no call to do what they did. There are so few people left. I can't understand why some are like that."

Porter motioned for Morgan. "Let's haul this garbage off. Do you have everything out of that truck we can use?"

Morgan noticed Porter's bloody pants leg. "Frankie, do they have any more friends who might come looking for them?"

"No, it was always just the seven of them with Cecil being the ring leader."

He pointed to the bandana around Porter's thigh and the widening blood stain. "Frankie, I'll haul off the garbage if you'll clean and patch up Porter's leg."

Frankie turned to see Porter's leg. "My Lord, why didn't you say something?"

"We were a might busy, Mam."

Porter thought *I'm starting to sound like old Indian Joe: a might busy?*

Morgan disappeared into the Duk and came out with a medical bag. "Frankie, this has everything you need to patch him up. If his wound needs stitches, just wait a few minutes for me to get back. Jimmy, you be her assistant."

Jimmy gave him a disappointed look. "I wanted to help you drag them off somewhere."

Morgan looked at Frankie who shuttered. "Sorry, son, I may need you to hold Porter down if we have to dig out a bullet."

Jimmy smiled at the prospect. Frankie led Porter into the kitchen and pointed to the kitchen table. "As soon as I get it cleared off, I want you to drop your pants and hop up if you can."

Porter listened to Morgan drive away to dump the dead. He loosened the bandana which allowed the blood to flow again. He dropped his pants, hastily replaced the bandana over the two holes and cinched it tight. She quickly cleared the table and covered it with a plastic table cloth. She took some of Morgan's moonshine and used it to clean the surface.

Porter commented, "At this point, I don't think we need to worry a whole lot about cleaning the table. The main thing we need to do is clean and flush out the wound. Save the whiskey to clean out the bullet channel."

He scooted onto the table, and Jimmie brought a

pillow for his head. Frankie grimaced at the clotted blood. Porter nodded at the jar of moonshine.

"Pour a little on my hands so I can help until Morgan gets back." Frankie wet a cloth with the whiskey and passed it to Porter.

He cleaned his hands and asked her, "Have you ever done anything like this before?"

She nodded. "Yes, I helped patch up some of the men from the Jonesville battle. I'll need to put a light turniquet above and below the wound; otherwise, it won't stop bleeding while I work on it."

She placed the medical bag on the kitchen counter and opened it. "My God, this bag has everything! Is this novocaine any good?"

"I don't know; you'll need to ask Morgan, but I don't need it."

"Is it still numb?"

"No, I don't need it. Just do what you have to do. If for some reason, I can't stand it; I'll let you know."

As she applied the tourniquets, Morgan came pulling

into the yard with the empty truck. They heard him cleaning himself up on the porch. Just as she was pulling the bandana off of Porter's leg, Morgan entered the kitchen.

"Do you need me and Jimmy to hold him down while you dig out the bullet? Jimmy, get on the other side of the table and hold his right arm."

Porter grinned as Jimmy grabbed Porter's arm with all his might. Morgan winked at Jimmy.

"If we're lucky, he'll pass out from the pain, and we can get a snack while your Mama patches him up."

Frankie gave him a dirty look. "Y'all cut it out! Is that Novocaine in the kit any good?"

Morgan picked up the bottle. "The liquid is still clear, but I'm sure it's out of date."

Porter insisted, "Just get on with patching me up; I don't need the Novocaine. Just do what you need to do!"

Morgan gave her a nod. "He's not kidding; he can take the pain. Let me assist. This isn't the first time I've helped work on a wound."

He cleaned his hands and filled a syringe with the whiskey. While flushing out the wound, Morgan remembered that alcohol on raw meat was excruciating. He saw Porter, who was remembering the horrible bullet wound through his shoulder, take his left arm and make a lazy circle over his head. Morgan shined a flashlight down into the hole from both sides to make sure there was no debris in the wound.

"Porter, I believe the bullet just knicked the muscle, so I think it will heal ok. It mostly damaged your hide; however, that wound is going to be sore for a couple of weeks."

"Good. Stitch it up so we can get some sleep."

Frankie passed Morgan a suture kit. After filling the wound with antibiotic ointment, he stitched it closed. They removed the tourniquets, wrapped the wound with gauze and put an Ace bandage around the leg to hold it all in place. Frankie brought out a pair of her late husband's jeans.

"These may be a little big in the waist, but they'll do until I get yours cleaned and mended."

Porter grimaced. "Thanks, Frankie. If I could get

that last piece of cornbread and a little milk, I'm going to retire to my bed in the Duk."

After finishing his snack, Porter, assisted by Morgan, went out to the Duk and retired to his bunk. Morgan made sure he was settled with fully loaded magazines in his pouch and his guns within reach.

"Porter, I'm going to make sure that Frankie and Jimmy are settled for the evening. They've had a stressful day, and Frankie is going to need help cleaning up after you bled all over the house."

Porter grinned and shook his head. "I won't wait up."

Morgan disappeared down the ladder as Porter switched off the lamp above his head. Even though the night was cold and his leg ached, he rested. This leg pain was no worse than what he had endured before, and it was nothing compared to his shoulder wound.

Morgan stepped on the porch and knocked on the door. "Anybody home?"

Jimmy, looking over his shoulder, answered the door. "Mom, it's Morgan; can I let him in?"

Frankie replied, "Sure."

"Jimmy, buddy, you are a big guy. Help me bring in these weapons so we can clean and store them away."

They spent an hour or so wiping down and stowing the weapons in a closet. Frankie kept a small .380 that would fit in the back pocket of her jeans. Morgan pulled out a shorty AR-15 from the cache and handed it to Jimmy.

"If it's ok with your Mom, I want you to have this rifle. The stock has enough adjustment that I can make it fit you, and it doesn't kick much. I think you can handle it."

Frankie asked, "Does it kick as bad as the AK-47?"

"No, he won't have any trouble shooting it. If he can handle the .22 rifle, he can handle this. I know he's young, but this is a new world. I'll spend some time with him early in the morning, and you can work with him once we're on our way."

Frankie asked, "How is it a young fellow like Porter can stand that kind of pain without flinching?"

"He's been through more than most. He was shot

badly when he was in Texas. In spite of injuries that would have killed most people, he managed to save his family and take out dozens of Chinese troops. When unspeakable things happen to people, they can go one way or the other. Many give up and die, and others just go crazy. Porter took it all inside where he keeps it until he needs it. He doesn't waiver; he just executes what needs to be done with nerves of steel."

"He took over the situation with Cecil without hesitation. Everything happened so fast; I could scarcely believe it. Does he always shoot them again after they're down?"

"That's what they say. I see his point. If things progress to the point that you've got to shoot them down, there's no point in trying to save them or keep them prisoner. I don't imagine there was much you could do with Cecil and his boys other than lock them up and feed them for the rest of their lives. If you let them out, they would simply come back and kill you for spite. I would say they needed killing."

"They needed killing alright. I wouldn't have minded shooting Cecil one more time just for making my life miserable all this time."

She looked around at Jimmy. "It's time for you to hit the sack; call Barney and y'all go to bed. Morgan and Porter won't leave until you see them in the morning."

Morgan asked, "Can I get a shot of some of that whiskey if there's any left?"

"Sure, we have about a pint we didn't use. Morgan, do you have a wife?"

"No, she was killed when 'the you know what' hit the fan. As far as I know, I'm the only one left alive in my family."

"Me and Jimmy are all that's left of mine. What about Porter?"

"Porter lost his parents and brother out in Los Angeles. His grandfather is Captain Cooney Jones. Porter was adopted by a family in Texas, but they all died from the plague. He does, however, have two wives and one that is still growing up."

"Two wives with one ripening on the vine? He's just a kid. How did all that happen?"

"Well, Porter saved them all, and they basically

decided that he was the man for them. I don't think he had much say in the matter. What young man would argue with two beautiful young women?"

"Morgan, I know there's plenty of available women. There are five or six, if not more, for every man running around. How come you haven't hooked up with anyone?"

"Well, Frankie, I couldn't get my little wife off my mind until today. Don't get me wrong. I'll never forget her, but it suddenly felt like it was ok."

"Morgan, the one thing I've learned, after living through all of this, is that you need to tell people what you think and how you feel. If you don't, there's a good chance you'll never see them again, and then's it's too late."

"After meeting you today, Frankie, I felt the same way." She dimmed the lights, and they kissed.

CHAPTER 7

Some people have recurring nightmares such as running from tornados, falling off cliffs or drowning. Others have happy dreams of fields full of flowers and puppies. Dix's recurring dreams all had the same theme: he dreamed of trying to save his dead family. This time, he was trying to perform CPR on his dying son Jake. A voice in the background said, "For God sakes, Fox, hold him tight. I think he's coming around."

The pain in his leg jolted him fully awake, and he realized that three men and two women had him pinned to the table. Jonas said, "Two more stitches, and I'll have him closed up."

Fox piped up, "Thank God, you got the bleeding stopped. If he had died, Rachel and my wife would never let me hear the end of it. They both gave me orders to watch out for him. I wish they had sent someone to look after me too. I'm not sure, but he may have winged me when those elk antlers fell off the wall and landed on him. I saw his pistol go off as he hit the ground."

Dix was staring up into the light that hung over the pool table that was now serving as an operating table. "I feel you working on my leg, but don't you think you need to be looking at my head? It feels as if it's about to fall off."

Jonas laughed. "That hard head of yours took a lick, but I had to stop this bleeding from your thigh. A piece of buckshot hit your femoral artery in your left leg. Another few inches, it would have hit your little brain. Folks let him up, and help me roll him over so we can look at his head."

Fox scrootched up his face. "I hope y'all don't have to shave his head again. He looks something terrible bald headed; all those scars and liver spots look butt ugly on him."

Dix winced as Jonas dumped some moonshine whiskey on the wound. "How bad is it?"

"You need some stitches. Hand me my knife so I can shave his head."

Fox handed Jonas the knife as Dix gave him a

disgusted look. "How long am I going to be laid up here?"

Jonas gently took the knife and tested the edge with his thumb. "The ATV should be charged up. I'll carry you back to my place where you can recuperate."

"Good. I need to call headquarters to report and tell the rest of my troops where to meet us."

Jonas looked over at Kitty who was watching while he shaved the hair from around the wound. "Kitty has a shortwave here; we can contact them on her radio."

"We have military radios that are encrypted. Can we attach her antenna to my radio?"

"Sure, we'll get it all hooked up once we finish stitching your head."

"What happened to Willie Ray and his boys? I seemed to have slept through most of it."

Hester asked, "You don't remember shooting Willie Ray right between the eyes?"

"I remember shooting at his head while we were both lying on the floor, and I remember Jonas upending the table. I don't remember much more than that."

"Oh, Dix, you should have seen it. Everyone was shooting, and the bullets were flying everywhere. One that went between me and Annie Ruth hit Old Bill's picture next to the cash register. One of the shots hit the elk horns, and they came crashing down on top of you. When you hit the ground, your gun went off and hit Fox. You rolled over on your back and tried to get up, but you fell back. The shooting slowed down because everyone, but Jonas, had been hit. Willie Ray rolled over on his back and was digging around for a gun in his shoulder holster when you woke up and started shooting at him. I could write a book about what I saw. Willie Ray and his boys are dead and are being hauled off right now."

"How bad did I hit Fox?"

"Not bad, it just took the hide off his stomach and tore a gash in his shirt, but he'll live."

Fox shot back. "Not bad, not bad? My modeling days are over! My once pristine body has been mutilated. I'm ruined. I just hope my wife can bear to look at me now."

Dix grinned. "If she can get past that slash you took when you lost your ponytail the first time, I think she can overlook this."

"We were just starting to date, and I was the only eligible bachelor around. Besides she helped patch me up."

"I think you hit the nail on the head; it was a toss up between you and Beagle, and you still have teeth."

Everyone laughed. When Jonas took out a suture kit, Dix had a sick feeling in his stomach.

"You didn't bring any of that Novocaine with you did ya?"

"Sorry, whiskey's all we got, but with that lick you took on the head, I wouldn't drink any of it."

"Start stitching; it can't hurt any worse than it does now." Once again, he was wrong.

After he and Fox were patched up, they waited as Jonas set up their radio and attached Kitty's antenna to the back. Dix put in his call to Cooney.

"Cooney, I hope you're near a radio; I need to make

a report."

Cooney came on the air. "Major, we were starting to get a little worried when you went silent."

"Sorry about that Captain Jones, we've been a little busy up here."

"You must be to start using military rank."

"I just want to impress all the folks here at the bar, they seem to like that kind of stuff. I need you to take notes and pass the info on to Colonel Miller."

"Sure thing, Porter and Morgan are on their way; they'll be coming by road and water in Morgan's Army Duk."

"He had that contraption up and running around before I left. Tell him the Jeep blew its engine. Are you ready to start taking notes?"

"Go ahead."

Dix spent the next thirty minutes giving him a blow by blow outline of what they found. He also gave him the names of the leaders in Pine Tree Mountain.

When they were finished, Cooney asked, "How many

men do I need to send?"

"At this point don't send any more. Porter and Morgan will do for now. I'm going to put on our newest officer, Lieutenant Jonas Hank, and he'll give you directions to relay to Porter and Morgan. I've got to lay up for a week or so until I get the stitches out of my leg."

Dix handed the microphone to Jonas.

"This is Captain Cooney Jones; tell him the best way for Porter and Morgan to get here to avoid confronting our friends in The Mountain."

"Jonas, did they tell you that there is no pay, no fancy uniforms, and you'll have to steal your gear and food?"

"Don't worry, Captain. I've got that covered; I won't be doing anything I haven't already been doing."

"There is one thing I want you to know. One of those men who is traveling to you is my grandson, so I don't want any screw ups or surprises."

"You won't get any from me. Write down the following towns and waypoints I'm going to give you.

When your men get to Bill's Bar in Briar Creek, the folks there will radio me that they have arrived. I hope you realize there is probably a lot of trouble waiting between there and here. You think those boys are up to it?"

Cooney laughed over the radio. "I expect those boys will thin out the bad guys on the way. Have Dix tell you about them. Now give me those directions, and, by the way,welcome to the Constitution Army."

After giving Cooney the waypoints and directions, Jonas signed off the radio and turned to Dix.

"The sooner we can get you moved and settled; the quicker you're going to heal. I have some pain meds back at my cabin."

Fox grinned. "Why didn't you say you had some pain meds. This is the first time I've been gut shot."

Everyone laughed as they rose to head to the door. As he started to get up, Dix's head spun, but Fox caught him when he began to crumple.

"Careful old friend. We'll carry you down in your chair. We need to get you in front of a fireplace or in a bunk until your head clears."

For the first time since he was wounded near Jonesville, Dix felt helpless. "I'm afraid I'm getting too old for all this."

"Since when? You still fight like you always have; you just feel bad cause you were conked out. By this time next week, we'll be struggling to keep up, cause you'll be thinking three steps ahead of everyone else."

"I sure hope so, Fox. I'm beginning to question my ability after almost getting us killed up on that mountain."

"This ain't the first time you almost got us killed; now shut up. You can wait to start all this thinking after we poke all your brains back in."

They arrived at Jonas's cabin at dusk. The cabin was a modern log home located on the side of the mountain overlooking the lake. Firewood was stacked on all the porches. With Fox on one side and Jonas on the other, they helped Dix up the stairs and into a recliner in front of a fireplace. A large wood stove sat in the corner. They immediately had a fire going in the fireplace and another one in the stove. A fire in the wood stove in the kitchen was lit as well. Dix sat quietly by the fire. His rifle was placed within reach, and his pistols were back in their holsters and secured on his body. For now, he was safe and warm. Jonas brought him some doxycycline antibiotics, acetaminophen and codeine capsules--all courtesy of the Pine Mountain pharmacy. Jonas heated up some cans of soup on the wood stove, and they ate. Soon Dix was asleep in the recliner with a couple of wool blankets over him.

Jonas spoke low to Fox, "He had one hell of a lick on his head; I don't think he needs to do much of anything for the next few days. He also lost a lot of blood before I got the bleeding stopped."

"You were pretty good patching him up back there. Where did you pick that up?"

"We were all cross-trained as medics. I've done my share of patching men up. I wish I had had one of my surgical kits with me like I have here and back at the cave, but I can only carry so much gear on my electric ATV. I have a truck that will run on alcohol, but it can't maneuver around on the mountain like the ATV."

"Let's face it. All of us have become somewhat

experts on 'ditch' medicine. Dix patched me up after I got hit down in Texas."

"Is it true what they say about him?"

"I don't know what they've been saying, but I can tell you one thing--he doesn't back down, and he isn't afraid of a fight. I think he has a tremendous amount of vengeance that boils up when needed. He is as easy a person as you ever want to be around, but he's also matter of fact and doesn't beat around the bush. If he says something, he means it, and if he decides that someone or something needs killing, he simply tends to business. I would be willing to bet that there is a plan circulating in his head on how to clean out Pine Tree Mountain. That look in his eye will tell you everything you need to know about his intentions. Once this is over, you'll see the other Dix. If he radios home to talk to his wife and baby, you'll see and hear it; otherwise, he'll solve this problem or get killed trying."

"Fox, let me show you your room. We've had a busy day."

"Jonas, you go on to bed. I'm going to sit up and make sure Dix is ok. That lick on his head has me

113

worried."

"No, you go on to bed. I was planning on sitting up to watch him. I think he's ok. I'm pretty sure it's the blood loss that has him down. Besides, old Willie Ray has a brother that may come calling."

"Thanks for telling me. Now I'm sure to get a good night's sleep with one eye open all night."

"Willie Ray and his brother weren't on the best of terms. Willie Ray was the black sheep of the family, so we may get a visit just to let us know that there are no hard feelings. Word is out that Dix Jernigan is here. They aren't going to want him gunning for them as well."

The mountain air was cold so Jonas put a large log in the fireplace and topped off the wood box in the heater and in the kitchen stove. The house was warm when Jonas settled back in a large leather chair in dark corner of the room. From this position, he could cover the room while being concealed from sight should someone manage to get through the door or look in a window. His feet rested on a large footstool, and he was covered in one of his mother's patchwork quilts. In fact, this one was the one she had used on his bed back home.

When a piece of wood popped in the fire, Dix awoke and took a moment to remember where he was. He watched the fire flicker and sizzle as a wisp of smoke came out of the end of one of the logs. An occasional coal would fall below the grate and send out a dusting of sparks that quickly disappeared on their way up the chimney. He couldn't help but think of his old life. He felt overwhelmed with guilt at having lost his family; he felt even more guilt at not having died with them. He then thought of his new family and realized that this was a good thing as well. Tomorrow, he would call Rachel and his little girl.

His success as a warrior stemmed from the countless, reckless chances he had taken. This scouting mission had turned into an offensive one. Some of the same people who brought on the nightmare he had lived through were living the life of Riley safe in their Mountain. These same people were indiscriminately killing anyone who ventured near. They were no longer above the law. Now that the word had gotten out as to who and what they were, their days were numbered.

The pain pills that Jonas had given him were starting to wear off. He reached over to the table next to his chair, shook several more into his hand and washed them down with water that had been left beside him. His head still hurt, but he had gotten full vision back in both eyes. Soon, he was lost in sleep.

The next morning, he was jolted awake by Fox's voice. "Jonas, Dix, we've got company."

CHAPTER 8

The crackling of the radio woke Porter with a start. Glancing over at Morgan's bunk, he realized that it was empty and apparently hadn't been slept in. Morgan's quilt was still rolled and secured to the bedframe. Porter couldn't believe that he had slept soundly all night. Usually, the only time he could sleep was when he was back at the ranch with the dogs at the foot of his bed or on the trail with Old Dollar and Ruth. Dollar was the best alarm to have around because nothing got past the attention of that old mule. He crawled out of the bunk and winced when he bumped his wound on the steel bar that supported the frame.

Cooney's voice boomed from the radio, "Porter, how's your trip so far?"

"We made about fifty miles yesterday;we'll be heading out in a bit."

"I can't believe you guys are sleeping in."

"I didn't mean to. We had a busy afternoon and evening. Morgan still seems to be enjoying his evening."

"Is there a girl involved? Never mind, I don't want to know. Did anyone get hurt?"

"Just the bad guys. The incident wasn't anything we couldn't handle. I can tell I was getting a little rusty. All this rest and relaxation put me off my game a little. I think Morgan has found a gal he wants."

"Hell, I knew it was just a matter of time before one snagged him. For God sakes don't get yourself killed. I don't know if I could put up with all your women by myself. Grab a pencil and take some notes. The Major called last night and gave me the directions he wants you to take and where he wants to meet you. Take your time. He and Fox had a little dust up as well, and the Major is doing a little recuperating while you guys catch up. Try not to do any more operating on him if you can help it."

"Y'all aren't ever going to let me forget about cutting off his toe and feeding him while he was gutshot."

"No, and you better not be operating on me either. Have you found a pencil?"

Cooney gave him the directions and a run down on what was going on at Pine Tree Mountain. While waiting for Morgan to show up, Porter made notes and circled the key spots on the map. From his vantage point in the Duk he had a commanding view of the area. He could see Frankie and Jimmy's yard as well as the overgrown field across the fence and the road in both directions. Suddenly, Porter heard a screen door slam at the house. Looking that way, he observed Jimmy and Barney come bounding down the front steps and heading toward the Duk.

Jimmy called out, "Are you awake?"

"I'm awake, kid. Where's Morgan?"

"He's helping Mama fix breakfast. Can I come up and look around?"

"Sure. Be careful on the steps."

Jimmy climbed in and proceeded to give everything a good inspection. He came over to the bunks. "Is this where you and Morgan sleep?"

"It sure is. Mine's the one with the blood stain on the sheet."

"Did Morgan make his bed when he got up this morning?"

"It sure looks like it, kid. He slipped out while I was still asleep."

"Does this thing really float like a boat?"

"Well, it has so far. What are they cooking?"

"Mama's making some pancakes. Morgan is cooking some eggs and ham."

"Tell them I'm on my way."

Jimmy disappeared down the ladder. Porter paused long enough to open the bandage on his leg wound. The area was deep purple from the bruising and every bit as sore as his previous shoulder wound. He re-wrapped it, and, as was his custom and ability, he buried the pain. So long as the muscles and ligaments were connected to bone and the nerves were intact, the leg would work, and that was all that mattered. He pulled on the oversized jeans, cinched up the belt and grabbed his rifle. His pistol was still in the shoulder holster that he had never taken off. After glancing around in every direction, he climbed down the ladder and crossed the yard. A few empty shell casings were still scattered on the grass and around the trucks that were still parked in the driveway. The second truck was shot up badly, but Cecil's truck was still in good working order. Frankie came out on the porch wiping her hands with a damp dish towel.

"Breakfast is on the table. You better eat it while it's hot."

"Don't worry; I'm not bashful when it comes to eating. I hope you did most of the cooking. I've had to eat Morgan's cooking for more than a few days. He is more concerned with quantity than quality."

"I kept my eye on what he was doing. I think you'll enjoy it."

Since the table was set, they motioned for Porter to take his seat. Frankie looked over at Jimmy.

"Can you say the blessing for us this morning?"

"Yes, Mam. Heavenly Father forgive our sins and accept our thanks for these and all other blessings. We ask in the name of Christ, Amen."

After eating, they cleaned the kitchen. Morgan spent

some time with Jimmy showing him how to run one of the AR-15's they had confiscated from the dead. With the stock in its shortest position, Jimmy was able to shoulder and fire it. Since Frankie still had her AK-47 and knew how to use it, both of them would be better protected. Morgan gave her a radio and set up an antenna using some antenna wire from a roll. While Morgan said his goodbyes, Porter climbed into the Duk and started a fire in the wood gas generator. Frankie gave Morgan a big kiss and a long hug. Jimmy covered his eyes and made a face.

Morgan climbed the ladder and said, "Looks like I'm settling down boss man."

Porter just grinned. "Don't you think this is a little sudden?"

"Maybe, but you've seen me in the daylight, and you've seen her in the bright sunlight, haven't you?"

"Yes."

"What do you think the odds are of a guy like me hooking up with a gal that looks like that?"

"You're probably right. She seems like a good

catch."

"As soon as we get back, I'm moving her over to the Natchez side of the river. This area flooded last year, and the water almost got into the house."

"Morgan, I think it's a good thing that you're getting back to living. Life is too precious to waste being by yourself."

Morgan poked his head out of the window and waved to his new family as they pulled away with a trailing column of smoke. Porter pivoted the captain's chair around so he could stretch out his injured leg. This also gave him a view of the road behind them in case anyone tried to overtake them.

"Morgan, after I talked with my Grandfather this morning, I circled the places on the map where we need to travel. The major has sustained an injury from a scrape they got into up there. We're in no real hurry because he needs some time to recover. Tonight, when we make camp, I want to radio my family back in Texas. Do you think our radio will reach that far?"

"I think so. We'll put up a mast for the antenna, and this is a full powered unit. Just realize that your home radio is a regular short wave frequency so the conversation won't be encrypted. We are only encrypted when we are talking to our own radios. How's that leg feeling this morning?"

"About like you'd expect. I can't believe old Cecil had time to get off a shot. It's all my fault. I should have shot him first instead of the one with the twelve gauge."

"All that easy living back on the ranch has made you soft."

"I should have just shot him when he drove up instead of talking with him. I guess I was hoping to bluff them down."

"That's not easy for you to do, since you don't look very threatening. That's both a curse and a blessing. The curse is that people will force your hand, but the blessing is they aren't prepared for what you can dish out. You know, with all the fighting we've done and our attack with the plague virus, we've killed a lot of people. Do you ever think about it?"

"Sometimes, but I didn't start any of it. I tried running and hiding, but that didn't last long. I think mostly about those poor, ignorant Chinese troops were here against their will, but that surely didn't stop them from trying to kill us when they had the opportunity. What we were doing is no different than killing roaches or rats. Are you going to fret about us taking out Cecil and his men?"

"Hell, no, you know as well as I do that it was just a matter of time before he raped Frankie, and his cousin molested Jimmy. No, he needed killing."

"You're right, Morgan. There's no excuse for anyone to do what they were doing. They had access to thousands of vacant houses, vehicles and everything else that was just sitting around to be used. With no-one left alive, other than food and good boots, there is plenty of almost everything, including clothes in all the houses and in a lot of the old stores. Look on your arm. You and I both are wearing Rolex watches. I noticed you had a first class collection of hand tools and equipment back at your shop. People like Cecil are simply on power trips; instead of being pillars of their communities, they are riding roughshod over them just for the hell of it."

They drove along in silence for a while. The road

was, by and large, free of debris. They encountered old abandoned roadblocks, farms and businesses along the way. Occasionally, they would spot someone traveling, but other than a wave, they received no resistance or threats. Sporadically, they would spot a working farm which was usually a very old house elevated above the spring flood levels. Morgan stopped and reviewed the map and his GPS.

"The GPS satellites are still working, but they aren't as accurate as they once were. No one is left to recalibrate or move them. Before long they will be just space debris."

Porter asked, "Do you think we can make it as far as Columbia today?"

"We should be able to make it that far. I don't think the bridge will be intact, but I am sure there's a boat ramp nearby."

"It's a shame we had to destroy all the bridges, but it was the only way to stop the Chinese and later the plague."

"I wish we still had a dose or two of the plague. It would sure come in handy if we could use it on Pine

Tree Mountain."

Morgan nodded. "It sure killed off those danged Chinese, but I was always scared to be around it. If we had made one mistake, all of us would have died too."

"I saw close up what it did to people; it would have been better to eat a bullet than to go through what I witnessed."

"As I understand it, Porter, we have a mountain fortress full of bad guys that we have to root out."

"That's about the size of it. They took a shot at Fox and the Major, and they've killed a bunch of our men who traveled through the area."

"I know the Major pretty well. My farm and shop are just down the road from his. After fighting by his side, I know one thing: if they tried to kill him and failed, he isn't going to walk away."

Porter agreed. "Yep, that old man is hard to kill, and he ain't afraid of nothing."

"I think he is raging with anger on the inside. All of us have lost family and friends, including him. He wants to cut out the cancer in our world. He's not going to stop until he runs out of bad guys, and I can't say that I don't agree with him. I kinda enjoyed killing Cecil and his men."

"Me too. I just wish I had shot him first."

"Well, we're back in the business of killing vermin."

"Yep, somebody's got to do it. Before long, they'll start moving out of The Mountain, and we'll have to handle them anyway."

As the big machine rolled down the old highway, the lugs on the tires let out a whine on the pavement. Porter found himself dozing. Intermittently, he would jolt awake when the Duk hit a bump that would send pain from his wound racing up and down his leg. They quickly made it to Columbia, Louisiana, and as they expected, found the bridge blown out.

An old man on a bicycle waved them down. "Where did you find that contraption, boys?"

Morgan smiled as he peered down from the driver's seat. "We made it from an old army Duk."

"Where you boys headed?"

"We're heading up into Arkansas on a little trip. Is there a boat launch on this side of the river?"

"There sure is. Just turn here and follow Pearl Street up to Wall Street, and you'll see the signs."

"Is there a landing on the other side of the river?"

"You'll have to go upstream for a couple of miles until you get to the locks. There's a landing on this side. The locks don't work anymore. A tow and barge have sunk and blocked them. There's a pretty big log jam behind them and the dam too. Mind if I follow you guys over there? I'd like to see that thing in the water."

"Sure thing. We'll wait at the landing for you to catch up."

As they drove down Pearl Street, they spotted the signs, drove over the levee and down onto the staging area above the launch. Porter sat with his rifle across his knees surveying the area. Morgan nodded at Porter's defensive posture.

"You expecting trouble?"

"If I were expecting trouble, I would insist that we proceed up the river, or I would be hiding where I could

129

shoot from cover. I call this condition Yellow. That's when I try to maintain a heighten awareness. Condition Green is when I am able to sleep. Condition Orange is where I have the safety off and my finger on the trigger. Red is when, well you've seen condition Red, all hell is breaking loose."

"I like condition Yellow a lot better. Here comes the old man. I don't see anyone with him."

The old man was huffing and puffing from pedaling the bike up and over the levee. "That old levee is getting a little steeper every year. Whew, I'm winded."

"You ready for us to hit the water?"

"You bet. I hope to see you again one day."

"With a little luck you will."

Morgan dropped the transmission into drive, pulled down the ramp and hit the switch on the dash activating the prop. The control valve was locked into the forward position but could be reversed if the need arose for them to back the Duk up in the water. As soon as it was floating, he bumped the transmission into neutral and let the prop push the Duk. When they were about a hundred yards from the launch, they heard one of the bildge pumps kick on to expel water that had seeped in from around the driveline seals.

Porter commented, "That this old gal doesn't ride this good down the highway is a shame."

"Eventually, I plan to put in an air ride suspension, a bathroom and a kitchen. When I finish it one day, it will be an amphibious motorhome."

"So far, it's made a good expedition vehicle. Once we get back on the road, I think we need to stock up with enough wood so, if necessary, we can run up the river past Monroe. At one time Monroe was good sized town. We can radio my grandpa to see if we have any Constitution Army guys up there."

"That's a great idea. When we get back on top of the levee on the other side, we'll see if we can reach him."

The trip up the short stretch of river was quiet and uneventful. When they reached the locks, they saw the tow and barges that were sunk right in the middle of them. A mountain of debris was piled up on the dam and behind the derelict vessels. The launch was clear so they had no trouble negotiating the ramp and driving up to the top of the levee.

Porter keyed the mic on the radio. "This is Porter calling Cooney Jones."

A few moments later the speaker crackled. "Porter, is that you?"

"Yes, Sir."

"How far have y'all made it?"

"We crossed the river at Columbia and are getting ready to proceed to Monroe. Do we have any people on the ground up there?"

"Sure, I have a good team up there. I'll radio them and tell them to expect you. You shouldn't have any trouble. I'll give them your frequency so expect a call from them sometime today."

"Thanks, Grandpa, Porter out."

"Be careful, boys."

"We will."

Porter clipped the mic on its holder. "I think we should hang out here on top of the levee where we have a view until we are contacted. Monroe is only about thirty miles away."

"That's a good idea. We need to do a walk around to make sure everything is still secure. We've been on the road two days, and this is the shakedown cruise so to speak. You stay up here and rest your leg."

"No, I'm going to keep using it. It won't do any good to let it get too stiff or too weak to use."

"Suit yourself, man. I don't know if I could do it."

"Sure you could. You have more grit in you than you know."

"I've been lucky. I received some schrapnel wounds when I was too close to one of my IED's that went off."

"Was it an accident?"

"No, I had just set it up when I was jumped by a squad of Chinese troops. I took off running and set it off to keep them away from me. It hit them, and me too. I didn't realize I was hit until it was all over."

"Thank God for adrenaline."

The radio cracked, and Cooney spoke, "Guys, just follow the highway north until you come to the I-20 cloverleaf. They have an outpost set up there, and they'll be expecting you."

Porter gripped the mic. "Thanks, Grandpa. We shouldn't take long to get up there, but I'm not sure how far we'll make it today or what the roads look like. Hopefully, we can get some information from our men in Monroe."

"Be careful, son. You too, Morgan."

Porter grinned. "Porter out."

They climbed down the ladder and did a walk around theViolet Marie. Morgan pointed to a hole in the rudder. "Looks as if she's been baptized by fire. Look at that bullet hole through the rudder. I know you seldom miss so it must have been a ricochet when we shot up the Cecil gang."

"At least we didn't hit anything vital. You'll have something to show your grandkids one day."

"Everything looks safe and secure. Let's put on some music and hit the road."

After putting on some oldies from the two thousand's and ramping up the radio in the Duk, they were underway. The sides of the highway were heavily overgrown with weeds and bushes. Small trees were already shoving their canopies above the briars and scrub. Berry vines spilled across the highway as nature proceeded to take back what was once hers. Local traffic kept the center of the road open; however, abandoned vehicles littered the road from time to time.

Along the way, they kept their speed down since they had encountered some wild hogs and loose livestock. Once, as they approached an overpass, they saw a pack of wild dogs that had a horse hemmed up under it. When Porter opened fire from the side window, the dogs scattered. The horse broke and ran leaving the rest of the dog pack behind. While exchanging the empty magazine in his rifle, Porter grinned. "I got three, but not sure about the others."

Morgan said, "You hit two more. I imagine the other dogs will eat them soon. I hate those wild dogs; they aren't afraid of people. I didn't realize there were so many Pits around. They seem to dominate the other breeds. I've killed dozens around my place, and anyone who has animals has to have extremely secure fences to keep them out."

"It's going to be bad when we run out of bullets one day."

"If Captain Jones is correct, we should find a lifetime supply in those Ozark caves."

"What do you think Major Jernigan has in mind?"

"I'm sure I know what he has in mind. I just hope we don't get killed doing it."

"I know what you mean. When all this started, I wasn't worried about getting killed. In fact, I think I was a little too anxious to kill. I've wondered if I wasn't one of those psychopaths you read about."

"Let's face the facts, Morgan. Normal people couldn't have survived. My Grandpa was a Ranger in Vietnam. I think I must have inherited some of his abilities. We are here because it was either do what we did or die."

"You're right. That's why we're heading off to do battle again."

They rode in silence the rest of the afternoon. Along the way, they had seen a lot of people who were armed to the hilt.

Coming upon an intersection, Morgan killed the music and slowed down. They noticed there was a sentry post located on the overpass. Porter glanced at either side and caught the glint of a sniper scope from the back of a van parked a couple of hundred yards away in a parking lot. Porter commented, "I think they've got their act together up here. They are positioned much like I would have done it."

Morgan nodded. "I'm glad they're on our side."

He pulled the Duk under the overpass where they were greeted by a man sporting an oilskin hat and packing an M4. "Y'all must be Morgan and Jones. Captain Jones said you'd be showing up in a floating motorhome. We weren't sure what to expect."

Morgan leaned out the window. "We're on our way to meet Major Jernigan up in the Ozarks; he's had a little engine trouble and needs a lift back."

"The Major and Lieutenant White came through here several weeks ago. They were pulling a trailer full of fuel and gear. I know where he was heading, and we have a squad missing that went that way."

Porter dropped the ladder and stiffly climbed down.

"I'm Lieutenant Porter Jones. What's your name?"

"I'm Sargeant Sal Griffin. This is the only outpost up here. There aren't enough of us left to do much more than have a warning network. Since everyone is busy at home farming and doing some hunting to feed their families, we try to keep quiet. Now, about sixty miles out in any direction, you will find a wilderness. A few folks are scattered around. We have had a report of some thugs operating between Columbia and Jonesville, but we haven't been able to catch them."

"Do you know their names?"

"All we know is that there is a joker by the name of Cecil running around calling himself the sheriff."

Porter reached into his coat pocket and handed him a shiny badge with a bullet hole through it. "You don't have to worry too much about Cecil and his boys anymore."

"How did you get him?"

"He decided to arrest us and confiscate our ride."

"Is that why you're a little gimpy?"

"I was a little too slow on the draw."

"Captain Jones said you and Morgan could take care of yourselves."

"I don't know about that. I've managed to get a few holes punched in my hide."

They laughed. Morgan peered out of the window. "Where's a good place for us to camp tonight? We want to travel until dark before we shut her down?"

"I would head toward the state line and camp near the Ouachita Wildlife Management Area. Due to flooding, there won't be many people living in the area. You shouldn't have any trouble, and there's some wild game if you need to hunt for food."

"How far can we go before we can expect trouble?"

"Y'all may can go the whole way. We just don't have anyone we can count on much north of the state line. We hear rumors, but nothing that would send us out that far."

"Sal, we'll give Captain Jones updates as we travel. I hope the rest of the trip will be quiet."

"Y'all will need to avoid the interstate. We trashed a lot of it to keep the Chinese from having space to land aircraft. Stick to the country roads. Take the long way whenever possible."

Porter climbed the ladder oblivious to the pain in his injured leg. "Thanks, Sal, we'll take your advice."

Morgan reloaded the wood gasifier and fired up the engine. "Where to, Porter?"

"Head north on Hwy 165, and when we get near the Ouachita Wildlife Management Area, we'll look for a place to camp and cut some firewood."

"Sounds good; we'll make final plans once we reach a camping spot tonight."

Most of the city had been abandoned. Neighborhoods and shopping centers lay derelict, and nature was relcaiming the city. The medians were overgrown and leaves filled the drainage ditches. Vines were overtaking the houses and buildings, and in their long, uncleaned gutters weeds and small trees were sprouting. One old man had still kept his house. His large garden filled his entire yard. Several large mongrel dogs chased the Duk as it ran up the roadway.

The old man smiled and waved; his wife stood behind him holding a shotgun.

Leaving the city behind them, they drove into the region of the Wildlife Management Area. They stopped a couple of hours before dark and used the time to cut wood for heat and fuel. The cold weather kept the mosquitos at bay, and after the sun set, they hooked up the radio and called Porter's home in west Texas.

Sandy answered the radio call. "Baby, when are you coming home? We sure miss you."

Porter grinned. "It's going to be several weeks before I can head home. Since we aren't on a secure radio, I can't tell you what's going on. Rest assured; I will be heading back just as soon as I can."

The other girls came in the room, and he was able to speak to each one in turn.

After Porter signed off, Morgan inquired, "How did you pull that off?"

"I'm still not sure what happened. One minute I was minding my own business heading across the desert trying to stay out of trouble, and the next thing I know I was killing bad guys and rescuing girls. While I was busy fighting, they decided to share me. The next thing I knew; I had two gorgeous naked girls throwing themselves at me. Sandy's little sister will probably join them in a few years. To be honest, I'm wasn't man enough to say ' no,' and I really like the situation if you know what I mean. So, I'm a family man, and I have a good life out in Texas."

"Porter, considering what you've lived through, you've made out pretty good."

"All and all, I've been very lucky."

The heat from the gasifier's fire box felt good. While they sat in the semi darkness, they munched on jerky and hard tac and waited for sleep to come.

Chapter 9

Elliot Planter sat behind his desk fiddling with his long wirey beard. His prayer rug lay rolled up next to the wall. He hadn't heard from anyone outside of The Mountain in three years. As far as he knew, he was the lone surviving leader of the government and the spiritual leader of the world. He tossed back a shot of vodka as he wrote down thoughts to add to his memoirs. Occasionally, he would add new passages to his book of scriptures. His interpretation of the writing of the great religions brought him great joy. The speaker came on as the second Morning Prayer was broadcast through out the facility. This particular crier was his favorite because he had just the right pitch and cadance.

A knock at the door brought his attention back to the matter before him. His personal guard cracked the door and clicked his heels. "Major Olsen is here for your meeting."

"Send her in and close the door."

Major Olsen entered. Even though she was wearing makeup, her heavy, shaved beard still gave her a five o'clock shadow. Planter motioned her to the chair. "Major, how are we coming on finding our lost trooper and catching the people who killed our other men? I also want to know who is at fault for our men being massacred."

Olsen fidgeted a moment as she gathered her thoughts. "Captain Harvey obviously underestimated the size of the enemy force. Fortunately, she was killed; otherwise, we would have had to court marshal her. After the dogs were killed, the backup team lost the intruders's trail, but we'll continue the search until we turn up something."

"I was thinking that we need to expand our perimeter. This was the third time people have showed up, and we've had to go after them. I wish we had held off sacrificing a couple of those men and found out from where they came. I want you to take one alive next time. I realize your guys enjoy the torture and the bleeding rituals, but we need to find out who they are."

Major Olsen fidgeted and crossed her legs. "How far out do you want to put up sensors and post guards?"

Planter walked over to a large map lying on the

conference table. The map was under a sheet of glass so that it was possible to draw and make notes on it using grease pencils. Three red X's with circles around them indicated where they had encountered armed men. Planter stroked his beard with one hand and pointed to the river valley that lay over the mountain ridge across from their Mountain. "What's going on over there?"

"There isn't much to see. I think some of our troops go over there from time to time to an old biker bar that has a handful of whores working."

"You don't think they're having relations with any of those women do you?"

"I don't think so, Sir. I spent a lot of time trying to weed out undesirables when I built this command."

"How many soldiers do we currently have on our roster?"

"Assuming that Corporal Edwards is dead, we have two thousand three hundred and forty troops and seven hundred twenty-three civilians."

"We'll have to assume that the three other men who were missing last year are either dead or have deserted."

Olsen fidgeted. "We quit sending out scouts by themselves after that; I doubt we'll have any more fly the coop."

"Is there any more trouble to report? Is everyone still happy?"

"The only trouble I see are from some of the men who are ready to venture out into the world. Several have hooked up with some of the women and want to start families."

"Did you explain to them that we have a plan? We have to start expanding our sphere of influence. We can start by trading for fresh vegetables and fruit."

"I don't think we are going to have a problem with your dictates that we convert to a vegetarian society, because we only have about two years' worth of frozen meat. We have plenty of canned meat, but the cans are quickly getting out of date."

"I told you. We are going to have to make a transition. You didn't think they would embrace the new world religion, but they are all praying five times a day and washing their feet, aren't they?"

"Don't you think cutting the rations of those not participating helped them to cooperate?"

"Sure, at first I had to be a little heavy handed," Planter explained. "But they seem to enjoy it now; you've just got to stay on top of any dissension. Let me know if I need to make an example of any of them. If we let things get out of hand, our New World Order will never stand."

"How long before we start letting the women have children?"

"I guess we can start anytime now. Have all the personnel completed their diversity and religous studies? We can't have any 'old world' ideas being taught to our children. This will be the first society on Earth where we take every child born and rear them in our ideals and beliefs from birth to death. We won't tolerate any more greed and prejudice. All will share and share alike. Besides, we'll need some fresh young blood for our transfusions soon. Our little orphans are all getting older."

"When are we going to open the doors and start

some colonies?"

"Let's move our security radius out to twenty-five miles. Any people we find will have to convert to our New World Order, or we will disposed of them. We will not tolerate dissent. We shouldn't have any trouble because this one episode is the only one where we have lost any men. Besides, the plague has done most of the work for us. All that's left is a bunch of hermits and those so called Prepper idiots running loose. We can just shoot them or make examples of them. Locate some abandoned farms and communities where our people can set up housekeeping and farming. Start infiltrating some of the locals by trading with them. When we find out who and where they are, we'll have a handle on what we're facing."

"I'll put together several teams to start."

"Make sure the officers or non comms you send are loyal."

"Don't worry, Sir. I've got some hand picked ones in mind."

"You need to be careful. Obviously, you are somewhat prejudiced in your choice of officers. I'm afraid you are going to create some resentment among the rest of the troops."

"When all this started, I only wanted people I could trust, and they, in turn, chose the people they could trust."

"Maybe you could promote one or two from within the ranks, and I don't mean just promoting women. Maybe promote one of each to start. Just make sure they are devout Gayan's and are devoted in their spiritual life. Our New World Order is going to revolve around our religion and not around government or profit."

Planter went to his desk, picked up a paper and handed a list to Olsen. "Since I am now the spiritual leader of the New World Order, I can't have people continue to call me Secretary Planter. What do you think of the titles on this list? I don't need a political title, but I don't want to appear to be a king either."

"How about Pontiff Planter, the First?"

"I like it. I have my Apostles, and we'll call their group leaders Pastors. Everyone else will be Pilgrims of the great Gayan religion."

"That sounds good, Mr. Secretary. I mean Pontiff Planter."

"I'll have those titles drawn up to be dispersed to the Apostles. We have to start using them. We can't just send a memo out and demand that everyone use those terms immediately."

"Have you had any more devine revelations lately, Pontiff Planter?"

"No, I need to summon my physician with my pipe and my Native American spices. The combination makes my visions and revelations very clear to me."

Pontiff Planter tapped a button on his desk, and his guard cracked the door. "Yes, Sir, what can I do for you Mr. Secretary?"

"No longer call me Mr. Secretary; you will refer to me as Pontiff Planter or simply your Holiness." He looked around at Olsen. "Are you ready for them to send in our tea boys?"

Olsen grinned.

Planter turned to the door. "Sergeant, send for my tea boys and my physician."

"Yes, Sir."

The guard closed the door and turned to the other guard. "Go round up the poor little bastards and get them in their costumes. Send for the Doc as well; he's feeling prophetic again this morning."

The guard walked down the corridor to the dorm room of the orphanage and flung open the door. "Troop B, get on your Peter Pan outfits. The snack tray will be waiting for you to push into the room when you get there. Remember; the sooner you please him and the Major; the sooner you can get back here and get cleaned up. Don't even think about running or trying anything. I don't have to remind you what happened to Chucky when he didn't play along, do I?"

CHAPTER 10

Dix winced as he pulled on the arms of his chair to stand. He felt Jonas's strong hand on his shoulder. "Here's your rifle; cover the door and stay seated. Me and Fox will handle this. I'll call if we need you. Just head out the back door and come around the side of the rock wall."

"Shouldn't I be heading that way now?"

"No, I don't want you busting out those stitches I put in your leg. There's no need for you to cripple yourself again unless it's necessary. I expect word has gotten out that you and Fox are here; it's probably people just wanting to see you in real life."

"Usually the only people who want to see me are trying to kill me. I didn't expect any of this other crap."

"Sit tight."

Fox came in with his old 30-30 Marlin. "Where do you want me?"

Jonas stood well back from the window and looked

down the hill at the men standing at the edge of the road.

"It's ok. It's old man Jack and his three boys. They live up the road a couple of miles. They have a good sized farm tucked way back in the hills. I go up there sometime to trade them sugar and stuff for fresh meat and eggs. They probably heard I was back and want to see what I brought back from The Mountain."

Fox laid his rifle back on the mantle and took Dix's rifle and laid it beside his chair. "Do they know where you get your goods?"

"I haven't told them, but they know I don't have to venure far or stay gone very long. They probably took some fresh meat to Kitty down at the bar, and she told them I was back."

Jonas opened the door. "Come on up, Jack. I'll put on some coffee."

Jack called from the road. "Don't shoot; we're coming up."

A few moments later, Dix heard the heavy footsteps of men and boots on the front porch. Four bearded mountain men came filing into the room and headed straight to the woodstove to get warm.

Jonas clapped Jack on the shoulder. "What brings you by, old friend?"

"We were at Kitty's when we heard you were back. I can't believe that bastard Willie Ray's finally dead. I've been hoping for a shot at him myself. I wasn't going to shoot him face on like y'all did."

"I didn't plan it that way. We could have just as easily been the dead ones."

Jack pointed to Dix. "Is that him over there in that chair? We heard that he was up here."

Dix couldn't help but grin. "I'm Dix Jernigan, and that's Fox White standing by the coffee pot."

"We were sure surprised to hear you were here, but after y'all kilt Willie Ray and his boys, we knew it had to be true."

"I don't know where you heard we were such bad asses. The fact we have not been killed is nothing more than blind luck."

"You can say what you want, but we've heard what you've done."

Jonas broke up the argument. "I'll rustle up some grub if you guys are hungry."

"No need for that, just coffee; we done et earlier this morning. Have you got anything you want to trade?"

"Sure do boys. If you look on the back my ATV, there's a blue duffel bag with coffee, sugar and some antibiotics. I knew your daughter-in-law was fighting pneumonia. Start with the Amoxicillin, but no more than three doses a day."

The old man nodded. "Thanks, Jonas, what do you want in exchange?"

"Just the usual, I'll need some fresh meat next time you start your butchering."

The old man turned to the youngest of the boys. "Bring up a couple of dozen eggs and some sausage."

Without a word, the young man left and in a little while returned with the food.

Without much fanfare, they each took turns shaking

Dix and Fox's hands. This was the first time they had met a hero. Dix humbly took their hands.

"Guys, I'm glad to meet you. I feel good knowing there are stong families rebuilding our country."

Fox and Jonas watched from the window and door as the men climbed into their truck and drove away.

Fox looked back at Dix. "You're sounding more like a politician every day."

"Hell, Fox, what am I supposed to do? Tell them that all this is nothing but bull crap, and I just like to murder bad people?"

Jonas turned from the door. "I hope somebody is writing down everything that has taken place. A thousand years from now, they will need to know what took place and why."

Fox pointed out. "Dix's wife Rachel and my wife Becky are keepng detailed journals. They are keeping them in fireproof safes in a secure concrete building along with history books printed before the book burnings and before the monuments were destroyed."

Dix sipped the hot black coffee. "We need to start

thinking about a strategy to take and clean out Pine Tree Mountain."

Jonas piped up, "I already know where they have an explosives bunker. Give me thirty minutes to set up charges, and I can bring the entire Mountain down on your order."

Dix grinned at the prospect. "As good as that sounds, I don't want to do that. There are things in there that people need. Imagine what all the medicine and other things could do for people like Jack's family. That's only one option. How many entrances are there to The Mountain?"

"The structure has one main entrance, two service entrances and a bunch of air shafts as well as other places for men to get out. One exit is under the fake pine tree and others are where they have sniper posts set up. Those are the reasons you can't get anywhere close to The Mountain."

Dix thought a moment. "How do they generate electricity?"

"They have six natural gas generators, so they can run The Mountain on any pair of them. The others are backup, and they rotate their use to insure that they are all working and reliable."

"What about the natural gas that powers their generators?"

"There are three lines heading into the complex. The well heads are inside sealed concrete bunkers. To blow them, we would need more explosives than I have access to. The pipe, bringing the gas from the well, enters into the facility about ten feet below the surface and is encased in reinforced concrete and buried under tons of limestone boulders. Not only would we need excavators and explosives, but the task would also take days to accomplish."

"There has to be valves, and I don't think they would have them underground in case there was a leak. They have to be able to turn off the gas in an emergency."

"The gas lines converge at a single point where a manifold is used to control which line feeds the complex. If one line fails, they simply close a valve and open another."

"I assume that point is well guarded."

"It is heavily guarded and fortified."

Fox finished his coffee and poured another cup. "Where do they get their water and fresh air?"

Jonas took the coffee pot and refreshed Dix's cup. "They have water wells inside the complex. The wells feed a large tank that acts as a reservoir at the uppermost part of The Mountain. The facility is gravity fed. The pumps only have to keep the tank filled. The only outgoing pump pushes water up to the gas valve facility and to some of the sniper nests. There are ventilation shafts with fans, but the fans aren't necessary; natural convection keeps the air fresh."

"We need to think of the rule of threes. Three minutes without air, three hours without shelter, three days without water and three weeks without food. We can't do anything about the shelter or the food so that leaves the air and water. If we can kill the water or the air, they'll have to come out."

Fox pointed out. "If they come out, what are we going to do? We only have the three of us, and when Morgan and Porter get here, there's only going to be five of us. I bet there are several thousand of them

159

holed up in there. I didn't bring enough ammo."

Jonas grinned. "I guess we could give them a chance to surrender."

Dix laughed. "They would if they knew what they were up against."

"How many men can your Colonel Miller come up with?"

"Maybe two hundred and fifty, if he's lucky. We'd have to be under full scale invasion for him to muster more. What we have now is a citizens' militia. If he gives the order, they will muster up, but if they get killed, the families left behind would be devastated. We've got to make do with what we've got and use our enemies' strengths against them."

Fox piped up, "You're kidding, aren't you? You expect the five of us to take on several thousand bad guys. Can't we at least call in one of the A10 Warthogs?"

"Fox, I don't think they have one that'll fly. I'm not sure they even have a working helicopter. I'm afraid we're on our own. Besides, the last thing they'll expect is five men attacking them. They are fully prepared to take on an army. We are not what they are anticipating, besides we don't fight fair."

Dix pointed at the radio set on the bar. "Can we fire that thing up? I need to hear my wife's and baby's voices."

Jonas hooked up the encrypted radio to his antenna and clicked it on. He handed the mic and headset over to Dix.

Dix keyed the mic and called, "I hope y'all can hear me."

Beagle answered, "I'm glad you ain't got yourself killed. We were beginning to wonder how you were doing."

"This is my first chance to get a signal out. Where's my family?"

"What do you mean your family? Are you saying I'm not family now?"

"Hell, Beagle, you know what I mean."

"Hold on; she's coming in the back door now."

Rachel came on. "Where are you and when are you coming back? I don't want this to be the first Christmas without you."

"I don't want to spend Christmas up here either."

"What's wrong? I can tell something's wrong by the sound of your voice. Have you been fighting?"

"We had a little dust up, but it wasn't anything we couldn't handle."

"How bad are you hurt this time?"

"It's all over, and I'm patched up. I'll tell you all about it when I get back, now put the baby on."

"You better be careful. You were just supposed to go look around, not go to war. Here she is."

While Fox and Jonas listened, Dix talked to his little girl. As the little girl's voice filled him with joy, they saw his harden features soften, thereby revealing another side of Dix Jernigan. Rachel got back on, "Please don't go and get yourself hurt, we need you."

"I'll do my best. Go get Fox's family. We'll turn the radio back on in an hour. We have to conserve power as we are running on solar charged batteries."

"We'll call back in an hour."

The hour went by quickly, and Fox got to talk with his wife. His little boy was too young to talk, but Fox could hear him babbling in the background and smiled. They signed off and clicked the radio off. They sat silently for a moment before they heard the approaching sound of a vehicle's engine. Jonas walked to the door and out on the porch. He looked back over his shoulder.

"This could be good or bad. We'll know in a few minutes. If I were you, I'd check my weapons."

CHAPTER 11

Porter and Morgan were jolted awake by the piercing sounds of a pig squealing in the early dawn's darkness. Somewhere off in the brush, they could hear the battle taking place between a pack of dogs and a wild hog. The hog ran into view and spun like a top hitting one of the dogs and laying its side open with a slash of its tusk. The other dogs backed away as the now emboldened hog turned his attention to them. The smell of blood drew more hogs to the battle so the two remaining dogs were forced to flee. The hogs quickly descended on the wounded dog and tore him apart in what can best be described as a feeding fenzy.

Porter looked at Morgan. "I would hate to be hurt in the woods without a gun. Radio Frankie, and stress to her that when they are outside the house, they are to be armed at all times. When they are inside, she needs to keep the hardwood door closed as well unless they are wearing pistols. The dogs and hogs will soon have absolutely no fear of men. They are apex predators, and now packs of them have never seen a man."

After Morgan got on the radio and warned Frankie about the scenario they had witnessed, he and Porter cleaned the ashes out of the wood gas generator, re-stoked the firebox and filled the fuel box. After the generator was up and going, Morgan hit the key, and the engine sprang to life. The Duk's frame creaked and popped as they traveled down the road. They stopped once to refill their water holding tank from a fairly clear running stream. A hand pump forced the water through a cartridge filter that removed most of the sediment. The water was ok for bathing, but it was undrinkable. A Berkely water filter was mounted in a frame on the counter in the area that served as their kitchen. Morgan filled it to capacity. The water now coming out of the spigot was filtered potable water. Morgan noticed that Porter limped a little when he moved about the cabin.

"How's the leg this morning?"

"It still works. It's just extra stiff this morning."

Morgan stopped the Duk and and killed the engine. "Let me take a look. We can't take a chance on your dying. Your grandfather would kill me."

Porter dropped his pants and pulled off the bandage. The wound was red and swollen. Morgan shook his head.

"I'm afraid it's infected."

"I've had worse."

"Did you have worse going into battle?"

"No, I had time to recuperate before."

"I've got a good supply of antibiotics in my first aid case. Do you know if you're allergic to anything?"

"Just knives and bullets so far."

They both laughed as Morgan pulled out his kit and fished around in it.

"Let's try some plain old penicillin; we'll start with three of these a day. Take two now, and then take three a day. If it doesn't respond by in the morning, we'll try something else. If it keeps swelling, I may have to open it back up so it will drain. You'll need to take these for a week. Now isn't the time to create a drug resistant strain of bacteria."

Morgan took Porter's temperature and found that it

was a little high. "Today should be an easy day. All we'll need to do is gather some wood before we shut down for the night."

"How far do you think we can get today?"

Morgan pulled out his road atlas. "I'd like to see how close we can get to Hot Springs. Of course, it all depends on the shape the roads."

"If we don't run across any blocked roads or washed out bridges, we can make it."

"Porter, why don't you hit the bunk and get that leg elevated. Maybe some of the swelling will go down. I don't think it'll be pleasent if I have to open it up to drain. If I need your help, I'll wake you."

Porter lay back in the bunk and placed his rifle in the rack directly above the window where he could grab it in one motion. Porter, who never removed his shoulder holster when he was on a mission, knew that his pistol was handy.

Morgan cranked the Duk and headed up the highway toward Hot Springs. After an hour or so of travel, they came to a small town named Strong. It was little more than a crossroads, but the road was blocked with farm machinery where a checkpoint of sorts was set up. When they were within a couple of hundred yards, Morgan pulled to a stop and called to Porter.

"Hop up, Porter, and dig out your long gun."

Porter was already up when he felt the Duk slowing. "What have we got ahead?"

"I'm not sure, but I don't like it."

Porter pulled out the rifle, dialed the scope up to nine power and steadied it by resting it across the back of the passenger seat. Through the scope, he could see a lot of excitement taking place. A number of men were scambling to get into position. Porter half expected to see red armbands, but none were evident.

"They're up to something; otherwise, they wouldn't be trying to block the road. I don't like it. Let's turn around and find another way around this place."

"I think you're right; I don't want to find out their intentions. I can't think of a good reason for them to have the road blocked out here in the middle of nowhere."

"I don't know about you, but I thought we would have run out of these characters by now."

"What do you think they want?"

"I can think of a lot of things. We have a lot of equipment including this vehicle that actually runs."

Morgan pulled over as far as he could in the weeds and vines and began to turn aound. At that moment, a large trailer was backed across the road behind them. They were trapped.

Porter said, "Kill the engine so I can aim steady."

As soon as Morgan killed the motor, Porter sighted across the bow of the Duk and centered the crosshairs on the head of the first man looking over the barricade.

As he was taking up slack on the trigger, a voice from a bull horn called out, "You in the military vehicle, stand down. You are surrounded, and you have nowhere to go."

Morgan glanced at Porter. "This thing isn't bullet proof, and if it gets shot up, we'll be on foot."

"I'm not going to give up even if I get killed. There's

a building with a plate glass window directly across from us on the left and there's an overgrown field on the right."

Morgan said, "I'll take the overgrown field to the right; you hit that building on the left. We passed a grain silo about two miles back; we can meet back there if we can't take'em out."

Porter grabbed his ammo pack and his bug out bag and headed toward the door with his AK-47. Morgan slapped the presciption bottle into Porter's hand.

"If you live through this, you're still going to need these."

"Thanks. Can you disable this thing so we can recover it later?"

"Good idea." Morgan grabbed a couple of radios and passed one of them to Porter. "Don't lose this, or we'll lose operational security. Put up a white flag until I disable the motor."

While Morgan pulled the ignition module and the distributor cap, Porter took a white pillow case, tied it to a broom handle and poked it through the roof hatch.

Morgan stuffed the engine parts into his bag and nodded to Porter. "Are you ready?"

"I was born ready. You hit the ground running. I'm going through that picture window and kill everyone in the building. Then I'm heading out the back where I can flank them. You concentrate on the ones behind us."

Morgan took a deep breath. "Go!"

Morgan, with his gear, rolled out of the window on the passenger side and bolted through the overgrown field. Bullets were cutting through the weeds as he dove into a small ditch and then chugged through the ditch to his right so that he was traveling parallel to the road behind him.

Porter leaped from the door, not touching the steps, and ran straight for the picture window. He squeezed the trigger on the AK-47 which was set on full automatic. Blowing out the window, he leaped through it. He dropped two men who were caught unprepared as he bolted through the window opening and continued out the back door. He was oblivious to the pain in his leg that had started bleeding again. When he stopped behind an abandoned car, he dusted the glass fragments from his hair and clothes.

Because this was the last thing they expected, the men at the checkpoint scattered. Morgan traveled several hundred yards through the ditch until he could climb out and work his way back toward the roadway. Keeping out of sight, he crawled through the weeds until he could see the large equipment trailer. Two men were hiding behind the diesel John Deere tractor hooked to the trailer. They were on the radio. Morgan could hear them say, "I don't know where they are." He couldn't understand what the other side was saying, but the guy said, "Ok, we'll see if we can find the one who took off across the field."

Morgan cut them down with seven quick shots from his AK-47. He stayed put in the field. Although he had good concealment, he had no cover. He could not afford to reveal himself because he would be a sitting duck if he were spotted.

Meanwhile, Porter replaced the empty magazine in his rifle with a fresh one. He took a quick glance around the car in time to see three men cutting between the buildings and ducking behind some vehicles. One of the men hid behind a pickup truck, and Porter could see his feet and legs clearly. He made a quick snap shot and cut the foot out from under the man who collapsed on the ground screaming in pain. A second shot through the man's midsection brought silence. He didn't wait for the others to spot him, but sprinted toward the dead man and dived under the truck shoving his back pack in front of him as he passed the still quivering body. He crawled on his belly toward an overfilled dumpster and peered around it from ground level. Once behind it, he paused and listened.

The radio on the dead man's body called out, "Eddie, are you hit?" Eddie didn't answer. He heard the two remaining yelling to each other. The one fartherest away said, "Can you see Eddie?"

"Yeah, I think he's dead. What do we do?"

The nearest man answered, "All this is Kevin's big idea. I'm getting outta here. I've got to take care of a family."

Porter spotted the nearest man and killed him with a shot through his head. The other man broke and ran, but didn't get far. A bullet between his shoulder blades sent him sprawling. Porter had no sympathy for these people. He had managed to live though the collapse without robbing a single soul. There was no need to do what they were doing. All these people had to do was trade or work for what they couldn't scavenge or make themselves. Porter was sure several more men were scouting around the area.

As he started to peer around the dumpster, a voice called out, "Don't move a muscle asshole, or I'll light you up. Lay your rifle down and ease that pistol out of your holster with two fingers."

Porter looked over his shoulder into a pair of sinister eyes. "You must be Kevin."

Kevin sneered. "How do you know my name, asshole?"

Porter looked up from where he was kneeling. "My name's not asshole."

CHAPTER 12

Just as Jonas had predicted, the snow came. Kitty was behind the bar bottling some beer when she heard a vehicle stop in the road. She walked to the window next to the double front doors and watched as three plain clothed men climbed out of the white SUV and headed for the stairs. They weren't in uniform, but she noticed their boots. She had seen them before. The SUV disappeared down the road as the three men ascended the stairs. Each was wearing identical Sig P320 pistols and had a Sig MP5 sub machinegun slung on his back. Their attempt to blend in wasn't working. They had Pine Tree Mountain written all over them.

Kitty called out to the girls, "Some of the Pine Tree Mountain boy scouts are coming in. Watch what you say; don't mention a thing about Dix, Jonas or Fox. You are only here to serve them and find out what they have to trade. Don't let them try to pay with money, and make sure you see what they've got before you feed them or give them anything to drink."

The men pushed open the door and removed their

sunglasses as they entered the dark bar. They all sported beards wtih their upper lips shaved clean.

Kitty called out, "Come on in, boys. I bet you guys could use a good cold drink; the first one is on the house."

The one in the lead answered, "That would be great. What do you have?"

"I have some sassafras tea, homemade beer, corn whiskey and butter milk. I'm out of fresh milk until our milkman delivers tomorrow."

He answered, "I guess we'll take sassafras tea."

The two with him looked disappointed. She nodded at the girls who immediately converged on the men while she opened a window behind the bar and retrieved a frozen ice tray. The girls knew their trade. Two of the men responded to the advances as most men would. The one who did the speaking seemed unmoved. Kitty soon had the ice broken up with an ice pick and had filled the glasses full of cold sassafras tea.

"Enjoy, guys. Let me know what you have to trade, and I'll let you know what you can buy. Do you boys have girlfriends?"

"Oh, we're here trying to locate one of our men who may have gotten lost. Have you seen any strangers lately?"

"We have a lot of strangers come through here. This is the main road along the river, and these are the only young sporting ladies in a hundred miles."

"We're looking for a guy around thirty who is probably wearing green army fatigues and goes by the name Edwards."

"I'd sure remember somebody dressed like that. He hasn't been in here. How long has he been missing?"

"He's been gone for a couple of days."

"I hope he's not hurt. The dogs and hogs will make short work of him if they find him helpless."

"You boys want to have a go with any of the girls or get a good home cooked meal?"

Hester kissed the one she was cuddling on the ear. "Whatcha say, handsome? You feel like a poke?"

Before he could answer, the one in command said,

"No, but thanks." Again the two men looked disappointed.

Kitty grinned. "What's the matter? Don't you like girls?"

The look on his face answered her question. Kitty grinned. "What's your name, honey?"

He turned to his men. "Let's have another glass of sasafras tea while we wait on our ride."

"Sure, honey. Whatcha got to trade?"

He reached in his pocket and pulled out a crisp $100.00 bill. Kitty shook her head.

"You've spent too much time in these mountains; not to know that those are only good for lighting fires or as toilet paper."

"We don't have anything else."

"How much ammo you got? A magazine of those 9mm bullets will get y'all three more drinks."

He reluctantly thumbed out a handful of the bullets and paid for the drinks. Kitty winked at the other two men.

"One of those pistols will get y'all three good pokes with the girls."

The white SUV that had dropped the three men at Bill's Bar was making its way down the road when they spotted Jonas's log cabin up on the hill. Smoke was coming from the chimney. Captain Naomi Carter was driving so she slowed when she came to the driveway.

"Let's make sure that Edwards is not holed up in this cabin beside a good warm fire."

Jonas looked around at Dix who had just checked to make sure that his rifle and pistols were fully loaded with bullets in the chambers.

"Looks like an SUV from Pine Tree Mountain. Do you want to kill them?"

"No, let's see what they want. I want to wait until Porter and Morgan get here before we go on the offense. I don't want to draw attention to this area. All they will do is come in here and kill everybody if we act too soon."

"Fox, you stay out of sight down the hall after you hide Dix's rifle under the couch. Dix, put your pistol

179

under the blanket where you can get your hands on it and pretend to be asleep."

Captain Carter came to the door and knocked in a commanding manner. Jonas answered the door. His pistol was in his waistband under his sweater.

Jonas whispered, "Who are you, and what brings you down here on the river road?"

Captain Carter, in her most commanding and official voice stated, "I'm Captain Carter with the U.S. Government, and I am looking for one of our men who has gone missing."

Jonas put his finger to his lips. "Please speak softly. I have a sick man here."

She asked, "What's wrong with him? It's not my missing man is it?"

"No, this is my brother Eddie. He got sick and took a tumble. He's real weak and is starting to develop a rash. He just got back from traveling down South. Do you have any idea what the plague symptoms look like?"

Her face grew pale, and she started backing down

180

the stairs. "Sorry your brother's not doing well."

"If I see your man, I'll send him on his way home."

Jonas reached up and pretended to scratch his neck as she scrambled back into the car.

After a long moment, she wheeled the SUV around into the road and gunned it back toward Bill's Bar.

Dix chucked. "I think they'll stay out of this valley long enough for us to get Porter and Morgan here and hatch our plan."

A few minutes later, the radio came to life. Kitty called out, "Jonas, are you listening?"

Jonas keyed the mic. "What's up, Kitty?"

"We just had three of the Pine Tree Mountain boys in here asking questions. They hung out until the SUV that dropped them off came up outside and honked the horn. They sped back toward The Mountain like they were on fire."

"Don't worry. They are running from some plague victims, and they've got to get back to report to their leaders."

"Plague? Is the plague back? What are we going to do?"

"There is no plague. I just let them think that it's back; that should keep them out of our valley for a while."

"I've got some bad news. Willie Ray's brother, Luke, and his boys are in here getting liquored up. They wanted to see the spot where Willie Ray died. They're crying over his death. I'm not sure if it's the liquor or if they are getting themselves worked up to do something. You might want to sleep with one eye open tonight."

"I've been half expecting something from those guys; call me back if you see that they're heading this way."

Jonas turned to Dix and Fox. "Does trouble follow you guys?"

Fox pointed at Dix. "I told you to drop him off up on the mountain, but it's too late now."

Jonas burst out laughing, and Dix shook his head.

"Who do I need to shoot now?"

"Willie Ray's brother, Luke, is down at the bar

getting liquored up and mourning the loss of his brother. Kitty's going to radio me if they get themselves worked up and head this way. In the meantime, I'm firing up the water heater, and we're going to get cleaned up. Then I'm putting you to bed, and Fox and I are going to take turns standing watch."

Dix looked at Fox. "Sounds like a good idea. Fox has started to get a little ripe now that we're hemmed up inside with him."

Fox grinned. "I'm surprised the paint hasn't started peeling with the three of us in here and the windows closed."

Dix asked, "How long before the stitches come out?"

"I'll take them out in a week. The ones I used on your femoral artery will disolve. I only had one set of the disolvable ones. I used one of the strings from the center of a piece of paracord to close your wound."

Although he was still getting dizzy when he stood up, Dix was moving around a bit. They helped him into the shower and helped him back to the chair when he finished.

Jonas and Fox in turn got cleaned up and took turns standing guard while Dix slept. A couple of hours later the radio once again came alive.

"Jonas, this is Hester, Kitty told me to call you and let you know that Luke is about to tear the place apart. He says its our fault that his brother was ambushed."

"Where's Kitty now?"

"Luke just punched her, and she's out cold."

"I'm on my way."

Jonas turned to Dix and Fox. "Luke just hurt Kitty. I've got to go."

Fox reached for his gun, and Dix started to rise.

Jonas gave Dix a stern glance. "Fox and I will take care of this; you are in no shape to fight. We can't look after you and fight at the same time."

They were out the door and barrelling down the road before Dix could argue with them. Fox and Jonas were in Jonas's trunk for this trip. They needed speed that the electric ATV didn't have. When they were within a hundred yards of Bill's, they pulled off the road and proceeded at a trot. Jonas carried an M4 with a thirty round magazine. Fox carried his 30-30 Marlin and wore the Colt 1911 pistol on his hip. They could hear glass breaking and cussing as they ascended the stairs.

Jonas spoke as he neared the door, "Kill anyone with a gun, or who wants to fight. This ends tonight."

As Jonas gave the front doors a mighty kick, Fox pulled back the hammer on his old rifle until it clicked.

CHAPTER 13

Porter woke with his hands tied behind his back and a headache that radiated down into his jaws. When he licked his lips, he could taste blood.

Kevin was on the radio. "Have you found the other one yet?"

"No, he killed Larry and Paul, and we're still looking."

Porter had no recollection after he told Kevin that his name wasn't asshole. He had to blink and wipe his face on his shoulder because blood was running down into his eyes. He glanced around and saw his Ruger revolver lying on the ground out of reach. Kevin was nursing a neck wound. He held a dirty rag over the wound with one hand and held the radio with the other. Porter thought *I must have miss-aimed. I wonder if I miss-aimed before or after I was hit in the head?*

He knew that there were at least two left--Kevin and the one on the other end of the radio. The smart assumption was that there were more men. At least they hadn't gotten Morgan. When Kevin walked over to Porter and kicked him in the stomach, Porter buried the pain again. The kick knocked the breath out of him, and he lay there suffering for few agonizing minutes until his breathing returned to normal.

The radio spoke again. "He's disappeared."

Kevin cursed. "Dammit, get back here and help me get this asshole out of sight."

A few minutes later a wild eyed man came running around the corner.

"What happened to you?"

"He got off a shot when I was trying to knock him out."

"Why didn't you just shoot him?"

"I want to make him suffer for what he did to us. I'm going to make an example of him. I want to crucify him and hang him on a cross as a warning for anyone else who thinks they can just come driving through here."

"Kevin, don't you think this is getting ridiculous? I'm surprised the New Constitution Army hasn't sent more troops up here since we killed that squad that tried to pass through here last month."

"You have your orders; get on the radio and find out if they've spotted the other one yet?"

"There are no others. It's just me and you; everyone else is dead."

"Go to frequency eight and get Marty and his crew over here."

Porter watcheld as the man switched the handheld radio and called, "Marty, Kevin needs you to get your men over here. Everyone's dead except me and Kevin."

A voice on the radio replied, "Melvin, is that you? What the hell happened?"

"Yes, it's me. We stopped an army vehicle, and these two guys were out and shooting before we could spit. We have one captured, and the other one is still running loose."

Melvin wandered too close to Porter while he was talking on the radio. Before Melvin could answer, Porter took both of his feet and with a sideways stomp, hit Melvin's knee from the side. The knee collapsed inward with a sickening crunch. It was dislocated and the tendons and ligaments were torn. With no modern medicine to help, Melvin would be permanently disabled if it weren't for what Porter did next. Melvin landed on his back. Porter swung his legs around and dropped his boot heel on Melvin's throat crushing his windpipe. Melvin could only clutch his throat. Unable to breathe, no sound came from his mouth as he suffocated. Kevin dropped the dirty rag he had held to his neck and grabbed his rifle. Just as he leveled it on Porter, a shot rang out. Kevin pitched forward landing on Melvin's nearly lifeless body. Porter took full advantage and kicked Kevin in the temple as hard as he could. Morgan appeared and shot both men.

Porter looked up. "Get me untied. There's more on the way."

Morgan produced a hunting knife and slit the duct tape binding Porter's wrists. Porter grabbed his weapons and checked the .38 revolver. Just as he suspected there was a fired cartridge under the hammer.

Porter wiped some of the blood off his face. "Do you want to take the rest of them out, or do you want to run?"

"I say, let's get moving. We can radio Captain Jones and let him know what's going on up here. They can come wind this party up quickly."

Porter spit blood. "I over heard them say that they took out one of the New Constitution squads that came through here last month. I'm afraid that the past couple of years have made us all soft. It's been three

189

years since our plague attack on the Chinese army down in Texas. Things quieted down after that."

"I think it quieted down as long as people thought they would get the plague. Let's get you back in the Duk. If we get away, I need to look at your head. You may have a new part in your hair."

"I think I have some broken or cracked ribs because it hurts when I breathe. The late Kevin evidently worked on me with his boots once I was out."

Porter again repressed his pain and climbed the ladder into the Duk. Since the wood fire was still going on the wood gas generator, Morgan reinstalled the missing engine parts, cranked the engine and headed through the gap between the farm equipment blocking the road. Porter kept a lookout and made sure they weren't being followed. He only stopped long enough to go to the sink and wash his face of the dried blood. One of his teeth was a bit loose but was still in place so he left it alone in the hopes that it would heal.

Morgan glanced in the review mirror. "There are some pain meds in the med kit."

Porter nodded. "I may take some at bedtime. I don't want to take anything until I'm sure we've gotten away."

The Duk didn't have the ride of a luxury RV. It had a truck's suspension and every bump in the road radiated through the vehicle and through their bodies. Morgan tried to steer clear of the worst of the holes and debris because he knew that Porter was in agony even though he didn't show it.

Porter gazed down the road. "I guess we've witnessed the worst and best of men."

"I'm about sick of witnessing the worst of men. You'd think that we'd run out of these bastards by now. I can't believe we've been fighting nonstop since we left."

"The past few years have been relatively quiet because we were in areas that we control."

"You know we can only dodge bullets for so long. I don't want to get killed before I can get back with Frankie. I've got a lot to live for now."

Porter chuckled. "Funny how a beautiful woman changes your perspective on life."

"Do you ever think about your life back home?" Morgan asked. "I have trouble remembering what my wife's voice sounded like sometimes, and I feel guilty."

Porter agreed. "I know what you mean. The main thing I remember about my folks is when I buried them.

I have nightmares about finding my dead little brother clinging to my mother's body. That's why I don't hesitate to kill these roaches when I encounter them. My only regret is that one of the ones that killed my family got away. I'm almost certain that I hit him. If my bullet didn't kill him, I hope the plague did."

"Knowing how well you shoot, I have no doubt he was packing lead when he left."

Porter kept his eyes on the road behind them. "Is this as fast as she will go?"

"It runs good at about forty-five miles per hour. I can get another ten or fifteen miles per hour out of it, why?"

"Glance in your rearview mirror."

In the distance they could see a vehicle following them. It wasn't catching up, only following.

Porter took out a small pair of binoculars. "They're in a dark colored pickup. I don't know if they are with the group that attacked us or just followed us when we drove through the gap."

Morgan kept glancing in the mirrors. "We're not going to get much rest tonight."

"Don't try to push our speed. They can catch us at any time if they like."

While keeping an eye on the truck behind them, they drove along in silence. Porter casually refilled the magazines for their rifles and replaced the discharged cartridge in the .38 revolver located in his back pocket.

"The way I see it is one: they are simply going the same way we are; two: they are following to see where we are going so they can attack later; or three: they've radioed ahead and they're bringing up the rear for the next ambush."

Porter studied the map. "I think we need to cut off to the right on this road coming up. We are going to head around El Dorado and take only the most remote routes toward Hot Springs. Once we turn off, look for a spot where we can set up an ambush. If that truck turns, we'll know they are up to no good."

The Duk made the turn, and they proceeded at a fast clip until they reached a fork in the road. In the middle of the fork, sat an old, long abandoned gas station. The old brick building was intact, and the pumps were still there but had not been used in years. They blocked the left fork with the Duk then took up positions in the woods and waited. The obvious place to take up a position would be inside the brick building. They knew that their pursuers would naturally assume that they were forted up in there. As they had anticipated, the truck came barreling down the road. When it was within thirty yards, Porter shot out the passenger's side front tire causing the truck to veer into a ditch. It flipped and flung the four passengers out and onto the roadway, ditch and shoulder. Porter and Morgan ran up to the disabled and dying men. They made sure the men were free of weapons before they proceeded. Two were killed outright. A third was out cold, but still breathing. The fourth had a broken arm and leg. He was in no shape to fight; however, he could tell them what they needed to know.

Porter walked over to the man who was still sprawled in the road. "Do you want to tell me who you are and why you guys were following us?"

The guy gave him a dirty look. "I ain't telling you nothin. You killed my brother, friends and cousins."

"Are you with the New Constitution Army?"

"Hell, no. We are with the People's Party."

With no emotion Porter asked, "Shouldn't you be wearing red arm bands?"

"We didn't need them until y'all started showing up."

Morgan winked at Porter. "Porter, this guy needs help; go get the med kit."

Porter played along. "Why? He's not going to talk."

"We're not like them. Get the kit, and let me help him."

Porter disappeared around the Duk while Morgan turned to the injured man. "Porter can get a little psycho if you know what I mean. I can keep him from skinning you alive, but I've got to have a little help from you. To start with what's your name?"

"Charles."

"Ok, Charles. I know you lost a lot of your friends and family today, but just remember, we didn't start this. We are under the command of Major Dix Jernigan."

The man looked up wild eyed. "We had no idea that we were fighting you guys; we heard that Jernigan had been killed."

"You heard wrong. Do you want to survive this?"

Charles nodded his head. "Yes, I don't want to die."

The pain was already working on him. Morgan moved his weapons out of reach and called back to Porter.

"Bring the med kit; Charles wants to cooperate."

Porter showed up with the kit and passed it to Morgan. He then went over to the unconscious man, tied his wrists behind his back and his ankles together. He went through his pockets and relieved him of his holdout gun and knife. Morgan cleaned out Charles's pockets as well. He opened the kit, produced a syringe and a small vial from which he withdrew a pale yellow liquid. He inserted the needle into a vein in Charles's good arm. Charles went limp. They gathered up some straight oak limbs and couple of boards from the old gas station. Morgan pulled the broken arm straight and with the sticks and duct tape fashioned a splint. He did the same thing with the broken leg.

Porter said, "Wouldn't it be better to just shoot them both and get moving?"

"We can shoot them after this one talks; turn that one over on his side so he won't smother."

While Porter repositioned the other one, Morgan broke a small vial and passed the smelling salts under Charles's nose.

Charles came around, and Morgan asked in a calm voice, "Charles, are you in any pain?"

"No."

"Good. Do you have any help coming, or do we need to carry you back to your people?"

"Marty was waiting to hear from us. They will come when we call."

"We are trying to help your friends. How many guys are with Marty?"

The man had dozed back off so Morgan passed the smelling salts under his nose again. Charles jerked his head.

"Tell me, Charles. How many guys does Marty have helping him?"

"He has eight besides us."

Morgan looked over at Porter. "What do you want to do?"

Porter said, "I'm in no shape to fight right now. We can shoot these two, or we can drag them out to the highway and leave them to be found. If we take them to the road, I think we need to at least cripple the other one so they will have two casualties to contend with."

Morgan looked back at the two of them. "Do you know what they would do if the shoe were on the other foot?"

They looked at each other and nodded in agreement. Two shots ended the dilemma.

Along with the gold and silver in the dead men's pockets, they gathered the ammo and magazines they could use and left the men where they lay. They climbed into the Duk and proceeded on their way. Porter sat in his seat and groaned when they hit a bump in the road. Morgan glanced his way.

"Are you ready for a pain pill or a shot of the yellow juice?"

"I'll take a pain pill. I don't want the yellow juice unless you have to operate."

"Look in the med kit. I have something better than a pain pill. I have some morphine that they used in the military. Wipe off your arm with some whiskey and jab one of those into your hide and squeeze. You'll be pain free in a few seconds."

Porter did as directed and soon relaxed as the pain faded away.

Morgan said, "Once we get further down the road, I'll stop and get you cleaned up and see about your busted head."

Thirty or so miles later they came to the driveway of an abandoned farm. They wheeled down the drive and pulled in behind the vacant barn where they were out of sight of the road. A rainstorm had been threatening for some time; it soon blew in so they settled in for the night. Morgan cleaned Porter's head wound and elected not to stitch it. Instead he wrapped it, gave Porter a sleeping pill and put him in his bunk. Before long, Porter was out of pain and asleep. Morgan set up the radio and called Cooney.

Cooney answered, "How far have you made it today?"

"We are still southeast of Hot Springs. We ran into a bit of trouble up here. We've been fighting for our lives all day."

Cooney Jones listened as Morgan gave him a detailed account of what they had encountered. Cooney absorbed the Intel and answered, "I'll send two squads up there and clean that scum out. I assure you it won't go well for them."

Morgan grinned. "If Porter hadn't gotten knocked in the head and had some ribs busted, we would've gone back."

"Try to stay out of trouble. If you need to hold up there for a couple of days, do it. Porter needs time to heal. Are you in a secure spot?"

"I think we're as secure as we are going to get. Since rain has started, there should be no indication that we have moved off the road."

"Good. Stay put and get Porter back on his feet."

Morgan opened the panel next to the wood gas generator and put some dry wood in the fire. The heat from the box warmed the cabin. A moderate wind that was blowing from the southwest carried any smoke away from the road. The rain came down heavy as he called Frankie on the radio to make sure she and the boy were ok. Since they wouldn't need a guard tonight, they both could sleep.

CHAPTER 14

Jonas was a big man. The heavy, size twelve hiking boots he wore violently drove the big double doors inward with his kick. One of Luke's boys was standing too close, and the big doors sent him crashing face first onto the floor. Several teeth skittled across the floor in front of him. Jonas's rifle barked as he placed a round into Luke who turned from the bar. Another one of the boys came running from the back of the bar drawing his pistol. At that range, Fox didn't need to raise and aim; he fired from the hip striking the oversize boy in his midsection. His feet went out from under him from the momentum of the bullet passing through his body. The pistol went flying across the floor. Luke cussed and made a grab for his rifle that was lying on the bar. Before Jonas could fire again, the boy who had been knocked down by the door turned and kicked at Jonas. That moment of distraction was all it took for Luke to grab his rifle off the bar and fire. He had the AK-47 on full auto, and the spray of ammo went between Fox and Jonas. In his haste, Luke accidently hit his own son who was still on the floor. Fox's 30-30 barked again and knocked Luke backward into the bar. He shucked the mechanism of the old rifle, and the spent cartridge hull flipped out of the gun. Fox had the action closed on a new round before the empty hit the floor. He didn't need to shoot again. Jonas had shot Luke through the head and had finished off the wounded son on the floor.

He called out to Hester, "Are there any more?"

Hester was stunned by what had taken place in the span of five seconds.

Jonas gave her a mean look and shouted, "Are. There. Any. More?"

"No, they are the only ones here."

Fox fished out a couple of cartridges from his pocket and replaced the fired ones from his rifle. "Are there any more brothers or sons running loose we need to go look up?"

"I think there are some cousins, but I doubt there is a man alive who will come looking for you guys after this."

Fox looked at the toe of his new boot. A neat hole had been blown right through the end just in front of his toes. "Might know my shiny new boots are shot to hell."

Kitty had started to come around. Jonas scooped her up and gently carried her back to her bed while Hester and Annie Ruth brought rags and an ice pack for her face.

Kitty asked, "What happened?"

Jonas gently wiped her bloody nose and applied ice to her swollen eye. "I'm afraid you lost three more customers."

"Hell, it's going to be mighty quiet around here without Willie Ray and Luke running loose. Did anyone else get hurt?"

"No, everything is ok now. I'm going to leave you with the girls. Fox and I will drag off the bodies."

They returned to the front room to find several of the local men were filtering in to check out all of the commotion. One of them went to work on the front doors while the other three helped Jonas and Fox drag the bodies out to Luke's truck. Jonas looked at the men who hadn't said much.

"Is there anyone who will be claiming the bodies?"

The shortest of the three was a man Jonas recognized as Randy Bastrop. He pointed up the valley. "We're not sure. They had some women, but they're a good ten miles away from here. We can take the bodies up there

203

in the morning and see what they want done with them. As cold as it is, the bodies will keep out in the truck."

"Thanks. Let me know if those women are in dire straits. We'll get them some food and supplies. They can't help it if their men were worthless. Stop at my cabin on your way, and I'll load them up with some staples. I don't want the thought of a bunch of widow women and starving children on my mind."

By the time they had gotten back up the stairs and into the bar, Hester and Annie Ruth had most of the blood mopped up and the floor disinfected with soapy water.

Fox sat at the bar, and the girls brought him a shot of whiskey. "I've spent the last three years tending my garden, hunting, fishing and helping Dix with the livestock. I haven't even had an argument with anyone, but my wife. In the last three days, I've done nothing but fight and kill people. All I agreed to do was come up here with Dix and look around."

Jonas looked over at one of the new girls, Doris Ann. "I think I need a shot of whiskey myself. I'm with you, Fox. I've managed to live a quiet life. I pretty much ignored Willie Ray and Luke. They were mostly just a bunch of horses' asses, but they started pushing people around. I can't understand why, with the shortage of people and the abundance of houses and equipment left, they had to act like they did." He tossed back the shot of whiskey and nodded for a refill. Doris filled both glasses and watched as the men tossed back their drinks.

Fox set his glass on the bar. "Maybe, I can get a night's rest for once. Is there anybody else I need to worry about tonight or can we go back and get some rest?"

"No, Fox. I think we've done about all the damage we can do for one day."

Without talking they went through the doors and out into the cold night.

"Fox, look up. Have you ever seen so many stars? On a cold clear night in the mountains, with no street lights around, you can see forever. More snow is coming; I can feel it in the air. It's snow cold; if you spend enough time up here, you'll know what I'm talking about."

With the moon peaking over the trees and with the snow on the ground, the reflected light enabled them to make their way without flashlights. Once they were in the truck, they had the heater running and were soon back at the cabin.

Fox called out to Dix as they reached the stairs, "Don't shoot. It's me and Jonas."

From his hiding place in the shadows on the porch Dix answered, "I knew it was y'all when you drove up."

"What are you doing out here in the cold?"

"Well, when y'all didn't show back up, I figured I would go down to the bar and help bury you. I assumed since you're here that the other guys are dead."

At the door, Jonas stomped the snow off his boots. "We won't be worrying about Luke or his boys any longer. With the way things are going, there aren't going to be any people left around here to worry about."

Dix limped into the room. "How many did you have to kill?"

Jonas stoked the fire in the fireplace. "Lucas and his two grown boys are dead."

Fox wiped the melting snow off his rifle. "My nerves are shot. Do you have any Pine Tree Mountain whiskey stuck back?"

"I think I can find a little something to calm you down. Are you a scotch man?"

Fox wrinkled up his nose. "I don't care for roach spray. Do you have any bourbon or Irish whiskey?"

"How about a little Wild Turkey?"

"Now you're talking. Give me a double then I'm turning in."

Jonas went over to his desk and pulled a bottle of Wild Turkey from the drawer of his credenza. "Dix, you feel up to a shot?"

"Why not. If I gotta die from something, I might as well die from drinking whiskey. I haven't had a pain pill since early this morning."

The only light in the room was from the fire in the fireplace. Since only two leather recliners faced the fire, Jonas pulled up one of the straight back kitchen chairs and leaned back balancing on the two rear legs with his foot on the coffee table.

All three sat in silence for a few minutes before Dix spoke, "Have you guys given any more thought on how we're going to clean out The Mountain?"

Dix sipped his whiskey and without taking his eyes off the fire pointed out, "I wonder if they realize that we have them surrounded."

Jonas gave him a puzzled look. "What do you mean?"

"They are all holed up inside The Mountain. You have the blueprints; we know where every door, hatch and vent is located. If we called the Colonel, I think we could get enough men up here to easily close or cover every single escape point. They would have to cut a new tunnel if they want to get out."

Fox pointed out the obvious. "Ok, we bottle them up. How many years of food and supplies do they have on hand?"

Jonas reached in his pocket and pulled out a pouch of tobacco. He also pulled out a chaw and tossed it over to Fox. "I figured you need a chew after tonight."

"Thanks, I can't tell you how much I miss my tobacco. Do you have any idea how long they could stay holed up in that Mountain?"

Jonas replied, "I'm not sure. Imagine the contents of a thousand Costco or Sam's Clubs neatly stowed away in those huge rooms that are all climate controlled. Let's assume there are four thousand of them in there. We are safe to say that they can stay tucked away in there for years and years. If we shut off the gas, they probably have enough flashlight batteries to last for years. Many of these huge rooms are stacked from floor to ceiling with soft drinks. Remember this facility supplied other warehouse facilities. If we shut off the water by blowing their water tank, it would take years for them to drink up the bottled water and soft drinks."

Dix scratched his newly growing beard. "We also have to remember that if they come out in mass, our puny forces would be overwhelmed in minutes."

Fox spat into the fire. "If we blew the main entrances, they could only send out a few at a time. In a coordinated effort, we could blow all of the exits at once, and they would be stuck."

Dix pointed to the rolled up blueprints on the kitchen bar. "Sanitation! Where do the sewage lines run?"

Jonas thought a minute. "I'm not sure, but I would be willing to bet they have a system in place that would prevent contamination of the local streams. We'll look at the blueprints and see where the waste water is being discharged."

Dix grinned. "If we stopped the sewer from flowing, things would get messy in there quickly. I figure we've got about two weeks, before their curiosity makes them come looking to see if we've starting dying from the plague. Porter and Morgan will be here soon. It's a shame we can't slip in there through Jonas's back door and do some damage."

Jonas rocked his chair forward and walked over to the fire and chunked in his chaw of tobacco. "We need to take out that idiot Elliot Planter and the top tier or two of his officers. If we retired them, things would start breaking down fast."

"We'll still have a big problem with thousands of heavily armed men who all think like that imbecile, Edwards, whom we captured. If they all think like that and have that attitude, what could they possibly contribute to our new society?"

"That's going to be a problem. They can't all be like Edwards, but you know, as well as I do, that they have all bought the communist fairy tale; otherwise, they wouldn't be in The Mountain that we all paid for."

Jonas noted that Fox still cradled the old Marlin 30-30.

"Fox, I don't remember you being that good a shot with your army issued Colt M16?"

"I could qualify with it on the range, but it just never felt substantial to me. I like the weight of this old 30-30 that I've carried ever since I was old enough to shoulder it. It's like a part of me; I don't have to think about it when I use it. It isn't fancy, but it hits where I aim, and that's all that matters."

Dix asked, "Where do you want me to sleep? I want to sleep in a real bed if there's one around here."

"You're in luck; you take the room down the hall in the mother-in-law suite. Fox, you know where your room is. I'm heading to the master suite, and as far as I know, no one will be gunning for us tonight."

Dix moved into the suite. There was no heat, but the bed had a large down filled comforter and big feather pillows. The room reminded him of the back bedroom at his grandfather's house in Catahoula Parish. The big old bed had a feather mattress, big feather pillows and patchwork quilts. The rusty old springs under it creaked when he climbed in and the big mattress enveloped him as he sunk into it. The one night he could vividly remember was when it was storming and cold. The rain on the tin roof and the wind blowing through the trees made him feel colder than he really was. Lightning lit up the room, but he was safe in the big bed. Just as on that night so many years ago in the drafty old room on the back of his grandfather's house, sleep came easily.

CHAPTER 15

Major Candice Olsen nervously sat in the chair across from Pontiff Planter's huge desk and awaited his arrival. She checked her nails to see how the new coral nail polish was holding up. Planter didn't keep her waiting long. The door opened, and a guard announced his arrival.

"Pontiff Planter has arrived."

Major Olsen jumped to her feet as he walked into the room. The Pontiff gave her a wave of his hand.

"Keep your seat, Major. What's the status on our plague victims?"

"I supervised the euthanasia of Captain Carter and her men, as well as the guard who stopped them at the gate. I stayed until their bodies were cremated, and the SUV was disinfected."

"Are you absolutely certain that they didn't come in contact with anyone else?"

"I'm certain, Sir. I took her report over the radio. I asked her to give the mic and headset to the guard who stopped them at the perimeter. I ordered him to kill them all on the spot, which he did. I then had one of our snipers kill him from a distance. A team in full hazmat gear took the bodies and gear to be cremated, and the area was completely cleaned. As a precaution, the hazmat team will remain in quarantine outside of the facility for two weeks."

"Does anyone outside of you, me, the sniper and the hazmat team know what has taken place?"

"No, Sir, everyone is being told that we were attacked, and that we lost some members of the team."

"Make sure the sniper and the hazmat team know what will happen to them if a single word of what's taken place gets out."

"I've already had that conversation with them. Do you think it was necessary to kill them without first waiting to see if they were infected?"

"Are you questioning my decision? Don't you think that I consulted a higher power before deciding what had to be done?"

"I'm sorry to have doubted you, Sir. It won't happen again."

"See that you don't," he snapped. "Is there anything else you would like to report?"

"Yes, we had a prisoner escape, and we haven't located him as of yet."

"Which prisoner escaped?"

"Charles Ward. You remember the boy they called Chucky, the one who refused to participate with us and the other tea boys?"

"Yes," The Pontiff snarled. "I remember the little bastard. He was the one who threw the saucer and hit me in the head. I had to have three stitches to close that cut above my eye. I remember having him caned fifty lashes and then thrown in the jail. How long has he been in there?"

"He has been in for two and half years."

"How did he escape?"

"He tunneled out through the wall behind his cell. He did it just like the guy in that movie. We let him have a poster for his wall, and he flushed his diggings down his toilet."

Planter ran his fingers through his beard with one hand and absentmindedly twisted at the corner of his eyebrow with the other. "How far did he tunnel?"

Major Olsen pointed to a diagram of level six that showed an exterior vent. "The tunnel was only about two feet into the equipment and armory room which was located just behind the jail. He spent some time getting his equipment and supplies together. We have evidence that he got into the outdoorsman, hunting and camping sections on level five. Since the hunting section is stocked with guns and ammo for hunters, he is well equipped and may be armed. We brought in dogs to track him. We believe he went out through this air vent shaft. The vent cap was damaged from the inside, and it was set back in place from the outside."

"How old is that boy now?"

"Our records indicate that he is sixteen years old."

The Pontiff scowled. "I can't believe that he didn't respond to the religious instruction. Were the Apostles giving him daily instruction? Which poster did he have on his wall?"

"Yes, they said he was making great progress. The poster that hid his escape hole was of you delivering the sermon for our first winter solstice feast."

"Oh, well, he probably won't be a problem. The plague will probably get him."

"We'd better hope so."

"How did he get past our sensors and snipers?"

"He knew where they were located because he was in the Youth Guard and part of their training was on the sniper teams. Our snipers and guards spend their time looking out and not so much looking behind themselves. He probably slipped through during shift change."

"I guess he was a little too old when we brought him into the fold, and if I remember, we bought him from a reliable supplier."

The major commented, "We'll have to take a chance on the plague. One untrained boy running loose in the mountains won't last long by himself, and if he finds anyone, he'll catch the plague. The best thing we can do is stay holed up in here for a few weeks. After that, we'll send out a hazmat team to check the surrounding valleys."

"Very good, Major. What time is the memorial service for Carter and her men?"

"It's scheduled for three this afternoon. Sargent Danforth's boyfriend wants to see you. I think he wants to pray with you; he took the news of the deaths really hard."

"Very well, have him come in, and we'll say a prayer. Since it is about time for the afternoon call to prayer, we'll knock both of them out at the same time. Have the foot washing basin brought in, and I'll let him wash my feet as well. That should bring him some measure of comfort."

Major Olsen left the room and stopped at the desk of Planter's Aide. "His Lordship would like to have his foot basin delivered. Once you have it in place, send in Danforth's boyfriend."

The Aide saluted. "Yes, Mam."
She paused where Danforth's boyfriend sat crying.

"Pontiff Planter will see you shortly; everything will be ok."

She caressed his shoulder and turned to see the foot basin being carried into the office. She turned and walked down the corridor to the main hallway and then out into one of the main tunnels. The facility was built like a giant parking garage. The main entrance was at the bottom, and the entire inside of The Mountain was a grid of chambers with doors where trucks could be backed up to the openings and unloaded. Each level had a ramp leading up to the next level. Level three not only housed huge storage rooms, but also housed the barracks, mess facilities and most of the mechanicals for the living section. It also housed private apartments, the armory, hospital and what could be best described as a cathedral. Originally, the cathedral was a huge conference area and gymnasium, but it was now the worship center. One corner could still be arranged for basketball and other activities, but now whenever necessary, Planter held his weekly sermons and tribunals. The Pontiff also conducted elaborate rituals and sacrifices in a chamber room next to his quarters and office. Level four housed the large natural gas generators and the electrical distribution panels.

A normal person would have difficulty in comprehending the enormity of the structure. The large Mountain was hollowed out with chamber after chamber of rooms and corridors. Level one was approximately fifteen square miles, and each subsequent level was slightly smaller in size as The Mountain was somewhat conical in shape. In the beginning, the company that owned and operated the facility was a shadow company created by the People's Party. The company received funding from the department of defense and various government agencies. With cooperation from some of the largest companies in America, it served a dual purpose. The company actually ran and operated as a wholesale distribution center for the major retail companies in the U.S., as well as hundreds of smaller specialty companies. Since the company was subsidized, the rent was practically free, and the warehouse was almost always filled to capacity. When the economy went sour, the government simply shut the doors and moved in the small army that was here now. The structure became a safe haven for their accomplices in the media and for some of the corporate big wigs that were the powers behind the scenes. While many of them were executed as soon as they outlived their usefulness, Planter did keep a few of them as adoring fans.

Most of the travel in the facility was in electric ATV's and golf carts; however, because walking the distances involved was impractical, bicycles and electric scooters were also available. Once it ceased to be used as an actual distribution center, gasoline and diesel vehicles were seldom used inside. Olsen made a point to visit every level at least once a week. She climbed into her personal ATV, hit the key and pressed the foot petal; it moved forward at a fast clip. The corridors were quiet as this was the third Prayer Hour. Everyone would be on their rugs bowing toward the west and getting ready to wash their feet. She thought about Danforth's boyfriend who was praying next to Pontiff Planter. The handsome young man might have to do more than just wash The Pontiff's feet.

The columns were numbered, and the corridors had street names. Originally, they were simply alphabetized, but someone felt that everyone would have a sense of normalcy if they were named. Many of the names were characters from the holy book of Gya that Planter was still revising. Other corridors were named after prominent politicians in the People's Party. The grand thoroughfare was named after the nation's first admitted communist president, Whitmore. The lights in the corridor provided illumination as she drove through the huge manmade caverns. She came up to Chairman Mau Square which was located at the epicenter of the complex. Here the two main elevators that went from the top to the bottom of the complex were located. Each was large enough to accommodate an ATV. Lesser elevators that allowed access between different levels were located in other areas. The lesser elevators were only designed to handle foot traffic. She pulled up to the nearest elevator and hit the button. After she waited a few moments, the door slid open, and she drove the ATV into the elevator. She hit the button to the ground level. The trip down was fast since it was only two levels below. Unlike the third level, this level was unlit until the light sensors picked up the transponder signal from the ATV. She sped toward the main entrance. The lights came on in advance of her arrival and went out a few minutes after she passed. She arrived at the main entrance just as the prayers were ending. The door guards were rolling up their prayer rugs and getting ready for the ritual foot washing.

Major Olsen pulled up and asked, "Any activity or anything to report?"

Both men popped to attention, and the older one answered, "No, Sir, I mean Mam, everything is quiet."

Major Olsen was obviously enraged by the guard's slip of the tongue. "Congratulations, soldier, you get to stand guard outside the door of my office for an additional shift for a week. Plug in my ATV charger and open the hatch; I'm going out for some fresh air."

Major Olsen walked out into the fresh air and squinted in the light. She looked back at the guard who was holding open the door.

"Hand me my weapon from the ATV. I'll be back in thirty minutes." The guard handed her the Sig MP5 that was on a rack in the ATV.

Major Olsen hiked down the road to a path that would take her to a point where she could look down the valley. She pondered *where would a sixteen year old boy with no outdoors experience go once he left the mountain?* She looked up the side of The Mountain in the direction of the vent that he used for his escape. She mentally imagined him heading down The Mountain and into the valley. That he climbed up The Mountain was unlikely because it had a covering of snow, and there was nowhere to go once he was up there. Unbeknownst to Major Olsen, Chucky had done the unexpected. His first impulse was to make his way down into the valley, but he knew that the snipers and sensors were looking down and not up. He wormed his way up and under the sniper nest located a couple of hundred feet above the vent. Once he heard the last Evening Prayer begin, he climbed around the platform where the two snipers were dutifully praying toward the west. The chant coming from the speaker masked the sounds of his movements as he worked his way above the snipers while they lay prostrate on their prayer rugs.

He was on top of the ridge by the time the snow started, and the moonlight reflecting off the snow allowed him to travel safe and secure. Two and a half years of sitting in his cell gave him plenty of

opportunity to plan his escape. His work details had
enabled him to know which store rooms held the items
he needed. A piece of limestone he had squirreled away
in his sock gave him his first tool to start chipping away
at the limestone in his cell. So, while Major Olsen sat
wondering how he disappeared, Chucky was working
his way down into the valley where Bill's Bar was
located.

CHAPTER 16

Porter woke when a clap of thunder rocked the Duk. He was unsure of the time, but it was daylight, and it was raining. "How long have I been out?"

Morgan, sitting in the passenger side captain's chair, was reading. "Take it easy. You've been sleeping for a day and a half. Your grandpa told us to stay put for a few days to give you a chance to heal a little. The major is still recovering as well."

"I can't remember the last time I slept this long."

"It's probably been some time since you were shot, knocked in the head and just about stomped to death. Do you want some coffee?"

"I thought you gave all the coffee to Frankie?"

"No, I held some back for emergencies."

Porter pulled himself to a sitting position. Dried blood was still on his clothes and in his hair line.

"Do you think I could get a shower and get out of these nasty clothes?"

Morgan smiled. "I think I can arrange that. There's a wash tub up on top. When we put it on the stove, I can fill it from the gutters by using a piece of hose. We can wash out our clothes in it, and the water in the reservoir attached to the stove is always hot."

"Let me get cleaned up. A hot shower will help me limber up. I'll take a shot at that coffee."

Morgan saw the intense bruising on Porter's ribs as Porter peeled off his shirt. "How bad are those ribs feeling?"

"I think I have several that are cracked; I can feel them clicking when I breathe."

"How about some pain pills or another hit of the morphine?"

Porter winced as he stripped down. "I hate to ask for it, but another one of those morphine shots the medics use would make this process a little more tolerable."

Morgan pulled out the kit and retrieved another of the morphine injectors. He wiped down Porter's arm and made the injection.

"Go ahead and get cleaned up. Then we'll get you dressed and fed so you can get back in the sack. I figure we'll roll in two more days."

Porter felt the pain easing, but he also felt weak from the injuries and the long bedrest. While Porter showered, Morgan opened a jar of venison stew and heated it on the wood stove. With a pot of rice, they had a hot meal. Porter clad in clean clothes returned to his bunk and lay down on fresh bedding. Using a plunger to agitate the water, Morgan washed the clothes in the tub, rinsed them and hung them on a line around the wood heater. They would be dry by morning. All Morgan had to do then was watch Porter recuperate. Making sure that Porter was resting comfortably, he opened the door, lowered the stairs and explored the area around the barn they were hiding behind. Although he could hear thunder in the distance, the rain had subsided, but he knew more rain was on the way. The back door of the barn was partially ajar so with his rifle at the ready he looked inside. The barn had been unused for several years. Mud dauber nests were in abundance on the walls and in the ceiling. Huge abandoned wasp nests hung under the eaves, and the holes of carpenter bees riddled the old beams. The heavy smell of old hay filled the air. The pungent smell of rat urine also hung in the air. The hay on the floor was practically dust, but the bales in the loft were still intact; however, he was sure they were full of mice and rats at this point. The decomposed body of a man was on the stairs leading up to the loft. The bones and clothes were scattered. Morgan poked around the clothes with a stick to see if there was anything in the pockets. He found a nice pocket knife and not much else. At one point in his life, he would have never taken anything from anybody under any circumstances, but times were different now; it no longer mattered. A quick walk around the old structure found a few items that he could use back at his place, but space was limited in the Duk, so he filed this location away in the back of his mind should he ever come back this way again.

The days came and went fast, and on the fourth day, they fired up the Duk, started back to the highway and headed toward Hot Springs. When they reached the area where the resort signs were advertising the long abandoned spas, they veered to the Northwest and skirted the city. They didn't run across anyone at all. The area was either devoid of human life, or the people chose to stay hidden.

Porter wondered aloud, "This area gives me the creeps. I bet people are playing it safe and staying out of sight. I'd be willing to bet that the people here are taking advantage of the hot springs."

Later in the morning, they met a man on horseback. He had a pack horse following; he waved as they stopped to greet him.

"Y'all must be with the New Constitution Army. We heard what took place back in Strong. Were you involved with that?"

Morgan leaned out the window. "No, what happened?"

"Well, that group that worked with the People's Party took over the area, and it's my understanding that they killed a squad from the New Constitution Army. The army got wind of it and sent in some commandos who shot them up pretty badly, and a couple of days later a couple of dozen more troops showed up and cleaned out the rest of them. They publically hung the ring leader and two of his men at the intersection of the highway. They used an excavator and just pulled them up in the air by their necks and let them dangle. As far as I know, that's where they left them."

Morgan looked concerned. "I would have liked to have seen that. We're heading up country. Is there anything up ahead we need to be on the lookout for?"

"I've come about a hundred miles from the direction of Eureka Springs. I have some brothers up there. I've been doing some hunting and fishing; that's about all I do these days. I don't have anybody, and I'm almost too old to worry about the ladies if you know what I mean. I just ran across a few people I've known for the past few years. You shouldn't have any trouble with anyone unless you get up to the east of Eureka Springs. The word is there are some bad guys up there. I know men who've gone up there and were never heard from again."

"We'll be careful; thanks for the advice."

The old man pointed to the Duk. "That's some contraption you have there. What are you're running it on? There aren't any gas stations around here anymore."

Morgan smiled. "This one is set up to run on wood gas."

"Imagine that. I guess necessity is the mother of invention. My grandfather told me something about using it back in the depression. I've gotten used to riding old Sparky here. We have reached an understanding you might say. I keep him from getting killed by the dogs and wolves, and he carries me where I want to go. Good luck, fellers. I want to get back to my camp before dark."

"Be careful, and we hope to see you if we pass back this way."

Morgan heard the safety on Porter's rifle snap as he flipped it back into the safe position. Morgan slid his pistol back into his shoulder holster as the man continued on his way. He eased off the brake, and the Duk pulled away. Morgan glanced into the rearview mirror at Porter who was still watching the man ride away.

"Whatcha think, Porter? Do you think we'll have smooth sailing the rest of the way?"

"I thought it was going to be smooth sailing when I left home weeks ago. I was supposed to just ride over and bring my grandfather back. Everything quickly went downhill from there."

"Other than stopping for some fuel, we should be able to get most of the way toward Eureka Springs by tomorrow. Depending on what the roads look like, and if we don't run into any trouble or have to stop and clear the roadways, we'll be in good shape."

They located a road leading through the middle of the Quachita National Forest. They took an open forestry road where they could gather firewood and remain hidden from the main road. No tire tracks or human tracks could be seen. Morgan dropped the ladder and took a look around. He looked back up at Porter.

"You stand guard while I gather the wood."

Porter put on his jacket, slung his rifle across his back and backed down the ladder. "I'll never be in fighting shape unless I get moving."

Morgan grinned. "If you get to suffering too badly, I won't begrudge your just standing guard. I need you well, not stove up worse than you are."

A large dead oak that had fallen near the road provided all the wood they needed. They quickly emptied the stove of the excess ash, and filled the wood box full of good dry oak. As soon as they climbed aboard, they restarted the fire, and got the wood gas generator ready to go. Morgan cranked the Duk and backed it out onto the main road.

"Porter, how you feeling?"

"About like you would expect. Everything hurts like the devil, but everything is working, and I think some of the soreness is gone."

They drove along in silence and slowed when a herd of wild hogs came pouring across the road. Porter pointed to the cause of the commotion. A tiger had a shoat down making a kill.

"Stop. I'm going to kill it. The last thing we need are more big cats running loose. We have enough trouble with all the wild dogs."

Morgan stopped the Duk, and Porter aimed from the front window with his .308 rifle. He squeezed the trigger, and the rifle bounced. When the bullet passed through its head, the big cat jumped about six feet in the air. It landed quivering, and its tail whipped around in spasms. They pulled up to the bloody scene. The shoat was dead, and so was the big cat. Porter climbed down with the AK-47 slung on his back. He leaned the rifle against the front wheel of the Duk and pulled the Kbar knife from its scabbard.

"In India, where they are from, people are on the menu. I hope we don't wind up with a breeding population. We have a bad situation now with all the wild dogs and hogs. I surely don't want to be looking over my shoulder for one of these."

Morgan joined him on the ground. "This shoat will be good eating. Let's get him gutted and skinned.

We'll quarter him out, and we'll cook him on the stove while we travel. I've got a large roaster we can fill with meat."

Porter said, "I'd like to skin out that tiger. Letting the hide go to waste would be a shame. Maybe we could use it as a rug between the bunks. I know that floor sure is cold sometimes."

Morgan shrugged. "Let's give it a try. If it starts to smell we can throw it out."

Porter's Kbar knife was razor sharp so he made short work of cutting up the young pig. Because the tiger was older, Porter had to take a bit longer to get the skin off. They finished the task within an hour and got back on the road. The road was in good shape. In a couple of spots, they had to drag away debris from fallen trees. By the time they started to look for a camping spot, Porter had finished scrapping the hide and had it spread out between the bunks. The meat in the pot smelled good when they pulled into an old rest area. They dined on the roast pork and used the pot liquor on their leftover rice. They looked over the map and determined that they should be near Eureka Springs by lunch the next day. They raised the tall antenna and called Cooney Jones.

Cooney answered, "Where are you men tonight? I hope you've had easier going since we last talked."

Porter keyed the mic. "We should make it to our first waypoint near Eureka Springs tomorrow. We're getting into the mountains, and the going is a little slower, but things have been quiet. We ran across a man travelling on horseback. He said that y'all sent a squad to take out the rest of the People's Party back in Strong."

"I contacted my men in Monroe, and they went up there and quieted the revolution with extreme prejudice, you might say."

"The word got out and raced ahead of us. I hope we didn't lose any of our men."

"We had one guy take a bullet in his arm, but they say he'll heal. I'll notify Major Jernigan that he can expect to hear from you the day after tomorrow. That should give you plenty of travel time."

Morgan took the mic. "We're getting into a little snow and ice up here. We'll let you know if we get delayed. We may have to put chains on the wheels, but so far, we haven't seen anything this vehicle can't handle."

"Be careful men. Cooney out."

They took down and stowed the antenna before climbing into their bunks. As they lay silently in the dark, they couldn't help but strain their ears listening for the sound of a big cat squalling in the darkness. Since they hadn't seen any evidence of recent human activity, they elected not to take turns guarding that night. Because the weather was cold, having someone adventuring far from a fire would be unlikely. They had been asleep for some time when all hell broke loose on the back of the Duk. Porter and Morgan bolted awake with pistols drawn.

CHAPTER 17

Jonas was up first and had the fire stoked and flaming in the wood stove. As soon as the house was warm, the wood stove would keep the main floor cozy. The bedrooms on the outskirts of the house were allowed to get cold because the beds were snug. The coffee water had just started to boil when the radio crackled.

"Jonas, are you listening this morning?"

Jonas recognized the voice of Kitty on the other end. "What's up, Kitty? You feel ok?"

"Other than being sore, I'm ok. The reason I'm calling is I've got someone here you need to talk to."

"Tell me who you've got down there."

"I have a young man who looks like he just stepped out of a hunting catalog. He has brand new clothes and equipment. He came in here early this morning and asked if he could warm by the fire for a few minutes. I didn't quiz him much, but I believe he came out of The Mountain. I have him eating some breakfast, and I have Hester's teenage daughter keeping him company so he's not going anywhere."

"Good, keep him busy. I'll get Dix and Fox, and we'll be there within the hour."

Jonas tapped on Fox's door.

"Don't shoot old man. It's Jonas. Roll out and get the Major up."

Fox opened the door scratching his short beard. "What's up?"

"We've got to run down to Bill's Bar."

"Darn, I don't like to go fighting without my coffee or at least a bite or two of breakfast."

"Hopefully, there won't be any fighting. Kitty has someone down there we need to meet."

Fox lamented, "You do realize that I haven't stepped through those doors without having to kill somebody."

Jonas started grinning. "I'll make sure they feed you before we start trouble again."

"What do you mean 'before we start trouble'?"

"I think this will be a good visit for once; get the Major up while I at least fix our first cup of coffee."

Fox tapped on the door to rouse Dix.

"Don't shoot; it's Fox."

Dix answered, "Fox who?"

Fox pushed opened the door and looked at Dix as he swung his feet out of the bed and onto the floor. Dix looked up at Fox.

"I hope you're telling me my coffee is going to get cold if I don't get up."

"I hate to get you up, but we've got to head to Bill's and meet somebody. The coffee's in the pot. Do you need any help?"

"I think I can make it. I hope I can get these stitches out today because they are starting to itch."

Very soon, all three of them were sitting in the cold electric ATV heading toward the bar. Fox was hunkered down with his coat collar pulled up around his neck.

"Tell me why we can't be riding in that good old warm truck instead of in this icicle."

They were laughing as they barreled down the road. The temperature had dropped in the night, and the new snow was like powder. The tires on the snow squeaked when they turned to go under the bar to the charging station. They got out and plugged the ATV into the charger before heading up the steps. Fox looking over into the back of Luke's truck saw the frozen bodies of Luke and his boys who were almost covered in snow.

Silently, they walked past the truck. This time they were fully armed with their rifles and pistols. The snow on the steps squished under their feet. Entering the dimly lit bar through the newly repaired door, they paused to let their eyes adjust.

Kitty called back to the cook, "Round up three breakfasts for these guys. Hester, bring us some coffee."

Fox grinned. "This is more like it."

Kitty's face was puffy, and one could see the bruising under her makeup.

Jonas gave her a hug. "I'm glad you are ok. I'm sorry I didn't come right away when you first called."

Kitty nodded in agreement. "I wish you had, but we had no idea he would go off the deep end so fast. I figured he would just get drunk and leave like he normally did."

Dix looked over at the young couple in the corner. "I assume that's the young man you radioed about?"

Kitty nodded. "That's him. He didn't say much, and he agreed to pay for his breakfast with 9mm ammo. He has an ammo pouch with a good supply of loaded mags for his MP5 and Sig pistol. All his gear and clothes appear to be brand new."

Dix glanced over at Hester. "Hester, what's your daughter's name?"

"Her name's Nadine."

"Can you ask her to come over for a second?"

"Sure."

Hester walked across the bar to the table where the young couple was sitting. Dix couldn't understand what she was saying, but he could see the young couples' eyes quickly dart to where he was standing at the bar. Hester stayed with the boy as Nadine hopped up and crossed the bar straight to Dix.

She stopped and simply said, "Yes, Sir?"

Dix tried to give her a pleasant grin. "Nadine, I'm Major Dix Jernigan, and I would like to meet and talk with that young man. I have no intention of hurting or even detaining him. Can you ask him if he would be willing to let us join him for breakfast?"

"Sure, I'll ask him. He seems really nice."

"Thanks."

Dix watched as she walked over to the table and sat down next to the boy. The boy looked up and nodded yes. Dix noticed that the boy's hand had fallen down to the pistol in the drop holster on his leg. Dix took out his pistol and laid it on the bar and left the M4 there as

240

well. He walked over to the table and offered his hand to the boy. The boy hesitated a moment and shook his hand. Dix grinned and clapped him on the shoulder.

"I'm Major Dix Jernigan. What's your name son?"

The boy looked up. "My name is Charles Ward; most people call me Chuck."

"Chuck, did you get enough breakfast?"

"Not really, I didn't want to spend all my ammo."

Dix looked over his shoulder. "Kitty, bring this man another breakfast; this one's on me."

Chuck grinned as Dix turned back to him. "Can Jonas and Fox join us?"

"Sure thing, tell them to bring your weapons over; I know you aren't comfortable with them out of reach."

"You're right about that. I can't even sleep unless I have a pistol under my pillow."

Jonas and Fox came over and joined them at the table while Kitty and Hester filled the table with food. Dix asked, "Are you a coffee drinker, Chuck?"

"I've never had it before."

Nadine piped up, "I'll bring him a cup."

They made small talk while they ate breakfast.

Once the boy had eaten his fill, Dix said, "Chuck, I want to tell you about Fox and Jonas and myself."

Chuck listened as Dix explained what had happened in the last few years and how they ended up sitting with him at a table in a bar in the Arkansas Ozarks. "Now, tell me about yourself."

As Chuck looked from one man to the next, Nadine slipped her hand into his left hand under the table.

"I don't know where to start. I was born in Huntsville, Alabama. About four years ago my parents were killed when everything started going crazy. While I was babysitting my little sister Ellen, a policeman came to the door and told me that our parents were dead and said that we had to come with him. We were separated, and I haven't seen her since. I was put in with a group of boys, and we were herded into an auditorium. They called us one at a time and had us stand on the stage. A few minutes later, we were led away in small groups. My group was put in a large van, and we were transported to a barracks where we were outfitted with clothes and received haircuts. From there, we were sent to The Mountain where we lived in a boy's barracks."

Dix knew in his heart what he was going to hear before the the words came from the boy's mouth. "Did they put you in school or provide any education?"

"Sort of, they made sure we could read and write and do basic math. They also put us in the Youth Guard and taught us how to use weapons and let us hang out with the snipers."

Dix pointed to Chuck's weapons. "Are you proficient with those?"

"Yes, Sir, I'm proficient with them. I scored top in my group."

"Tell us some about your life back at The Mountain."

Chuck continued, "Well, they taught us a lot of things. We had to memorize passages from The Pontiff's scriptures. We were taught to act out scenes from the book and how to dance in celebration. He referred to us as his tea boys."

Dix could feel the hair rising on his neck as he anticipated the rest of Chuck's story.

"Continue."

"Every week or so we would have to go have tea with Pontiff Planter and Major Candice Olsen or sometimes other important men who also live in The Mountain. Sometimes, they were accompanied by women, and I know there were some girls they brought in as well. They would have us get into different costumes with different themes, and we would have to entertain them by singing and dancing and serving them tea and snacks. The adults would pass around a vessel that had a frothy pink liquid. We were told it was blood, milk and other things. They would let us join in eating and drinking, and some of the boys would get real silly after they drank the tea. I wouldn't touch the blood and milk or the tea. I just pretended to drink the stuff. Usually at that point, they would send some of us back to the barracks. After a while, the other boys would be brought back, and they would all feel bad and were really quiet for the next few days."

Dix hated to ask. "Did they ever try to make you drink the tea?"

"They tried once, but I realized what was taking place. When I refused, Major Olsen slapped me, and I threw a saucer at her but missed and hit Pontiff Planter in the head. They called the guards, and I was thrown in jail. I was sentenced to fifty lashes with a cane and thrown back in a jail cell until I escaped."

"How long were you in jail?"

"I'm not sure; I think it was almost three years."

"What did you do for three years?"

"I had to memorize Planter's book of scripture, pray five times a day and work on the labor gang."

Dix asked, "How many more people are on the labor gangs?"

"I only know of seven more besides me. There were four men and three girls that I would see from time to time. I think I was the only one that was put on every work detail. Pontiff Planter took great offense at my resisting their advances."

Dix shook his head in disgust. "I don't know what to say. I am speechless at what I'm learning. I knew there were rampant rumors that the People's Party leadership was involved in sex slaves, pedophilia and the Occult. Unfortunately, another conspiracy theory has turned out to be true. I know you've had a long time to think about this, but I want to point something out to you. I believe you and your sister were kidnapped. I don't have any idea if your parents and sister are still alive, but we have put together a common database to help families find one another. Have you heard about the plague?"

"I thought about being kidnapped, and I realized how stupid I was to just go with the police, especially when my aunt and uncle didn't come to get us. I had given the police their names and numbers, but that was the end of it. I heard the guards talking about the plague, but I heard very little. They were under strict orders to only talk to me when it pertained to my duties on the labor gang."

Jonas and Fox had sat silent the whole time. Obviously, they were fuming over what they had heard from Chuck. Dix proceeded to explain in detail what the plague had done and how few people were left in the world. Chuck listened and said, "What you're trying to tell me is that I have almost no chance of finding my family alive."

Dix almost had tears in his eyes. "That's what I'm trying to tell you, son. I also want you to know that you are not alone. You have a place with me and Fox if that's what you want."

Hester also spoke up, "There's room for you here as well."

Nadine grinned when Chuck looked over at her.

"Thanks, I wasn't sure what it was going to be like out here."

Jonas said, "It won't be easy, but after what you've been through, I think you'll survive."

Dix looked around the table and back at Chuck. "I originally came up here to find some of our missing people; I now know what happened to them and what is taking place in that Mountain."

Chuck interrupted, "You don't know the whole story. I'm pretty sure your people weren't just killed. Some were tortured to death for sport, and I know of several who were used for sacrifice. I think that was where they got a lot of the blood they are drinking at their meetings and religious ceremonies."

Dix sat silent for a moment because he had known most of the men who had come up. Several of them were men he liberated from the communist jails back home. These were men who physically carried him when he couldn't stand. He knew their families; he would be seeing the widows and orphans when he returned. The deep abiding hate that was always lurking just below the surface was back. Looking at Jonas, Fox, Hester and Kitty, he knew that they felt the same way.

Dix peered at Chuck. "How bad do you hate those men in The Mountain?"

Chuck's hands were clenched into fists. "I hate them with every fiber of my being. I started to try and kill them once I was out of my cell and equipped, but I knew that I could only do so much by myself. Besides, getting to Pontiff Planter would have been difficult, so I just ran like a coward."

Dix grinned. "I was almost killed a dozen times because I ran head first into battle, but since then I've learned to fight smart. There's no shame in sneaking out when you had the chance. In fact, if you are willing to help, we'll see if there's a way to help them meet the Deity they've been worshipping."

Chuck asked, "Can I join the New Constitution Army?"

Dix nodded. "Of course, son, but I want you to think about it before you do. When you join, you are in it for life. We receive no pay or uniforms, and you have a good chance of getting killed. You probably don't know much about the constitution that was written by the founders of the United States, but that is what we pledge to uphold."

"My dad taught me about the constitution when the People's Party pulled the old history books out of our school and took down all the statues in Washington."

"I'm glad; he gave you a great gift when he gave you knowledge about our once great country."

Chuck smiled. "Can I join or not?"

"Do you swear to uphold the original constitution and agree to be in the army for the rest of your life?"

"I do."

"Congratulations, Private Ward. Jonas, do you have another spare room?"

Jonas nodded. "Yes, I do. I have a basement suite with a warm bed."

Dix looked around at Chuck. "Private Ward, I hold the rank of Major; I'm the highest ranking officer here so that puts me in charge. Fox and Jonas are both Lieutenants so you will answer to them as well. We have two more officers who will be here in a day or two. Right now you are the low man on the totem pole so to speak. As soon as I can get a couple of us killed, we'll get you promoted."

Fox piped up, "He ain't kiddin kid. You've never seen so much fighting and killin that can take place around one man. I hope you can stand up to all the blood and guts you're going to be seeing."

Jonas broke out laughing. "Chuck, you're in for an adventure."

Nadine nodded in agreement. "Things can get pretty exciting around here sometimes."

Jonas asked Chuck, "Can I look at your weapons?"

Chuck handed him the MP5. Jonas pulled the slide back and realized that there wasn't a round in the chamber. "Your first order is to keep this weapon loaded and in battery at all times. You don't want to have to take the time to charge it if the shooting starts. The only time I want to see it unloaded is when you're cleaning it. The same thing goes for your pistol. I can outfit you with an M4 if you want something with more range."

"Thanks, I'll take you up on the offer. I never shot these more than about thirty steps from a target."

Fox pointed out. "I don't like to get that close to people I'm trying to kill. Also don't ever let them get the first shot and make sure you're aiming. Don't just blast away unless you're just keeping their heads down while someone is getting in position. There's no shame in shooting them in the back either."

Dix asked, "I know you've been all around the complex in The Mountain. Do you think you can help us with the layout and tell us where things like the sniper nests are located?"

"I'll try. I can draw you a map of a lot of it. Much of the complex is unlit except when they are actually in the area. The lights only stay on 24/7 on level three and a small part of level four. I slipped around in the dark, and I knew my way by counting my steps when I was on the labor gang. I located the store rooms for some outdoor companies. Once I got into the rooms, I turned on the lights after I closed the door. The individual rooms don't have video or alarms. Cameras point down the corridors, but the rooms don't have any. The guards spend most of their time and energy looking out, not looking in."

As they were sitting and talking, they heard footsteps on the stairs outside. Instinctively, they reached for their weapons. Fox assumed his position by the juke box. The door opened, and the light streamed in from the outside. The men almost fainted when they walked in and realized that four rifles were pointed at them.

The one in the lead raised his hands. "Don't shoot, fellers. It's just us."

Jonas recognized them as the men who had helped drag out Luke and his boys from the night before. Jonas lowered his rifle.

"It's ok. They're friends; sorry we're still a little jumpy."

"We just came to carry Luke and his boys back home."

Jonas pointed toward his cabin. "We're going to head that way in a few minutes. When you get there drive around back, and I'll load y'all up with a barrel of food for their families. Just back up to the big barn door."

He stood up and walked over to the bar where Kitty was sitting on a stool.

"You need to go get some rest; in the meantime, I need you to do me a favor."

"I'll do anything for you."

"Is Nadine starting as one of your working girls?"

"Hester would kill her before she'd let that happen."

"Good, I think Chuck likes her, and I don't want him worrying about this girl. After what's he been through, he has had a hard enough time. He's got a lot on him right now, and he's had to digest a lot of information today. A cute little girlfriend will help keep him grounded."

"No problem, I think Nadine likes him too besides he's the only young bachelor round here."

Dix looked over at Fox. "You ready to hop back on the icicle with us and head back?"

Fox frowned and reached in his pocket and put on his gloves.

"Let's get it over with."

Jonas motioned for the men. "Give us about a fifteen minute head start. Your trucks will run faster than my ATV."

The trip was cold, but fortunately, it didn't take very long. The men from the bar driving two trucks and carrying the dead arrived right behind them. Jonas hooked the ATV to the charger in the barn and opened the big door. He took a large plastic barrel with a screw on plastic lid and filled it with rice, beans, salt, pepper, sugar and various can goods as well as other items until it was packed full. They rolled the barrel into the empty truck.

Jonas told them, "That should feed them for a couple of months. Don't tell them I gave it to you. Let me know if I need to send more."

Dix and Fox went into the cabin, but Jonas stayed outside and watched as the men drove out of sight down the valley road. Even though the dead were bad guys, he knew it wouldn't be easy delivering the bodies and news to the families that remained.

CHAPTER 18

The noise of the pot falling off the stove had Porter and Morgan on their feet with pistols pointed into the darkness toward the noise.

Morgan whispered, "Ready for the light?"

"Hit it."

The beam from the Q Beam hit the rear doors and windows like a torch. A large raccoon that had overturned the pot quickly ran from sight. Porter sat back on his bunk.

"I jumped up so fast I think I busted a stitch."

Morgan laughed. "Don't worry; I've got plenty of needles and thread. Anyway, we probably need to yank those stitches in your leg when it gets light enough to see in the morning. You stay put. I'll dump out the rest of that pork. I don't want to eat after a raccoon, unless you want to."

"No, that'll teach us to put away our food instead of being lazy."

Morgan slipped his pistol back into the shoulder holster.

"Thank God, we didn't shoot up the gas generator. If one of us gets up to go to the bathroom we need to turn on one of the floor lights so we won't shoot each other."

Porter nodded in agreement. "I have to admit I've been jumpy after what we've gone through on this mission."

He glanced at his watch, the illuminated dial showed 4:00 am. He thought about his dad's watch that he had worn after his parents were killed. It was back at the ranch in his desk drawer; its battery long dead. This watch was a Rolex with a self winding mechanism. He looked up from the watch.

"Morgan, after all that, I'm awake; let's eat and get this show on the road."

"I agree; I'll get the stove cooking."

They were underway before the sunrise. Since they were in the mountains, they traveled in darkness through the valleys but climbed into the light as soon as the road meandered up and over the ridges. To their amazement, the road was clear. Apparently, the locals were keeping it open. In some places it was only one lane, but since they were the only traffic, they encountered no problems. Suddenly, they came upon an old wooden building with a long porch on the front.

Prior to the crash the structure had apparently been an antique store or flea market because an abundance of old and decaying items were scattered about the yard. The chimney located in the middle of the roof had a column of smoke pouring from it.

A middle aged woman came to the front steps and called out, "Stop and sit a spell. We don't get much company."

Porter looked at Morgan. "What do you say we visit for a minute and see if we can get any information? We are not far from Eureka Springs, and our first waypoint." Porter rolled down his window on the passenger side.

"Howdy, Mam. How are you doing?"

"Oh I get by. What brings you boys up here in that contraption?"

"We're with the New Constitution Army. I'm Porter Jones, and this is Hunter Morgan. We're on a scouting mission to locate some of our people up this way. We report back daily our position and findings. If for some reason we don't report, several squads will show up looking for us."

She grinned. "Hop on down, boys, and I'll let you meet my man."

Porter and Morgan checked their weapons, slung the rifles on their backs and backed down the ladder. They climbed the front steps and followed her to the door. The rusty old screen door's spring sung out a screech as she pulled it open. There is no other sound like that of an old screen door spring. The screen had patches stitched on it from years of use. The house had the smell of old wood smoke, and the wood floors creaked with their steps. She led them into the old parlor that was still cluttered from its days as an antique store; however, many of the old items were finding new life. An older man was sitting in a chair. His crutches were lying within arm's reach of his chair. His leg was amputated just below the knee.

He said, "C'mon in, boys. My name's Gord Holmes, and this is my wife Nellie. We don't get much company. Where you boys traveling from?"

Morgan walked over and shook his hand. "My name's Morgan, and this is Porter. We're officers in the New Constitution Army."

Gord grinned. "We heard what happened down in Strong. We've been expecting to see you guys starting to come through here. How many more guys do you have coming behind you?"

"They don't tell us that. Our mission is a focused one. If they need us to wait or meet up with other squads, they'll let us know."

Porter, who had been silent, realized that they were being picked for information, so he changed the subject.

"Mr. Gord, what happened to your leg?"

"I lost it in a battle with some of the People's Party who came through several years ago. A group consisting of myself, my brothers and some neighbors had to confront them. They kept coming by and confiscating our food and supplies. They made one run too many."

Porter glanced at Morgan. "We've run across a few of them ourselves.
A lot of them had government jobs prior to the collapse; now most of them have a sense of entitlement. How bad did the plague get up here?"

"It got bad until we just isolated ourselves. All of us in the area stopped it by halting all traffic and having absolutely no contact with anyone outside our own households. We maintained the quarantine for ninety days. After that we had contact only with the people in our community for another year."

Morgan warmed his hands by the fire.

"That was smart of you. I've seen people suffering from it, and that's not something you want to catch or see firsthand."

Nellie asked, "Boys, we haven't had any coffee in years, but can I fix you some dandelion or sassafras tea?"

Morgan smiled. "Thanks for the offer Mam, but Porter and me need to get back on the road."

Gord said, "If you see Major Dix Jernigan, tell him old Gord says, 'hey.'"

Porter looked surprised. "How did you come to know the Major?"

"I was a scout up here for the Constitution Army before I got myself crippled. I'm a Captain under Colonel Miller; I've spoken to the Major several times giving him updates when I was in the field."

"Do you have a radio up and going?"

"Sure, you'll want to verify with the Colonel or Captain Jones that I am who I say I am."

"I hope you don't mind, sir."

"Not at all; Nellie, get that radio uncovered and hook up the battery."

Nellie crossed the room. Hidden among the clutter was what appeared to be an old Singer Sewing Machine.

She pulled off the cover and revealed one of the military radios. When she clipped the little alligator clip to the positive post on the battery, the radio came alive.

The frequency was already set so all Morgan did was key the mic. "This is Morgan. Captain Jones, do you have the radio on?"

Cooney Jones came on. "What's up, Morgan? Any problems? Y'all usually only call at night."

Porter took the mic. "No problems, grandpa. We are up here at the home of Gord and Nellie Holmes. I just wanted to verify who they are."

Cooney came back on. "Put that one legged old coot on."

Porter handed him the mic. "What do you want me to do with these two deserters?"

"Don't shoot'em. I want to do that myself if they get back. You can give them all the information they need; they're meeting up with the Major and a couple of other men."

"I assume they are going to that Mountain fortress near the state border?"

"How did you find out?"

"There aren't a lot of us left, but we stay in touch. I know the Major has been doing a little house cleaning up here. That Mountain is the only place nobody comes back from. We figured something was going on up there. He's going to have his hands full in that Mountain if all the rumors are true. They've been poking their heads out of The Mountain in the last few months. We just beg them for food when they show up. We haven't had to kill any of them as of yet."

"Gord, try to keep that other leg, and don't let Nellie work you too hard. Is there anything that you need?"

"If you can find me a wooden leg, I would appreciate it. We are in good shape for food and equipment, but some coffee and tobacco would come in handy if you can send me some. Here's Porter."

Porter took the mic. "We're going to get back on the road. We'll be making the turn to the East soon, and then we'll work our way across to the valley where we'll be meeting the Major."

"Be careful, son. Gord will let you know if you need to lookout for anything."

"We'll watch ourselves. Porter out."

Gord sat grinning in his chair. "You boys are good; I couldn't squeeze any information out of you. I figure you are going to meet up with the Major in the valley where Bill's Bar is located."

"That's correct, Sir. We are going to radio him once we reach the bar."

"You shouldn't have any trouble unless you have a weakness for the ladies."

Morgan and Porter looked at each other and grinned.

Morgan said, "Let me answer that. Our weakness for the ladies has already crippled both of us."

Nellie grinned. "That's what I figured; there are some working girls over there so hang on to your valuables."

Porter cocked his eyebrow. "We're pretty much broke. All we have are our weapons and gear, and besides the Major will be keeping us pretty busy as he usually does. What can you tell us about The Mountain?"

"People who venture up there disappear. Nellie, bring me the map."

Nellie brought out a state map and handed it to Gord. He unfolded it and motioned for them to look.

"I want to show you these points around The Mountain."

They watched as he pointed out a highlighted line around The Mountain.

"If you venture past this line, you'll probably disappear."

"Well, I'm certain the Major will have us inside that line pronto. If we don't see you again, I'm glad I got to know you. If we find some coffee and tobacco, we'll drop if off if we come back through."

Nellie took them by their arms and walked them to the door.

"You boys, be careful. We can't afford to lose any more good men."

Morgan and Porter climbed into the Duk. As they pulled away, Nellie and Gord waved from the porch. Morgan steered the Duk down the road and up and over the next mountain pass.

"I don't know about you, but I don't like the sound of what I'm hearing about that Mountain."

Porter had his pants off and was looking at the stitches in his leg. "The Chinese down in Galveston Bay looked formidable as well; they are all now a bunch of skeletons lying around."

"Yeah, but we had a secret weapon they didn't know about."

"I'm sure the Major has a plan, or there would be more than just the two of us coming up. He always points out that we don't fight fair. When you get tired, pull over so we can yank these stitches. These things are really bothering me."

"I've been tired since about an hour after that raccoon got us up."

Morgan pulled to the side of the road, and removed Porter's stitches in a few minutes. Porter's scalp wound looked better so they left it open to air out and just added some more antibiotic cream to it. Morgan wiped his hands on his pants.

"Pull up your shirt; I want to get a look at those ribs."

Porter pulled up his shirt.

"They aren't hurting as badly, and they don't click anymore when I breathe."

"You may have dodged a bullet and only cracked them. I kind of like the way the purple fades into green and yellow. You are naturally camouflaged now; that might come in handy."

Porter pulled the shirt back down.

"Let me know if I can help you with your camouflage."

"Thanks, pal."

They roared with laughter. When they were back on the road, Morgan looked in the rearview mirror at Porter.

"Check that map. We don't want to miss our cut off."

"I don't think we can miss it. According to my notes, its right past a rock slide that almost covers the road."

"We've passed three in the last two days; I hope it's a little more detailed than that."

"The road we are looking for is Lazarus Road which will take us down some winding roads and over what looks like three ridges. I think we need to put the chains on the tires. I'm sure we'll be getting into some ice."

They stopped and laid the chains out in front of the wheels where they could drive over them. Morgan cranked the Duk and pulled forward on top of the chains. Once they had them centered, all they had to do was wrap the chains from both ends and clamp them tight. The chains on the tires made a terrible racket as they dug through the snow on the road and hit the pavement beneath. Morgan drove the Duk down the winding road. As they were descending, the Duk slipped once and touched a guardrail on a curve. The chains bit when Morgan put the Duk in reverse and backed away from the guardrail.

Porter said, "Let's take it extra slow going down these roads."

Morgan put the Duk transfer case into low range and pulled the transmission down into low gear.

"We are in tractor mode; we'll keep it dead slow until we get out of these mountains. This was designed to operate on unimproved roads and swamps; not on ice covered mountains. This is kind of like Hannibal bringing his war elephants through the mountains."

Porter leaned his hands on the dash in front of his chair as they went downhill.

"We won't be getting out of these mountains today. When we stop tonight, we'll radio the Major and tell him that we won't be arriving until tomorrow."

They made it around three more turns before coming to a long downhill straightaway. The road was completely covered with ice and snow to the point that the shoulder was invisible. Morgan aimed the Duk down the center.

"We either go for it, or wait to spring."

Porter swallowed. "Go ahead; we'll just pretend we are on a ski slalom."

About a hundred yards down the slope the Duk lost all traction. Morgan tried to keep it centered.

"Hold on."

CHAPTER 19

The fog from Jonas' breath lingered a moment before it dissipated in the cold mountain air. He shivered as the sound of the trucks grew quieter and finally faded away. Jonas turned and went into the warm room. Dix was back in the chair, and Chuck and Fox were still warming themselves by the wood stove. Fox pointed to the stove.

"I hope you don't mind that I put on some more coffee."

Jonas went over to the fireplace and punched up the few remaining coals from under the ashes and added some kindling before stacking on some bigger logs.

"Make yourself at home. Chuck, that door under the stairs goes down into the basement. At the bottom of the stairs to the right is a bedroom; there's no heat, but there's plenty of cover for the bed. The only rooms heated in this house are the living room and kitchen. The bathroom you can use is up here and down the hall. Do you have any more clothes other than what you're wearing?"

"Yes, Sir, I have another full set in my backpack as well as extra socks and underwear. I also have a shaving kit."

"Good for you. Did you bring Planter's book of scriptures with you?"

Chuck grinned. "I sure did; it comes in handy for toilet paper."

Everyone burst out laughing. Dix wiped his eyes with his handkerchief.

"I needed that laugh. Jonas, pull out those blueprints and show them to Chuck. Let's see if he can help us understand the layout a little better. I know you know a lot about it, but maybe he can tell us about some of the places you haven't been able to explore. I'd like to have a good understanding of the complex by the time Porter and Morgan arrive."

Jonas cleared off the kitchen bar and rolled out the blueprints. The blueprints were laid out with one page per level. The bottom four levels also had more detailed pages beneath them as they were too large to illustrate with just the one page. This set of blueprints were not fully detailed but gave the dimensions and distances of all the corridors, the locations of the vents, passageways and elevators. Chuck took a moment to orientate to the drawing.

He said, "Let's start with level three. That's where I became accustomed to traveling to and from."

He pointed to the chamber where the prison cells were located.

"The prison cells were added to this corner when the People's Party moved in. My cell was approximately here, and this is the wall I dug through. I wound up in this chamber where I was able to access the entire facility. This chamber had all the spare uniforms, armory and gear. I simply put on a uniform, complete with boots, belts and cap. All I had to do was keep my head down and avoid everyone. Since it was night, I never saw anyone. If someone had been looking at a monitor, all they would have seen was one of their own people walking down the corridor. I counted my steps down to the chamber where the outdoor and sporting goods chain had their inventory warehoused. I went in, flipped on the light and outfitted myself. Their firearms inventory was housed in a locked cage. I simply took one of their multi tools and cut through the wire on the cage. The MP5 is almost identical to the ones the troops carry. It is semi-automatic where theirs are all automatic. I completely outfitted myself with everything I thought I needed or could use. Then I walked down to the elevator, went up to level five and got out into the darkness."

Jonas flipped the pages as Chuck showed him the path that he took.

"Once I had all my stuff put away and had put on my new clothes, I ditched the uniform, killed the lights and went back down the corridor to the service door next to the elevator. There's a ladder in the service area alongside each elevator that runs from top to bottom. Several of the air shafts are located in the elevator shaft so that the air pressure can be equalized as the elevators move up and down. The air shaft I was looking for comes out just above level five and runs on a forty-five degree angle to the outside. I was sent in once to clean it out. Some squirrels had managed to get in and made a nest, and all the debris from it kept getting into the elevator shaft. I tied the cap back on from the inside so I knew how to get out. The shaft is just big enough for a man to crawl through. I knew there was a sniper platform just above it, because they lowered some water down to me when I was working on it. It was just a matter of being quiet and waiting for the Morning Prayers."

Dix looked at Jonas.

"Jonas, show us where you enter the facility."

Jonas flipped the drawings back to level four, pointed to a chamber on one side and pulled out a map of surrounding countryside.

"You will notice the electrical panels and boxes are located in the chamber. They are not up against the wall because the ceiling slopes a little and that leaves a space large enough for a man to walk behind it. About ten feet into that dark space is a door. If you go through that door you will be in a natural cavern. The door is locked and barricaded from the cave side, and in order to go through it someone would have to reroute all the electrical conduits, connections and electrical boxes and bring in some equipment. If they happen to get through, the resulting explosion would collapse the cave and probably the electrical room with it."

He pointed to the map.

"You will see that on the eastern side of the mountain there is a ridge than runs down above the valley. That valley is on the other side of the range where this cabin sits. About two thirds of the way down, you'll see a huge pine with the top third missing. If you use that as your mark, all you have to do is follow the trail behind it about fifty feet to the entrance. I have it covered with dead limbs."

He pulled out a map of the cave.

"Either memorize or copy this map of the cave. You'll need to carry flashlights or a lantern and follow the rope. You'll need to use the map to locate the booby traps I set up and know how to disarm them. I'm sure you and Fox remember what happened to Trooper Edwards."

Dix scrutinized the map.

"How did you to get around in there without being discovered?"

"I did the same thing that Chuck did. I managed to obtain a uniform from one of the men that I had the good fortune of interrogating back in my lair. He didn't need it any longer. I keep it stashed back in the cavern behind the switch panels."

Fox cocked an eyebrow.

"It's one thing to walk down a corridor, and yet another to haul stuff up and down the corridor. How did you manage to do it?"

"I studied the blueprints so I basically knew the layout of the fourth floor and the third floor. I knew they had a control room on the fourth floor not far from where I was going to enter. I also figured that they would have a break area with a coffee pot. So I slipped in and located everything. The break area was just around the corner from the control room. The control room had a small conference table and against the wall were the computers and monitors. Only four of the monitors were on, and the images would cycle from one camera to the next. Most of the cameras were dark as the caverns were not being occupied. There were two troopers on duty in the room playing cards and not paying any attention to the monitors. I went back to my secret entrance and left The Mountain. I returned the next week with a bottle of Benadryl. I slipped in the same way and stopped in the coffee room, dumped a handful in the coffee and swirled it around until it was dissolved. I went back to my secret entrance and took a nap. Three hours later, I slipped back in; it was 4:00 am. I peeked around the corner, and they were leaned back in their chairs and were snoring. I made a quick run through the fourth level, located the various rooms and got some idea of their contents. I located the pharmacy supply and loaded up on a treasure trove of narcotics. With what I found, I could keep the coffee pot spiked forever. I carried the narcotics back into the cave for future use. Over the next year, I would slip in once every two weeks, and I gradually explored a big part of the facility. Sometimes I would get a guard that didn't drink coffee, but more often than not, they went right to sleep. I looked at the shift schedule posted on the wall. They have three shift changes: seven am, three pm and eleven pm. I didn't spend any time on the third level because that was the one where there was always activity. Besides, there was so much to steal in the rest of the facility; it was pointless. I could steal a lot of stuff in three or four hours. I'd stow it all in the area where my uncle and his buddies smoked their dope. There are still lawn chairs and tables where they used to kick back and relax. I'd then spend the next couple of weeks packing the stuff out and over the mountain where I could bring it here and store it. I've made a pretty good living trading what I stole for odds and ends."

Dix pointed out. "You have probably helped more people than you traded with. Other than some fresh meat and vegetables, I don't see where you needed to trade for anything."

"I guess my secret is out. I tried to do what I could for the few people who were left."

"That's the reason I want to take that facility without destroying it or its contents. Imagine what just the medical supplies alone could do for people?"

Dix looked around at Chuck.

"Are there any doctors and nurses in there?"

"Yes, they have a full medical clinic with three doctors, several nurses and a small completely equipped hospital. Some of the rich big wigs had all that installed before the collapse."

Dix turned to the page showing level three.

"Can you show me how the barracks are laid out, and where the apartments and private quarters are located?"

Chuck pointed at the various chambers.

"The barracks are situated down the north side of the level. It's broken up into semiprivate modules, but every twelve modules share a common bath and shower area."

Jonas studied the drawings.

"Are there separate barracks for the men and women?"

"No, Sir, Pontiff Planter says there is absolutely no difference between men and women."

Fox piped up, "I can tell you one thing: Pontiff has never laid eyes on Dix's wife Rachael or my wife Becky."

Dix raised his eyebrows.

"No truer words have ever been spoken."

Jonas pointed at the drawing.

"This section down the east side, middle and south side must be the apartments and officer's quarters."

Chuck looked where he was pointing.

"Yes, the units on the east side are for single officers, the larger ones are for the officers who have partners and the big ones are for the invited big shots."

Dix noted the large elevators.

"Are there access ladders alongside all the elevators?"

"Yes, you can go from the top to the bottom by ladder if your legs hold out."

"Show me the one where The Pontiff lives."

Chuck took a moment and pointed. "The Pontiff lives in the one down here on the end. He has the biggest because he has a large ceremonial room where only he and a very select few have their most secret ceremonies. It's there that he always reveals his latest prophecy."

"How do you know about all this?"

"The guards talk, and I've been on the labor detail cleaning up the place. Evil rituals take place in there. It's a bloody mess when they conduct their sacrifices."

Fox spoke up, "I'm afraid to ask what is being sacrificed."

"Mostly animals, but about once a month they conduct a human sacrifice. There's a large flock of goats maintained down on level one. The human sacrifices are usually prisoners or captives. Four or five of your men died in there. I was forced to help clean up what remained."

Dix looked around at the others who all had a sick look on their faces.

"I guess we all know the reason we have to clean this mess up. I'm almost inclined to blow the entire Mountain at this point."

Jonas took a deep breath.

"I had no idea; I knew they would shoot and kill people just like when they tried to kill you and Fox. I didn't interfere because everyone knew better than to go up there. We gave a warning to anybody we ever saw."

Jonas looked at the plans.

"Looking at this from a tactical standpoint, I think that, other than the snipers and perimeter guards, everyone we need to kill spends every night on level three. We ought to think in terms of trying to isolate that area. Disabling the elevators would be easy. We could even take out a section of the ladders so they couldn't climb up or down. If we had the time to set charges, we could collapse the roadway going through there as well. Chuck, are all those caverns with the barracks and apartments behind doors?"

"Yes. They have regular doors, but they have steel doors that can be closed and locked to cover those doors. Rather than do away with the large industrial steel doors, they simply left them open and installed the nicer residential doors inside the openings."

Jonas grinned and said, "If we can close and lock down those steel doors, they wouldn't be getting out quickly. If I remember correctly, the hinges are on the outside of the doors. Chuck, how are the people armed in the facility? I know the troops on the outside are all armed to the teeth."

"Only the guards are allowed to be armed inside the facility. I think some of the officers are armed, but none of the troops or civilians."

Jonas asked, "How many guards would you estimate are on duty?"

"I'm not sure, but if you add the ones on the outside, probably twenty-five at any one time. They probably have half that many on the late shift."

Dix looked over the plans and questioned, "Where is the armory located?"

Chuck pointed.

"In the center of level three is the great auditorium, hospital, cafeteria and various shops and things like the barber shop and dentist's office. You will find some bars, spas and a number of bath houses. Here, in the area at the rear of the room I broke into, is the armory. The men who are going outside check out their weapons and return them upon their return. I'm pretty sure Major Olsen is armed, and I'd bet that Planter has a weapon stashed somewhere as well."

Dix smiled and replied, "That simplifies matters a lot. Several men with suppressed pistols could easily shut that place down, especially if we can isolate the armory and get most of the steel doors locked and closed. The problem I see is that it's like a rat warren in there. If things don't go exactly as planned, an assault would go to hell fast. The five of us could pull it off if everything went as planned, but y'all know as well as I that as soon as the bullets start to fly the best planning is over."

Fox pointed out, "Several thousand people aren't all going to be fast asleep in their little beds. Some are going to be awake; others will be heading to the cafeteria at all hours. I bet they have some sort of food service twenty four hours a day, not to mention all the sneaking around that's taking place for late night rendezvous. I don't like it, maybe if we had twenty of us, we could pull it off."

Chuck interrupted, "Can I be part of the assault?"

Dix clapped him on the shoulder.

"You're already part of the assault by just being here and helping us devise the plan. How many men have you killed Chuck?"

Chuck stammered, "I, I've never killed anyone."

"You don't need to be embarrassed. Each of us have killed hundreds of men. Fox and I have killed many hundreds. I'm not proud of that fact, but four years ago I had no choice, and I haven't looked back. Even if you never pull a trigger, you will be just as responsible as any of us here for the inevitable deaths that are going to take place in that Mountain. Everyone has their strengths. Morgan knows gadgets and how to make booby-traps. He understands electronics, and yes, he has killed and helped killed many hundreds. Porter's skill is that he doesn't miss and doesn't have a moment's hesitation when it comes to taking action. Porter is the one who goes in first, and unless someone shoots him in the back, they're dead. I won't send Morgan in first because that's not his strength. Your strength at this moment is your detailed knowledge of the facility and the people inside. Your knowledge makes this assault possible and will probably keep some of us alive. You'll get your chance to pull the trigger, but not until I tell you or you have no choice. At this moment your weapon is what's between your ears." Fox interrupted, "Chuck, believe me when I tell you this. You will be in the thick of it. Shooting someone is unavoidable if you hang out with the Major. If he goes out for popcorn, look for the blood on it before you try to eat it."

Dix just shook his head at Fox and said, "It's not quite that bad. Chuck, do you have any friends in there?"

"My only friends are the people that were with me on the work details. They'll be easy to find because they'll be in the other prison cells if they're still alive."

"I'll try not to get them hurt, but it may be unavoidable. Are there any children in the facility?"

"Some of the civilians have children and grandchildren, but they'll all be in the apartments. We won't find many because a group fearing for their safety left one night with their kids. The guards they bribed to get out ended up in the cell next to mine. They were both bled for weeks and were finally sacrificed."

Chuck rolled up his shirt sleeve and showed them the needle scars in the crook of his elbow.

"They bled me once a month; I was told I have good veins. Pontiff Planter received transfusions from me and several of my teenage fellow prisoners. I think it was for his health, and they usually drank pure blood as part of their rituals."

Jonas opened the drawer on his credenza.

"I could use a drink. This gets more bizarre by the minute. I know what the other men drink. Have you ever had a shot of bourbon, Chuck?"

"My Dad kept a bottle in his pickup truck, and I stole a sip once."

"Well, how did you like it?"

"I didn't, but I'll take a shot of yours. I believe that I'm going to be doing a lot of things that I'm not accustomed to."

Fox lamented, "You got that right, boy; you've got that right."

Jonas poured four double shots.

"Here's to putting Pontiff Planter's head on the end of a pike."

CHAPTER 20

Pontiff Planter took a long draw from the stem of his hookah. The rich smoke could be felt all the way up into his sinus cavities, and the rush made the ends of his fingers and toes go numb. A moment later, a sensation of tingling started on his ear lobes and then moved to the hairs on his head. He turned to the pages of his text and recited the words from a long dead language that he had been attempting to interpret. Another draw from the pipe helped him focus on what the god of his scripture was attempting to say to him. The red brown mixture in the liquid of his hookah made strange pink bubbles as the smoke from the mixture in the pipe bowl bubbled through it. His physician waited patiently on the side lines to make sure that The Pontiff was not overwhelmed.

He turned to the man that was tied to a massive stone table in the middle of the room. The altar which dominated the room was a thick granite slab that had veins of what appeared to be gold running through it; thereby, giving it an otherworldly appearance. This room was a rock grotto that was cut into the side of The Mountain. At one time, it was used for records storage.

The room was lit by hundreds of candles. Their soot trail led to a vent that had been cut into the rock of the grotto. This allowed the smoke to exit the room. The floor was stained a deep burgundy around the granite slab. Brass loops were located on the four corners where affixed chains secured the naked man who laid spread eagle on his back. Behind the massive altar, stood the face of Gya who looked down in silence. The stone carving had come from a photo of the original that was taken before the idol was destroyed by Islamists deep in the Afghanistan Mountains. Its goat shaped head was adorned with horns covered in gold leaf. The Pontiff chose to remove the passages concerning the forbidding of images before incorporating it into the good book.

The Pontiff, staring at the soon to be sacrificed man, thought that he appeared to fade away and return. He turned to his costumed guards.

"Call in my Apostles and Pastors; the ceremony is ready to begin."

The visions were coming fast as his faithful surrounded him.

He called to the guards, "Leave us until the sacrifice is silent."

Sitting on the altar chair, he watched as his clergy each smoked from hookahs reserved for them. They started to rhythmically chant in time with the beat of drums carried by several of the faithful. Their hookahs did not have the same mixture as that of The Pontiff, because the visions could only be seen and interpreted by the one and only spiritual leader. He started praying out loud and referring to his scriptures as his faithful surrounded the granite slab.

Major Olsen walked down to The Pontiff's apartment, but stopped short of entering. She could hear the muffled screams of the man being sacrificed, and in her mind, she could envision the naked, blood covered bodies of the Apostles writhing and undulating on and over the dying man. The light from the candles would throw dancing shadows over the room as The Pontiff, reciting passages from his book, would enter into a deep trance. Soon, the faithful would collapse from the effects of the concoction they were smoking and the exhaustion that came from the physical exertions. She could visualize, as she had witnessed before, the sacrifice lying in a pool of blood, urine and semen. She remembered being mesmerized by the blood dripping from the nipples of the women participants. Afterwards, The Pontiff would be gently led away to his pool where the guards would clean him up, dress him and put him to bed. The Pontiff's four wives would dutifully standby should he need anything before he awoke in the morning. Tomorrow, the prisoners would get to clean up the mess and haul out the pieces. She turned and walked down to her apartment. Tomorrow would be a very busy day. The Pontiff would be full of information from all his visions. If she were lucky, he might even call out the tea boys. She dismissed the guard who had been doing double duty as punishment. She went in her apartment, drew a bath and while the tub filled, shaved her heavy beard. For a few minutes she had forgotten that she was now a woman; she thought *these things take time even for me.*

The next morning, just as she expected, The Pontiff summoned her to his office. When she came in, The Pontiff was excited to see her.

"Olsen, have a seat. I can't wait to tell you what was revealed. I saw great cities with golden streets springing from the ruins. Our new world is going to be fabulous!"

"I'm so happy to hear the news. Was there anything else?"

The Pontiff looked down at his notes.

"I had to write it all down. We are not going to wait to see if the plague is taking hold. We still have hazmat trained troops outside in quarantine. I want you to pull out two additional twelve man squads and make sure they are hazmat trained. Set up a camp some distance away so we can supply them without taking the chance of contamination. Gya told me that we should immediately expand our perimeter as we have discussed before. I think two hazmat squads should have no trouble cleaning out the valley, and I want one of the three teams heading down toward Eureka Springs as well. Once we clean out the area, we can move north. By then we should know if the plague is actually back or not. For all we know, Captain Carter could have been wrong."

"I already have six squads trained for just such an emergency. I can have them in the field this afternoon. I'll have my officers gathered in the conference area in a couple of hours. Will you want to address them?"

"No, that won't be necessary. I've got to get all my notes consolidated for the prophecy chapters I'll be adding to the good book."

"Very good, Sir. I'll keep you apprised of our progress."

The Pontiff was so engrossed in his work that he didn't notice that Olsen had left the room.

Olsen went to her office and summoned her aide.

"Summon the senior officers for a meeting at 11:00 am in the conference center. I'll prepare the agenda and email it to you for printing."

"Yes, Mam, is there anything else?"

"No, I'll call you if I need anything in the meantime. Oh, on second thought, send someone to bring me some coffee and some sort of pastry."

"Yes, Mam." The aide saluted and left.

Olsen walked over to the map and contemplated how they could systematically sweep the area so that no one was missed. She had a nagging feeling in her gut that it had been a mistake to have taken out the New Constitution Army squads. Surely, they would send someone to investigate. Two men were missed by the snipers, and she had to assume that these two men had the skills to kill a dozen of her best men. She also had to assume that they had had an opportunity to interrogate Edwards. The Pontiff may not have an understanding of what they could face. He seemed to believe that Gya would intercede as needed.

Olsen walked over to her desk and thumbed through the most recently issued copy of the Gya good book. She realized that The Pontiff was a psychopath. Yet, eighty percent of the troops were true Gya believers and Pontiff followers. She watched as the officers and men in her command actually had study groups where they discussed the good book. She had observed as they composed hymns and how some of them actually cried during the daily prayers. The Pontiff supplied them the communist dream of caring for their needs and the spiritual comfort of having a deity. Because most of these people had been living on the fringe of society, they felt right at home with the people who had been brought together under this command.

Olsen opened her laptop and pulled up her list of carefully chosen officers. These officers had handpicked the non-commissioned under them, and those people had in turn chosen their squads and squad leaders from their commands. Men and women who had families were not chosen. She was surprised that some of the men and women in The Mountain had paired up anyway. They had to have children in order to maintain the People's Party and the Gyan religion, but she was surprised at the large number of the people forming opposite sex couples. They had tried to dissuade the troops from forming family units because they wanted them to think of the community as their chosen family. Children would be raised by the community as a whole. The concept of mother and father had been eliminated, and use of the terms had been omitted from the good book. When the trooper arrived with her coffee and snacks, she completed the agenda and sent it to her aide for the meeting.

She finished her coffee and went down to the conference room. Her officers were already filing into the room. She could readily determine the faithful. The male officers present had beards with the mustache area clean shaven, and the female officers had head scarves that only revealed their faces. Of the twenty people in the conference room, only two people did not have the beards and headdress of the faithful. Olsen waited until everyone was seated. She looked around the room and asked one of the men to lead the group in prayer. The prayer went on for about five minutes, and she made a mental note to herself not to ask him to pray at any future meetings unless The Pontiff was present.

She looked around the room.

"Pontiff Planter has received a revelation from our Lord Gya for us to send out hazmat teams to eradicate the existing population of people living within twenty-five miles of this facility. As you know, they are all infidels and may be plague infected. We will be putting them out of their misery. If you will look on your agenda, I have assigned the officers who will lead the three squads. Squads B and C will join Squad A that is already set up outside of the facility. Squads A and B will travel down the valley shown on the map and systematically sweep every roadway and driveway that has evidence of human activity. Resistance should be minimal. Simply go in, kill them and leave them where they lay. If you find any evidence of the plague, you're to report it immediately. Squad C will head toward Eureka Springs. Again you should find little or no resistance. All female officers, non-comm and troops will refrain from wearing the full headscarves that cover your ears. I understand that it is cold, and you will need to cover your ears, but realize this also impairs your hearing. So until further notice, traditional religious headgear will be limited to when you are off duty."

Olsen turned to the second page.

"Troop C and D will set up the camp outside of the facility in the former parking area just south of the main entrance. This will be the home of troops A, B and C for forty-five days after this operation is over. I want troops A, B and C prepared to stay in the field. You will be resupplied as needed. I want support vehicles traveling with the troops as they sweep the valley. This is a full offensive operation. You may meet resistance, but these people are basically civilians with hunting rifles; however, they should be no match for our troops. I want the squads to head out in two hours. As you know, we have vehicles already provisioned for just such an expedition. I want your temporary quarters set up in the parking lot before dark. In the name of Gya, good hunting. Meeting dismissed."

They all shouted, "Gya is great."

CHAPTER 21

Bob Cartwright was at his workbench cleaning his favorite shotgun when his six year old girl came running in.

"Daddy, there are strangers coming down the road."

"Where are your mother and brother?"

"They're watching from the wheel house."

He pointed to the hutch in the corner.

"Get in the hole while I see what's going on."

Without hesitation the little girl tugged on the hutch, and it pivoted out of the way revealing a passageway into the stone foundation of the building. In three steps, she was inside, and the hutch closed behind her. When Bob started up the stairs to the wheel house, he met his wife and son coming down fast.

"There are at least twenty Pine Tree Mountain troops, and they are fully armed with backpacks."

"Let's get in the hole. We can't fight that many."

In less than thirty seconds, they were in the hole with the hutch closed. A half inch thick steel plate rolled over the opening from behind. The steel plate was set in a groove cut into the rock floor and slid into a corresponding groove in a rock boulder to the left of the door. A heavy steel bar wedged on the opposite side would keep it from ever being opened should someone happen to discover the hole behind the hutch. Once inside, the passage led downhill through the foundation of the old water mill. When they first came to occupy the site, the Cartwrights blasted into the rock face that formed one side of the passage and created an alcove where they kept emergency provisions, including an emergency radio. He opened up the water tight ammo box that housed it and connected the antenna wires that led to his big antenna on top of the building. This was not the first time the family had retreated to their bolt hole. Everyone knew to be quiet. He was wearing his sidearm as was his wife Lucy and his twelve year old son Mike. He flipped open another case and pulled out an assault shotgun for himself and a couple of AR-15's for Lucy and Mike. They were well trained in their operation. Once they were armed, he turned on the radio and called down to Bill's Bar.

"I hope y'all are listening."

The radio crackled in the bar and at Jonas's cabin. Jonas looked at Dix.

"That's Bob Cartwright; he wouldn't be on the radio if it wasn't important."

Jonas keyed the mic. "What's up, Bob?"

Bob recognized Jonas's voice. "We've got at least twenty fully equipped Pine Mountain Troops coming down the road outside."

Jonas keyed the mic again. "Are you secure at this time, or do I need to come running."

"We're safe at the moment."

"Call out if you need us to respond." Jonas called out, "Kitty, are you hearing this?"

Kitty who had been listening came on. "What do we do?"

"Grab your bug out bags and gear and head up the back trail like I showed you. I'll try to raise Jack and his boys. Don't think about what you want to take. Get on your winter outdoors clothes and boots. Put on your pistol, and get your rifle and bug out bag. Have the girls and the cook do the same. Do it now; tell the old boys that hang around there that they will be killed if they don't leave right now. We'll meet on top of the ridge. You know the spot. I want y'all on the trail in five minutes. Now go!"

"We're as good as gone."

Jonas tried to call old man Jack but got no answer.

"Darn it. They don't keep their radio on. Ok, guys, gear up. Chuck, grab your stuff. Fox and Dix, you know what to do."

Dix grabbed his Springfield and the bandoleer of cartridges. He was already wearing his pistol. He hid the M4 that Jonas had given him under the couch. Fox, who had disappeared down the hall, appeared wearing his backpack and handed Dix his pack. They were always ready to leave at a moment's notice. After pulling a stocking cap over his still sore scalp, Dix put on the pack.

"Darn it. I was sure hoping to get those stitches pulled today."

Fox grinned and quipped, "Don't worry; we can pull them after we're through putting in new ones later today."

Chuck appeared at the top of the stairs ready to go. As he was cinching up his backpack, Jonas gave him a glance.

"Have you had any training using the M4 carbine?"

"Yes, Sir, I am proficient with them as well."

Jonas pointed under the couch where Dix had stashed his rifle.

"Grab that rifle and the pouch of loaded magazines under there and leave your MP5. I want you to stay with Dix, and if he needs backup, you're it."

As they were heading out the door, they heard gunfire echoing from up the valley. They ran to the barn and flung open the big door. Jonas pointed to the shelves on the back wall.

"Grab four cases of MRE's, those two rifle cases and those three ammo boxes beside them."

Jonas also grabbed a chainsaw case, a gallon of gas and a can of oil. Once they were loaded on the cargo bed of the ATV, he covered it all with a net and secured it. They went out the door, turned behind the barn and headed up a seldom used trail. About thirty minutes later, they arrived at a point where a four foot tall cairn was located. No one in the area knew who built it, but it was the location where Kitty and the girls were supposed to meet him. Jonas parked the ATV and hopped out and listened. He heard gunfire in the direction of Bill's Bar.

"I was afraid of that. They dragged their feet and didn't get out in time."

Fox recognized the look that Dix had the look on his face.

"Jonas, this is your battle ground; we'll follow your lead."

Jonas turned his cap around backwards and shucked his backpack. All he carried was his weapons and ammo.

"Follow me and spread out. I'll take the point. Fox, I want you behind me, and I want Dix and Chuck to bring up the rear."

Everyone followed his orders and watched as Jonas took off at a trot. Fox gave him about ten seconds and followed. Because his leg wasn't healed enough for him to be trotting down the mountain with a full load of weapons and ammo, Dix started walking at a quick pace. Chuck brought up the rear.

The trip down the mountain trail went quickly Other than ice on some the exposed rocks, the footing was good. Jonas angled off the trail so he could look down onto the valley road next to Bill's. Several troopers were scattered out and shooting up the trail. Jonas spotted a couple of bodies on the ground. He pulled up his rifle and spied the men doing the shooting. He put the crosshairs on the first one he noticed and squeezed the trigger. Without waiting to see if the bullet connected, he cycled the bolt and found his next target. He heard Fox's rifle barking to his right, and he saw men around the bar scrambling for cover. He turned to the vehicles on the road and shot the drivers standing near their vehicles. Dix eventually came to the point on the trail where Jonas and Fox veered away. As bullets dusted the ground at his feet, he spotted Kitty and her girls scrambling up the steep trail in his direction. Someone was shooting at them, and the ricochets were almost hitting him.

"Chuck, get over behind those rocks and spot for me. Tell me when you see the shooters and their position."

Chuck moved to the spot as directed and said, "I see two of them shooting from the wood shed which is located to the right of the Bar."

Dix was on his belly sighting over a rock. He put the crosshairs on the spot where a man would rise up and shoot. The instant he saw movement, he squeezed the trigger. The old rifle bounced, and less than a split second later the man fell backward out of sight. The other one he couldn't see was still shooting.

Dix called over to Chuck, "Try to shoot that son of a bitch if you can."

Chuck opened fire on the man and made him dive for cover. That was the opportunity Dix needed. The man was down behind the wood pile, but Dix could see his hip. A 150 grain 30-06 bullet through the hip is not an easy way to die. The man landed on his side screaming. Dix could have finished him, but the psychological distress caused by a man dying a horrible death can be very distracting to his fellow combatants.

Kitty and the girls reached the spot where Dix and Chuck were shooting.

Nadine was crying, "They killed my Mama."

Dix commanded Kitty, "Get the girls up the trail and hide when y'all get there."

They could hear Fox's old Marlin 30-30 barking as he spotted targets. Jonas arrived in time to see Kitty and the girls heading up the trail. Dix shook his head.

"I think they killed Hester."

Jonas angrily shook his head and replied, "We're not letting them retreat. I killed the drivers, and I put rounds through the air brake control units on both vehicles. Those bastards are on foot just like us. They don't know the mountain, but I do."

Dix saw movement off to the left.

"They know where we are. I suggest we hightail up the mountain. It's going to be night soon, and it's going to be cold. With their vehicles disabled, they will have to stay in the bar unless they call in help."

Jonas thought a minute. "I'll get Fox. Y'all head up the trail. I'll set some IED's and be right behind you."

Dix and Chuck climbed to the top where Kitty and the girls were waiting. Nadine was crying, and Chuck tried to console her.

"I'm sorry about your mother."

She hugged his neck and cried.

Dix turned to Kitty in a low voice, "Are you sure Hester's dead?"

Kitty had a mean look on her face. "I don't know. I saw her go down, and she wasn't moving. I told Nadine that she was dead. If we had stopped or gone back, we'd all be dead. Several of the men who hang out at the bar thought they could fight them off. Most of them have been shot or killed as well."

Jonas and Fox appeared. While Jonas was unpacking his IED's from the ammo boxes, Dix explained what had happened to Hester.

Jonas said, "I'll head down and see if I can get her if she's still alive."

Dix shook his head.

"No. Here's what I want you to do. Cover our back trail with your IED's. How far does this trail go?"

"It's a hiker's trail that follows the ridge of the mountain for miles. We can take the ATV about three miles. I know where there is a shelter for the backpackers about two miles from here. I'll take the ladies there."

"I'm assuming we can walk down the side of the mountain to the valley road from there."

"Sure, but it won't be easy. You'd never make it in your weaken condition. You haven't recovered enough to handle that trip. Fox and I can carry the chainsaw down and drop a tree across the road a couple of miles up. That will slow down any help they've called and will keep them on the ground where we can get at them."

"Ok, then. You get the IED's placed. Let Chuck help; it's the only way he's going to learn."

Jonas pulled out six of the devices which were made from hand grenades with motion detected electronic triggers placed inside GI canteens. "This trail and the one coming up the mountain will be impassable in ten minutes."

Dix looked down the mountain.

"I'm not going to leave Hester down there. Those idiots could decide to conduct a sacrifice with her, and that's not going to happen on my watch. The plan has changed. I'm going to go down in advance of your IED's and hide. When they get past me, I'll slip down once I hear the first explosion. That's the last thing they'll be expecting."

Fox was listening and stated, "I'll go with you. They won't be expecting two of us within their lines. Once the sun goes down, they'll have out their night vision goggles so we'll have to stay hidden."

Dix called Chuck over and instructed, "You stay with Jonas and do exactly what he orders. Fox and I are going back down and hide until the IED's start going off."

Fox grinned at the boy and joked, "I told you that you would be in the thick of it before you knew it. You didn't even get to try out that warm bed."

Chuck nodded in agreement.

"I won't say anything to Nadine; I don't want to get her hopes up."

Dix and Fox hid about a hundred yards off into the woods where they were in a position to slip back down the side of the mountain. They heard Jonas and the ladies moving up the trail. Jonas would have to take a couple of trips to get them all moved to the shelter. They had Kitty, Annie Ruth, Nadine, and the three working girls: Doris, Lyn and Elsie. Unfortunately, the cook lay dead back on the trail.

As soon as Jonas had them relocated to the shelter, he dug out his radio from the third ammo can and set up an antenna from a coil of wire that was also stored within. Once he had it hooked to the battery in the ATV, he fired it up and contacted Cooney Jones.

"Captain Jones, this is Jonas Hank. I'm one of Dix Jernigan's new recruits. If you remember, we spoke earlier. We have a situation unfolding."

"Tell me what's going on."

Jonas went through everything that had taken place and explained their immediate situation.

Cooney absorbed the info and answered, "I'll notify Porter and Morgan to be on the lookout. Chances are they will head into danger as well. Keep me posted, and I'll be back in touch."

For a long time, Dix and Fox sat quietly and waited in the shadows. They stood out against the white snow, but they were far enough from the trail that no one would spot them. Suddenly, the first IED went off, and the detonation was so intense they felt the shock wave and were startled by the sound.

Fox commented, "I may have wet myself a little."

They both grinned, and Dix nodded.

"It's show time."

CHAPTER 22

Porter braced himself against the handholds on the dash. "I wish you had installed seat belts in this rig."

Morgan stood on the brakes. "I didn't think I would be getting into a wreck since there aren't any cars on the road any longer."

The Duk slid sideways toward the left edge of the road, where the shoulder disappeared into the seemingly bottomless abyss. Just as they thought they would slid over the edge, the chain on the passenger side rear wheel bit through the ice for a moment. That action didn't stop their runaway ride down the mountain, but it caused the Duk to pivot in a clockwise direction. After several complete, slow motion, pirouettes, they found themselves sliding down the mountain backward and gaining speed. A crash at this speed would destroy the Duk and probably kill them both. Morgan in a moment of desperation punched the accelerator pedal and released the brakes. The Duk was still sliding backward, but the wheels on both axles were spinning forward. Precisely at the moment they thought they were doomed, the chains started to bite when they hit a spot where the ice was thin. The chained tires found traction, and the big rig shuddered and bounced as the chains bit and slipped. When they were no more than ten feet from a plunge into the river below, the Duk started to pull its way back up the mountain. Morgan looked over to see Porter punching the air.

"Yes."

Morgan kept the wheels turning and let the chains do their job.

"I'm not going to stop until we are back on top of the mountain. I can't believe that we didn't go off that cliff. I bet there's damage to the drivelines after all this. We'll have to check it out once we're safe to stop."

The moment they were back on top, Morgan pulled over. Porter walked over to the door and got ready to lower the steps.

"I think I'm going to kiss the ground after that. You know that the only way we're going to make it down that road is by tying off the winch line and letting the winch lower us a hundred feet at a time. Maybe Gord Holmes knows a better way around."

Before he could lower the steps, Morgan pointed.

"Look."

From their vantage point they could see the winding road leading down to the long straightaway where they had almost died. They could also see the winding road on the opposite side leading back up and over the mountain. At the very top of the mountain there were three military vehicles. Two were the large armored personnel carriers, and they were followed by a third truck pulling a fuel trailer.

At that moment the radio came on. "Morgan and Porter, this is Cooney Jones. Where are you?"

"We're sitting on top of a pass looking at a three military vehicles on the opposite pass heading our way."

"I've been trying to call you. The rats are coming out of The Mountain, and Major Jernigan is under attack in the river valley where Bill's Bar is located. That group, heading in your direction, will be trying to kill the civilian population in your area. You are going to have to stop them."

Porter keyed the mic. "If they reach the bottom, they aren't going to make it back up the mountain. We were almost killed on the slope, so unless they have steel studs or chains they'll be trapped there. It's so icy. We may have to abandon the Duk back at Gord Holmes's place and proceed on foot or by alternate transportation. I have a box of armor piercing rounds for my .308 rifle. Not sure if I can stop the trucks with them, but I'll try."

Cooney keyed his mic. "I'll get word to Gord, and see if I can get you some backup. Colonel Miller is putting together a task force to head in that direction, but they can't get there in less than a week."

Porter answered, "There can't be more than a dozen in this group, and I don't believe they have the drive lines armored on the vehicles I'm looking at."

"Just be careful, and don't get yourself killed."

Porter replied, "We'll try to avoid the getting killed part. Porter out."

Porter removed his long gun from the rack and replaced the cartridges in it with armor piercing rounds. "I don't think these will penetrate the windows or the body. Since you know more about these vehicles that I do, where should I direct my fire?"

Morgan was looking through his binoculars.

"I would wait until they are at the bottom and are attempting to come up the icy incline. You will notice that the drive train is not protected as well as the crew compartment. Don't try the tires because they are all the run-flat type, and an onboard compressor keeps them inflated. Aim just beneath the front bumper below where the winch is mounted. You might get lucky and hit the bottom of the engine or the oil pan. The four wheel drive system and drive shafts are down there as well."

Morgan drove around the bend of the road out of sight where they could wait behind some boulders that had been placed on the turnout to keep cars from running off the road and down the cliff. As they watched, the vehicles below were soon bunched together at the bottom of the incline. The lead vehicle was helplessly spinning its wheels. Porter waited until the men started piling out of the vehicle before he fired. Morgan held his M4 and looked through his ACOG scope.

"Porter, I'm estimating that they are about four hundred yards away. I'll try and spot you before I start shooting."

Porter dialed the magnification up to nine power and located the differential chunk on the front axle. He raised the crosshairs over the chunk an estimated twelve inches. He held steady, and just as his breath exhaled, but before he started to inhale, he squeezed the trigger. The rifle discharged, and he cycled the action.

Morgan said, "You hit the differential chunk almost at the bottom."

Porter aimed a little higher and squeezed. The rifle bounced again.

Morgan shouted, "Dead on; tear it up."

After Morgan joined the shooting, they had men scattering. Some of them were trying to jump behind boulders while others were attempting to get back into the safety of the vehicle. When several men started returning fire, bullets began to hit and ricochet off the nearby boulders. Morgan winced and cussed as a rock splinter cut a gash high on his cheek bone.

Unfazed by the bullets and rock fragments, Porter fired three more rounds into the drive train of the vehicle and reloaded.

"I think the lead vehicle is disabled. I'm going to hit the fuel trailer next. With any luck, I might set it on fire."

His next five rounds went through the fuel trailer. Although he could see fuel pooling under it, he knew that he couldn't ignite the diesel fuel without tracers. He switched back to full metal jacket ammo and joined Morgan in shooting at the men who were firing from cover.

Porter called over to Morgan, "Can you run a magazine of your bullets into the pool of fuel under the trailer? I would sure like to luck up and get a fire started."

Morgan replaced his magazine with a fresh one and in rapid succession fired thirty rounds into and under the fuel trailer. Against all odds, the fuel caught. Porter dropped a man who ran over trying to put it out, and they kept firing on the men who were helplessly trying to stop the growing flames. Before long, the inferno engulfed the trailer and the truck pulling it. Suddenly, the truck carrying the ordnances ignited and the weapons started to explode. A crate of hand grenades cooked off and blew the truck into smithereens. The men scattered and tried to flee the conflagration. Several men escaped by going over the edge and down into the river basin below. Meanwhile, the middle vehicle started to smolder from the intensity of the burning truck and fuel.

Morgan and Porter reloaded their weapons, and kept an eye out for anyone poking their heads up. A few troopers were trying to use, for cover, a huge fallen pine tree that was lying beside the mountain road. The full metal jacket bullets from Porter's rifle blasted through the wood, and sent up showers of bark and white splintered wood. One guy, who was hit and dying, grasped the trigger so tightly on his automatic weapon that he stitched, in a wide arc, a pattern of the bullets in the snow and blew small rocks off the side of the mountain.

While he was peering through his scope, Porter spoke, "I know I hit three. How about you?"

Without taking his eyes off the trucks, Morgan stated, "I put four on the ground, and I know three went over the edge after the truck exploded. So, we know seven aren't going to be in the fight, and we have the three that went over the edge. There could be several more dead, hiding or wounded down there in that mess. What do you want to do?"

Porter couldn't see any movement.

"The way I see it we will be sitting ducks if we try to go down that hill. Those three in the river bottom will take at least two or three hours to work their way up to where we are, if they didn't break their necks on the way down. Those other two vehicles will probably burn up so they are all stranded in the dead of winter with only the clothes they are wearing and their weapons. I think we should hold out here until all three vehicles are on fire, and then high tail it back to Gord's and work on plan B.

In forty-five minutes all of the vehicles became fully engulfed in flames. While they waited, Morgan and Porter, looking for movement, carefully scoped every square inch of the road and mountain. All of a sudden, the intense heat caused a trooper to break and run back down the mountain. As he dived for cover, Porter was able to hit his leg when he tried to scramble behind a rock. In his panic, the trooper went too far, and Porter hit the man's exposed arm. If he didn't bleed to death, or die from exposure, he would probably never fight again. About that time, Porter and Morgan heard the ammo in the trucks cooking off, and in a few minutes they saw the vehicles' doors and windows explode.

Porter and Morgan stayed out of the line of sight and ran in a crouch toward the Duk. Once they were out of sight of the road, they climbed into the Duk, stoked the fire and replaced the wood in the gasifier. While the gas pressure was building, they fired up the radio.

Porter keyed the mic. "Grandpa, we stopped them, destroyed their equipment and killed most of them."

Cooney Jones answered back, "I hope there are no new holes in your hide this time."

"No, not this time. The road is impassable because of the ice and the destroyed vehicles blocking it. We're heading back to Captain Gord Holmes's place to figure out where to go from here."

"Ok, men, keep me posted. I think Gord's men can take care of the ones that are left. I need you to figure out how you are going to reach the Major."

"We're heading to Gord's place now."

The Duk cranked, and they traveled back the way they came. Morgan couldn't detect any damage to the driveline. His upgrade to the axles and drive shafts from the military vehicles had paid off. When they arrived at Gord's home, he directed them to park in the small pasture behind the house. They climbed down and joined him and Nellie in the parlor. Gord had his map unfolded on the coffee table.

"Show me where you hit the People's Party."

Morgan ran his finger down the road and showed him where the burned out vehicles were still smoldering.

"The three troopers that we know escaped went off into the river bottom here as well."

Gord looked over at the radio.

"They won't get far in this weather. Hand me the mic."

He keyed the mic. "Conway, are you listening?"

"Yes, I've got some of the guys on their way."

"Great. Do you know that long straightaway in the middle of Lazarus Road where it bottoms out above the river?"

"Yes, I know the spot."

"You'll find three burnt out vehicles and a bunch of dead bodies. Three People's Party troops went over the edge toward the river, and there may be some more wounded or hiding around the vehicles. See if you can kill the bastards that are trying to get away."

"We're on our way. I'll get Raymond and Gary to come in from the north side."

Gord looked at Morgan and Porter while he keyed the mic again. "Good hunting boys. Let me know what you find."

Porter pulled the map out of his pocket and showed Gord where they needed to go.

"Major Jernigan is in a fight, and Morgan and I need to get there as quickly as possible."

Gord spread out the map.

"As you know most of the roads that you could have used in the past are not passable using a vehicle. It would take you a full day to go back and cut across on the southern route. Your best bet is to go one mile back up this road until you reach an overlook. Opposite of that overlook is a hiker's trail that heads up into the mountain. The trail is well marked, but it won't be a cake walk. There will trees and rockslides you'll have to go over and around. I suspect that you'll have a ten mile hike. Once you reach the top, you'll hit a trail that goes down the spine of the mountain. There will be a cairn at that point. It will be a pile of rocks about four feet tall. If you turn south on that trail, you will be heading parallel to the river and a road which leads down to Bill's Bar. In about three miles, you'll come to another cairn. When you reach the next one after that, you'll be directly above Bill's Bar. The walking will be easier once you get on the spine of the old mountain. That first ten miles will be mostly uphill, but you guys are young; you can handle it."

Morgan shrugged and declared, "The sooner we get moving; the sooner we can get there."

Nellie headed to the kitchen.

"While you guys get your gear together, I'll have you something hot to eat."

Morgan nodded and smiled.

"Thanks, Miss Nellie, that would be great. In the meantime, we'll go out to the Duk and get ready."

They dumped out their packs on their respective bunks and stripped them down. Since weight had to be at a minimum, they would carry nothing that wasn't essential. Morgan paired down his first aid kit to the basics. From this point on, he would be practicing 'ditch' medicine.

Porter reached down and grabbed a large butterfly bandage and insisted, "Go put this on your cheek; that's a wicked cut."

Morgan stepped over to the mirror behind the wash basin. He winced as he applied some moonshine to the wound. "It looks like it was sliced by a knife. Hand me the super glue."

Porter brought the super glue over, applied it to one side of the cut and squeezed the two edges together.

Morgan closed his eye and admonished, "Careful; I don't want your finger glued to my face."

"That might be an improvement."

As soon as they had patched Morgan, they went back to repacking their backpacks with emergency food rations, water filters, etc. They would leave their sleeping bags and take only the clothes they wore. Morgan had his M4 and a pouch containing ten-thirty round magazines. Porter had an AK-47 and ten-thirty round mags in his pouch. Years before he left California, he had taken the gun from a dead Chinese. Porter also carried a Kbar knife and pistol that never left his body. He did fish out two extra magazines for the Beretta 92 that he continued to carry. These magazines would fit on the outside of his shoulder holster which was concealed under his coat. He put the suppressor for it in the pack in case he had to do some close up work. When they were loaded, they climbed from the Duk and headed into the house where Nellie had cooked some eggs, ham and corn cakes. Knowing that this could be the last meal for a while, they ate all they could hold.

Porter looked up from his plate.

"We each have a handheld radio, but the batteries aren't going to hold up if we leave them on. We'll radio in when we reach the first cairn."

Gord shook their hands and instructed, "About two-thirds of the way to the top there's a hiker's shed that has an old wood heater, and there may still be some dried wood around. There could be a bear in there as well. Y'all just be careful. Let me know so I can relay your information as needed."

They cinched up the packs, clicked the straps across their chest and headed out. Morgan leaned forward a bit.

"I may have to stop and get rid of some more stuff; this is going to get heavy by the time we reach the spine of this mountain."

They reached the trail head and looked up.

Porter rubbed his head and remarked, "I know what you mean. My head is already sore under this stocking cap, and the straps of my pack are already digging into my shoulders. I just hope the wind doesn't come up. If it does, it's not going to be pleasant. I hope we make the shelter before dark, 'cause there's no way we can travel this trail in the dark."

As they started their ascent, they heard the echo of gunfire from back up the mountain to the north.

Morgan commented, "It looks as if they are starting to clean up the mess we left."

CHAPTER 23

Olsen threw her coffee cup across the office. It shattered when it hit the door behind her aide.

"What do you mean we've lost contact with all three squads?"

The aide stood wide eyed and stuttered, "M...M...M...Major Olsen, we lost all contact with all of them. They don't answer their radios. They missed their mandatory check in communication."

"Did you check our radio?"

"Yes, Mam, that's the first thing I had them check."

Olsen turned away from the aide and absentmindedly bit the knuckle on the index finger on her right hand. She turned quickly and asked, "Has The Pontiff been told any of this?"

"No, Sir, I mean Mam."

While the rage boiled up within her, Olsen closed her eyes and silently counted to five.

"Summon Nichols and Wilson; do not notify The Pontiff; he doesn't need to be bothered."

Nichols and Wilson were the only two on her team who were not religious zealots.

The aide had to spend some time searching before he located Nichols and Wilson. They had been off duty so they looked disheveled when they entered Olsen's office. Olsen pointed to the chairs at the small conference table. "We have a problem; we've lost contact with all three squads."

Nichols slicked back her hair and insisted, "That's impossible; we must've had a radio glitch."

Wilson spoke up, "There was a radio in each vehicle. Do you think that we've had five radios suddenly fail?"

Olsen, visibly flustered, exclaimed, "Hell, no, we haven't had five radio failures, and besides the squad leaders have personal radios. Eight radios didn't all fail at the same time. Something's happened."

Nichols looked at Wilson.

"People, we've got a problem," Olsen restated. "We all know why we're here. So unless you two can grow beards in the next ten minutes, we'll be on that granite slab if we can't get this resolved."

Olsen knew that her aide was listening at the door.

"Crofton, get in here. I know you're eavesdropping."

Crofton came in and joined them at the table. Olsen looked at the three of them.

"Mobilize four squads; I want two sent in behind each of our lost squads. Nichols and Wilson you will each lead a group. No slip ups; do you understand?"

They all nodded in agreement.

"Crofton, if any of my other officers have questions, don't say a word; just refer them to me immediately. Do you understand?"

"Yes, Mam, do you mind if I start growing a beard?"

Scowling, Olsen admonished, "Don't be funny. I want your squads to be in the valley and in Eureka Springs by 9:00 am in the morning so get your non-comms in line tonight. If anyone asks, you're going in strictly as backup support units. We aren't using all hazmat trained units because there is no indication of the plague, and this will serve as a good training exercise. Remember this has to go off without a hitch. The Pontiff does not accept failure. He will look on this problem as an affront to Gya."

After dismissing the three, Olsen stormed around the room. She ran through her mind all of her available options. She had been by The Pontiff's side and knew how precarious her predicament was. The Pontiff would never accept responsibility for his mistakes. She had executed his orders on so many occasions that she knew he would look for a scapegoat. A failure this big would require a big head to roll. She would notify him in the morning after she knew for sure what had actually taken place. In the meantime, she had to have plans B and C in place.

She went to her apartment and entered the storage closet where she pulled out a large tote that contained the clothes she wore when she identified herself as a man. She inventoried the clothing and put her field clothes into a laundry bag. She returned to her office and pulled up the facility's inventory logs. She quickly located the levels and floors that would have the items she needed in order to make her escape. She hopped in her electric ATV, went down to the motor pool and drove around until she came to the room that held the vehicle for which she was looking. Parked inside, was an older Jeep Wrangler Unlimited that someone had extensively accessorized.

The previous owner had spent a fortune installing a lift kit, off road tires, rims, winches, roof rack, and trailer hitch on it. The engine had been upgraded to a Cummins diesel. Behind the Jeep was a matching off road trailer with an extra fuel tank and fuel pump. When Olsen found the Jeep downstate, she had the motor pool mechanics service and maintain it. Normally, she would call down and have it delivered to the front door so that all she had to do was go out and get in it. The fuel tanks were full, and it was ready to roll. If she pulled out this time, she wouldn't be giving anyone prior notice of her planned departure.

She hopped back into her ATV and drove up to the same room that Chuck had used to outfit himself. Once she was inside, she turned on the lights and prepared two backpacks with everything she would need to hike out. One would stay in her apartment, and one would be in the Jeep. That way regardless of her mode of escape, she would have a bug out bag with her. Down the corridor in yet another storage cavern that had belonged to a large home supply chain, she found four wheeled waterproof plastic storage cases. She also selected a tool box that she filled with mechanic's tools. She loaded the cases and tool box onto the ATV and proceeded to the storage room of the Outdoorsman where she filled one of the boxes with freeze dried food and the other with items such as a rocket stove, lanterns, flash lights and every other camping item she could conceivably use. Being a high end outdoors store, she found coats, hiking boots, pants, shirts, sweaters, socks, hats, stocking caps, gloves and the latest camping gear. Her last items were a high quality tent, sleeping pad and an all season sleeping bag system. In the hunting and shooting section, she located the cage that Chuck had broken into. She dug out a Ruger .380 LCP for her back pocket. She also found the Sig handguns, a Ruger Scout rifle, an MP5 carbine, magazines and ammo. The two rigs were now complete and ready to store in the apartment and in the Jeep. No matter which way she chose to run, she would have weapons ready. She heard movement behind her and spun with her newly acquired pistol in her hand.

Crofton jumped back and exclaimed, "Major, it's just me."

Olsen gave him a stern look and inquired, "Are you following me?"

"No, I'm doing the same thing you're doing; I'm getting ready to bolt out of here if I have to. I have no intention of being bled for three or four months and then being sacrificed."

Olsen stared at him a moment. She knew that denying what she was doing was useless.

"Get your gear together. I don't want to know your plans, and I'm not telling you mine. Fair enough?"

"Fair enough, Major."

Crofton proceeded to arm up.

"I'll see you in the morning, Major. I would appreciate your giving me a heads up when you see things getting bad."

"I will."

She walked back to the ATV leaving Crofton to gather his gear.

Before morning, she would have everything loaded on the Jeep and cinched down with straps. If she escaped from the facility, she could live in the field until she located an abandoned home or farm where she could set up housekeeping. If she had to make an escape, she would go as Charles Olsen. Then her hopes of making the transition would be dashed.

She dreaded breaking the news to The Pontiff once the new teams reported back in the morning. He wouldn't take the news lightly.

CHAPTER 24

Dix and Fox trotted toward the trail well below the point where the IED exploded. They found seven troopers that were disoriented: three were down on the ground, two were wounded, but on their feet, and two were cautiously approaching the scene of the carnage. The two unharmed men spun and fired at Dix and Fox, but their aim was disrupted by the thirty caliber bullets that passed through their bodies. Fox stroked the lever on the Marlin and Dix cycled the bolt of the old Springfield. Fox was first to fire again hitting one of the two wounded who were still on their feet. The other trooper had one arm broken and couldn't get her hand on her pistol fast enough. Dix and Fox both fired at the same time dropping her just as the pistol cleared its holster. Dix pulled out his pistol and double tapped them all before turning to Fox.

"Let's find Hester."

Fox bent over and retrieved a radio from one of the dead.

"Must have been an officer; maybe we can listen to what they're saying."

They turned and headed toward the bar. Once they were within sight of it, they saw three troopers running down the steps and up the road. They didn't slow down as they passed the disabled vehicles. Fox raised his rifle to shoot.

"Don't waste your ammo, Fox. Besides, it's too long of a shot; they're heading back to the mountain. We'll get them in a few days."

Fox ran ahead, and Dix followed at a fast walk. He was still favoring his wounded leg. When Fox reached the bar, he ran up the steps and kicked the door open. He was fully expecting a shoot-out. One of the troopers was laid out on the floor with a gut wound. Fox popped him through the head, and when his eyes fully adjusted, he saw Hester tied to a chair.

"Hester, can you hear me?"

She opened her eyes, and in her delirium, repeated over and over again, "I ain't telling you nothing; I ain't telling you nothing…." Her head dropped back to her chest.

Dix came through the front door.

"I heard that 30-30 from outside. Are there any more?"

Fox had his knife out and was cutting the bindings that held Hester.

"That was the last one. Help me get her back into her room."

He scooped her up and carried her to the room with her name on the door. He laid her on the bed. Dix came in with a wet towel and a glass of water. She was bleeding from her nose and one ear. A large bruise in the shape of a hand was forming on her throat. Dix wiped her face and encouraged her to take a sip of the water. She choked from the trauma to her throat.

"Take is slow, Hester."

Dix looked around at Fox and complained, "They have no sense of decency, and we've got to cut this cancer out of that Mountain. Something is bad wrong with those people. I'm surprised Chuck is not scarred for life."

Fox stood out in the hall where he could see the front door. "You know he is. He's just like you and me and every other person alive. I know I'll never get over what has happened and what I've been forced to do."

Hester asked in a raspy voice, "Nadine?"

Dix quieted her.

"Nadine's fine. Jonas and Chuck have her and the others in a shelter up the mountain. You need to sit and be quiet while I find a first aid kit."

Blood was dripping down her neck from a wound on the back of her head. When Dix gently moved her head, he saw that a bullet had grazed her skull and knocked her out. That she was alive was a miracle.

Fox handed him the first aid kit and explained, "I knew where they kept it from when they patched you up."

Jonas heard the explosion and the gunshots that followed. He turned to the ladies.

"That'll be Dix and Fox. Don't worry; just get inside, and we'll start a fire in the old wood heater."

Kitty pointed into the shelter.

"Ok, girls, it's not a mansion, but it's out of the wind and snow. Get your packs in and check your pistols. Then I want you to gather some wood. It's going to be dark and cold soon, and I don't plan on sharing my sleeping bag with anybody."

Jonas turned to Chuck and instructed, "Get a fire started in the stove. Find that old aluminum pot that a hiker left, fill it with snow, and get some water boiling. I'm taking the chainsaw to get the road blocked with trees in case they send more troops down. Your job is to protect the women, but I don't expect any more troops to be coming up the trail from the bar."

Chuck replaced the magazine in his rifle.

"I'll do my best."

"I know you will, son. If I don't make it back, remember to disable those IED's we set before trying to go back down that trail. Don't get yourself killed. Porter and Morgan are on their way; however, I'm not sure how or when they'll arrive. If for some reason the Major, Fox or I don't come back, don't come looking for us. Your orders are to protect these ladies. Scout the area before you try to go back to the bar or the cabin."

Chuck watched the ladies gathering wood.

"How long should I wait?"

"The decision will be made when you run out of food. Remember; the New Constitution Army will be sending in a lot of firepower. They aren't going to let those communist perverts exist, so if you can hold out until then, y'all will be ok. There is a lot of food and provisions back at the cabin, and you have all the MRE's here on the ATV; not to mention what they may have in their bug out bags. All these women, but

Nadine, are tough old gals, and they all have pistols. I assure you they won't go down without a fight."

Jonas shouldered his rifle, grabbed the chainsaw and disappeared down the mountain. The going was difficult, but he managed to make his way into the valley. He heard the loud boom of a shotgun firing from up the valley. Finally, the going got easier when he came to a trail that led in behind the burning remains of a homestead belonging to one of the men who helped around the bar. The man's family lay beheaded in the yard. The man's daughter and son were both bottomless; it was evident what took place before they were beheaded. Jonas felt his anger boiling over. Their idea of war was no different than the people he had fought in North Africa when he was dealing with the Islamists. He thought *they aren't even in the same league as rabid animals. At least a rabid dog has an excuse.*

He could do nothing here so he turned with renewed strength in his body and jogged toward the Cartwright's water wheel.

Meanwhile, back at the bar, Fox called out, "I hear a vehicle on the road. Get your gun ready."

Dix turned from Hester and said, "We're sitting ducks in here; Fox, get out of the building where you can shoot."

Without a word, Fox was out the front door and down the stairs.

Dix looked back at Hester. "I'm going to back up Fox: will you be ok?"

She could only nod yes.

He grabbed his rifle and headed for the door when he heard the vehicle turn in and stop. He heard Fox talking so he went to the front door and walked out.

When Old Man Jack and his boys got out of their truck, they were armed to the teeth. The old man looked up.

"What's going on, Major?"

"We've been hit by the Pine Tree Mountain animals."

The old man grimaced and remarked, "I figured something was up when nobody answered their radios. What can I do to help?"

Dix pointed behind him.

"Hester's been beaten; can you take her back to your farm? It's not safe here."

One of his grown boys went under the bar where a SUV was parked. He cranked it and brought it around.

"This one has enough gas to get her back."

The old man pointed up at the bar.

"You boys, get up there and help the Major. I'm going to check on the Cartwrights and the other families."

On the way over he had seen the bodies of his neighbors lying in the blood stained snow. As he climbed into his truck, he gave Fox a look of disbelief.

Fox called up to Dix, "I'm going with Jack; I'll be back."

Dix turned to help get Hester moved.

"I'll be here waiting."

Bob Cartwright saw Jonas coming and came out brandishing his assault shotgun.

"I saw what they did to Mac's family. Three came running through here an hour ago, I killed one, and I think the others may be packing some buckshot."

Jonas pointed to Bob's ATV.

"Can you run me up the valley? I want to drop some trees across the road and slow up their reinforcements when they arrive. I'm sure they'll be sending more soon."

337

They turned their gaze back down the road in the direction of the bar and Jonas's cabin. The sounds of a vehicle could be heard coming. Jonas sat the chainsaw in the back of the ATV, unslung his rifle and walked to the edge of the road where he could see the approaching truck. Bob was beside him and pointed.

"That's Old Man Jack; don't shoot."

Jonas slung his rifle back over his shoulder.

"I tried to radio him, but they never turn on their radio unless they need something."

Jack pulled up and killed the engine. Fox saw Jonas.

"Hester's alive. They beat her, but I think she'll be ok. They're taking her back to Jack's farm. Dix is waiting back at the bar."

Jonas pointed to the chainsaw on the ATV.

"We need to go up the valley and drop a tree or two across the road in some tight spots to slow them down when they come back."

Cartwright headed over to the ATV and said, "I'll drop the trees if y'all want to check on the rest of the families."

Jonas nodded and exclaimed, "That would be great; you don't want to know what they did to Mac's family.

I don't want to guess what we'll find at the other homes."

Jonas turned to Jack and inquired, "Can I use your truck? I'm going to prepare a welcome for those bastards when they come back."

"Sure thing, I'll help Cartwright. We'll come find you when we get back."

Dix built a fire in the bar's wood heater and found some cold leftover stew that had been left on the cooking stove. He sat in the dark with his rifle leaned up against the table next to him. His leg and head wounds were hurting along with every square inch of his body. He thought about going into one of the bedrooms to rest, but he had second thoughts *I've never been in a cat house bed, and I'm sure not going to start now.* He was lost in thought when he heard Old Man Jack's truck return. He was too tired to get up and look, but had his pistol ready should the wrong people come through the front door.

Fox and Jonas entered through the door opening, and looked at Dix who was putting his pistol back into his shoulder holster.

"Men, I don't think we've killed them all. Do a body count. Bob Cartwright thought there were at least twenty, and I know three that got away."

Fox said, "Two got away; Cartwright stopped one."

Jonas looked over at the dead trooper on the floor.

"Fox, help me drag this corpse out to the truck. I want to prepare a pile of these dead troopers out on the road for the ones who will be showing up soon to see. Coming upon that scene will have a strong psychological effect on them. It should leave them shaking in their boots."

They spent a couple of hours dragging up the dead and creating a pile of bodies about a mile or so north of the Cartwright's water wheel. They could hear the chainsaw further up the valley where Cartwright and Old Man Jack were dropping a tree across the roadway. After a while they had a pile of seventeen dead troopers blocking the road. Jonas and Fox walked down to the river and washed their bloody hands in the cold water.

Fox labored as he climbed up the river bank to the road.

"I'm about fed up with all this mountain fighting. I am a flat land fighter."

Jonas hopped into the driver's seat of the truck as Fox climbed in the other side.

"We almost have them licked Fox; there's only about three thousand or so left. I bet we'll have them killed, and you can get back to flat land fighting in no time."

Fox dug around in his pocket feeling for rifle cartridges and remarked, "I'm going to need more ammo. I only have a handful left."

"Don't worry there's plenty of 30-30 ammo just waiting up there in The Mountain."

Fox grinned and stated, "I've got quite a shopping list if I survive long enough to get in there."

Before they closed the doors, they heard the distant boom of a heavy rifle from the direction of Bill's Bar.

They both looked at each other and spoke at the same time, "Dix!"

As they were jumping into the truck, they heard the sound of Willie Ray's motorcycle racing down the road in their direction. One of the troopers was on the bike with his rifle slung in front of him. Fox and Jonas fired in unison. The bike's front wheel went into a wobble, and the rider couldn't hold it. He was flung over the handlebars, landed flat on his back in the road and slid to within twenty feet of Jonas and Fox. He sat up. His rifle was gone, and his hands were raw from the road burn. Fox aimed his rifle at the man's chest.

Jonas caught the barrel.

"Let's see what he has to say."

He told the stunned trooper, "Lock your fingers behind your head."

The man did so without question or pause. Jonas unhooked the man's gun belt that held his pistol, holster and knife.

"We heard some shooting. What happened back there?"

"Me and one of the guys slipped back to the bar to steal a ride. We found two motorcycles under the bar. Someone from the bar killed my friend as we were heading out to the road. I kept going until you guys shot my ride."

Fox said, "Today's your lucky day, friend; we were shooting at you, not the bike. How many more of you are there left back there?"

"There are three more wounded guys back in the woods behind the bar. All of them are badly wounded and can't walk; we were going for help."

As they were talking, they heard three loud booms that could have only come from Dix's rifle.

The guy looked terrified. "What are you going to do to me?"

Fox spit and glanced at Jonas before addressing the man, "We know what you guys do to the men you capture, and I assume by the beard you are sporting that you are member of the religion that is housed in that Mountain."

The man started chanting, "Gya is great, Gya is great, Gya is.............."

He was unable to finish the sentence as a round from Fox's rifle passed through his skull just above his right ear.

Jonas grabbed him by his vest loop and pulled him over to the truck. Together, they dumped him into the back and drove back to the bar, Jonas suggested, "Let's load up all the dead ones that Dix has waiting, add them to the pile and get some rest. I have a feeling that tomorrow is going to be a long, busy day."

They arrived at the bar as Dix was climbing the steps. He came back down and pointed out behind the bar.

"There's this one in the road and three more are just behind the bar out in the woods. You can't miss them."

Fox said, "Relax until we get back; this won't take long."

Dix climbed the steps and made his way back to the chair beside the wood heater. He added a few sticks of wood, laid his head on the table and rested.

CHAPTER 25

Captain Wilson pulled up on the crest of the mountain and looked down on Lazarus Road. At the bottom of the hill sat the three burned out remains of the Troop C vehicles. He could see several bodies lying in the snow. Captain Wilson keyed the mic and raised Captain Nichols who was heading toward the valley river road.

"Nichols, can you hear me?"

Nichols answered, "I hear you. Have you found anything?"

"I found Troop C. Their vehicles have been destroyed, the road is blocked by the vehicles and I see a number of dead."

Nichols keyed her mic. "We've come to a spot where a huge tree is across the road. We aren't going anywhere until we get the road cleared."

At that moment, the two troopers who had been with troops A and B appeared from the mountain side to report to Captain Nichols.

Nichols keyed the mic. "Wilson, hold tight. Two of our men just showed up from up on the mountain. Let me find out what they have to report."

The squad leader led the men to the vehicle where Nichols was on the radio.

"Captain, they have been up on the mountain all night. You'll want to hear what they have to say."

Nichols looked around at the men in the armored personnel carrier. "Open the back door and set up a perimeter. This could be an ambush. Get those two men in here so they can warm up and give me their report."

She looked around at the two men and inquired, "Before you say a word, are there any enemy forces that you know of in our immediate vicinity?" They both shook their heads no. She looked at the names on their uniforms and directed her question to the one called Ladner.

"Ladner, tell me what has taken place."

Ladner glanced over at his comrade, Leblanc, before turning back to Captain Nichols.

"We were systematically going from house to house and farm to farm cleaning out the hostiles. When we came to Bill's Bar, we encountered strong resistance from the locals there. Until that point, we had easily overcome everyone that we had encountered. The inhabitants of the bar escaped up the mountain. When we tried to pursue and kill them, we came under superior fire from somewhere up on the mountain. Most of our people are dead. We barely made it out alive. Leblanc has a piece of buckshot in his arm."

Nichols called out through the back door, "We need a medic in here."

She turned back to Ladner and asked, "How many do you estimate were firing on you?"

Ladner glanced again at LeBlanc.

"It had to be twenty or more; our men were dropping like flies."

"How did you guys escape?"

Leblanc stammered, "We retreated once we realized that we were about to be overrun."

Nichols motioned for the medic to look after LeBlanc and looked back to Ladner.

"Did any of our people survive?"

Ladner glanced away and then back.

"I don't know. We left one wounded in the bar; however, I doubt they'll let him live. I'm not sure about all of the others."

Nichols keyed the mic. "Wilson, we have an estimated force of twenty who've wiped out the two squads; Olsen is going to be pissed."

Wilson paused a moment.

"The only thing that's going to save us is going in and cleaning up this mess. I can't proceed with the road blocked. What do you suggest?"

"Are you looking at your map?"

"Yes, I have it pulled up on my laptop. What are you thinking?"

Nichols drew a circle around her location on the map and another at Wilson's location. He was at the peak of the mountain where the hiking trail that followed the ridge culminated.

She keyed her mic. "Do you see the trail head that should be close to where you are sitting?"

Wilson blew up the map and spotted the trail head and replied, "I see it; it's a mile or so behind us."

"Park your vehicles, leave guards and proceed with the rest of your troopers down that ridge. I'm showing that it is only about fifteen miles or so down to where we are on the road. We should be able to surround them. If you encounter them on the mountain, we can respond from below, and if we are hit, then you can move in from the top."

Wilson motioned for his squad leaders as he keyed the mic. "I'll radio you once we are on the trail. Wilson out."

Nichols fumed for a moment. She certainly wasn't looking forward to reporting to Olsen.

She changed the frequency on her radio and keyed the mic. "This is Nichols; get Major Olsen on the radio."

The operator answered, "Right away, Captain."

Olsen was in her office looking at maps when Crofton came in with a handheld radio.

"Nichols's on the radio."

As she keyed the mic on the radio, Olsen had a sick feeling in her gut.

"How bad is it?"

She knew that the radio operators would be eavesdropping, but getting around the truth at this point was impossible.

The radio cracked as Nichols called back, "We have a complete massacre. We only know of two survivors at this point. We have an opposing force of at least twenty down in this valley. I don't know about the force level on the road to Eureka Springs."

Nichols proceeded to explain their planned strategy to Olsen.

Olsen consulted her map and stated, "I agree with your plans. Take and secure the river road out twenty-five miles, and maintain forces on top of the mountain and the road. Once you've secured the valley, proceed in the direction of Eureka Springs."

Olsen marked her map with circles and arrows.

"Proceed and keep me posted. Let me know if I need to send reinforcements."

Olsen looked up at Crofton who had been listening.

"I'm going to inform The Pontiff of what has taken place, and if I don't come back, that will be your cue to disappear; understand?"

Crofton nodded as Olsen walked past him out into the corridor and hopped into her ATV. He watched as Olsen disappeared in the direction on The Pontiff's office.

Olsen rubbed her chin and realized that she had forgotten to shave, but going back to shave was too late now. She pulled up to the door and saluted the guard as she entered Pontiff Planter's offices. She was surprised to see that The Pontiff's new receptionist was Danforth's old boyfriend. She thought *the foot washing must have gone well.* Olsen waited until she was introduced. As the guard held the door for her, she anxiously entered the inner sanctum. The Pontiff was sitting at his desk with hands clasped together and resting on top of the desk in front of him.

Before Olsen could speak, The Pontiff sternly asked, "Is it true what I've heard?"

Olsen looked The Pontiff square in the eyes.

"I'm not sure what you've heard, but here is what I've determined. We've lost thirty-five men and six vehicles. I have ordered forty-eight men and support vehicles into the valley."

Without giving The Pontiff a chance to speak, she walked over to the map table. The Pontiff followed her to the table and listened as Olsen pointed out on the map where the resistance existed and explained their planned action to attack.

The Pontiff stiffly walked around the room and called to his guard,

"Bring me my pipe."

He then turned back to Olsen and demanded, "What excuse do you have for us getting caught off guard?"

Olsen knew that The Pontiff was looking for a scapegoat, and she was fully prepared to cast the blame elsewhere. Olsen made it a point not to lose eye contact with The Pontiff.

"Your Holiness, the officers and squad leaders were obviously not up to the task. I can only assume that they were not sincere in their relationship with our Lord Gya. I have no other explanation. The powers of darkness must be with the resistance."

The guard brought in the hookah and stated, "Your physician has already filled the bowl. Do you wish me to light it your Holiness?"

The Pontiff pulled out his lighter.

"I can take it from here; you're dismissed."

He lit the bowl and drew a deep draw from the mouthpiece. The white smoke bubbled in the water bowl as The Pontiff inhaled. He held the smoke in his lungs, leaned his head back and let the smoke from his lungs exit through his nostrils. The two sat in silence while The Pontiff contemplated the situation. Scratching at the scar over his eyebrow, he expounded,

"Olsen, Gya may require another human sacrifice. Those two troopers who survived the attack and retreated will be next. How long has it been since we had a double sacrifice?"

Olsen felt her stomach muscles tighten.

"It's been quite a while. Let's wait and see if they are able to capture some of the hostiles."

"What about the plague, Olsen?"

"There seems to be no indication of the plague at this point."

The Pontiff motioned for Olsen to come over to his writings.

"Look at this, Olsen. Several texts I have been reading and interpreting state that the truly faithful eagerly give up their lives for their lord. There is some indication that when they die, they are even more powerful and can wage war from the other side."

Olsen realized that the concoction that The Pontiff was smoking was having a profound effect on him. He pointed to another line in his newest chapter of the good book of Gya.

"We are going to add a sacrament to our daily prayers. This sacrament will be in the form of wine which will represent the blood of the sacrificed. To prove their faith, our followers will have to drink it even if they believe it is poisoned. We have to make sure that only the most devout are walking among us."

Olsen nodded her approval.

"I only wish that I could achieve your level of devotion so that I could receive a tiny share of the prophecy that the lord Gya gives you in his infinite wisdom."

The Pontiff reached up and placed his hands on either side of Olsen's face and pulled her face toward him. He kissed Olsen on the forehead.

"You will one day feel the connection with our lord, my daughter."

Olsen gave him a thoughtful look and bowed.

"If you will excuse me, I want to closely monitor the progress of our assault team. Please ask for Gya's blessing in the Morning Prayers."

Olsen left the office, hopped into her ATV and headed back to her office all the while thinking *what a lunatic. I should have just shot the crazy bastard through the head.*

When Olsen came back through the door, Crofton was waiting at his desk. He gave her a questioning look.

"What did he say?"

"He was on his Indian tobacco. Don't drink the wine when they start the sacrament this week."

Crofton gave her a puzzled look.

"You'll see, don't drink it unless they're holding a gun on you."

Olsen mentally went over her escape plans. Plan A was to simply drive out the front door and disappear in the mountains. Plan B was to go out by way of the door leading up to the fake pine tree antenna array. Plan C was to go out the way Chucky escaped. She had no intention of drinking the wine. She heard the morning call to prayer, but since she and Crofton were the only ones in her office, she didn't bother to roll out her prayer rug.

The Morning Prayer and sermon from The Pontiff was long and convoluted. The Pontiff, under the influence of the magic drugs, was sinking yet further into his delusions. Before long, he would believe that he was himself a man/god walking on Earth.

CHAPTER 26

Porter and Morgan had spent a miserable night in the mountains. They hadn't made it very far up the trail before they were overtaken by the darkness and cold. They found refuge from the wind in an alcove that had been created by an ancient rock slide. They piled rocks around their fire to radiate the heat back toward them. Their backpacks served as pillows, but the hard ground was unforgiving. A layer of pine boughs and leaves gave them some padding and insulated them from the cold ground beneath them.

Morgan screwed the lid back on his canteen.

"I don't know about you, Porter, but I'm ready to kill those Pine Tree Mountain folks and head home. No offense, but I had rather pile up in bed with Frankie than lay around in the cold forest with you. I half expected a bear to show up after Gord warned us about one being in the hiker's shed we didn't get to."

Porter rolled to a sitting position.

"I don't know; you are starting to look pretty good to me. I especially like the four day beard and the dirt and leaves in your hair. The way you cook up hard tack and jerky makes me realize what a great little wife you'd make."

As he opened the bags of tack and jerky, Morgan just shook his head.

"Here you go, sweetie, bon appetite'."

"Ah, breakfast in bed; that's sweet of you."

With a piece of jerky clenched firmly in his teeth, Morgan shouldered his pack.

"I believe this thing is heavier than it was when we started."

"It's going to be a lot heavier by the time we reach the top of this trail."

The trail which zig zagged up the mountain side had deteriorated from neglect and lack of use. They had to climb over and around obstacles of trees and rock slides. As they progressed, the straps from the backpacks, rifles and ammo packs began to dig into their shoulders causing them to labor under their load. Porter glanced back over at Morgan.

"If the fighting starts, we're going to have to ditch these packs. There's no way we can fight in the mountains and maneuver under this load."

Morgan pointed ahead.

"I think I see the hiker's shelter ahead. Let's see what we can unload from these packs. We can eat as much of the food as possible. That way at least, it's stored inside us and will take some of the load off our shoulders and back."

Porter agreed, "Let's use the shelter to stash some gear. We can always come back and retrieve it. We're not that far from the Duk, and unless we're wounded or injured, we can get back to it in half a day. It's all downhill from here."

They came to the abandoned shelter. After peering into the building, they ducked and went inside. The sun streamed into the shelter from the opened door. An ancient candle sat in a tin can with the front cut out so that it could be used as a lantern. There were several sleeping platforms against the wall, and a fire pit was next to the opening. They went through their packs separating out what they needed. From this point forward, they would be in combat mode. They would carry their rifles, pistols, ammo, knives and canteen. Porter had a small pair of binoculars, and Morgan had the ACOG scope on his rifle. In their packs, they had a change of socks, underwear, a first aid kit, water filter, folding multi-tool, flashlight, para cord, duct tape, zip ties, candle, fire starter kit, gun oil and a bar of soap wrapped in a face cloth. If they needed anything else, they would have to come back to the shelter or scavenge off the dead. As they were leaving, they were munching on hard tack and jerky. When the food in their hands had been consumed, they would go hungry.

Porter repositioned his ammo pack and exclaimed, "This is more like it. I can move now. A heavy pack is ok for a mile or two; but we'd have been sitting ducks if we ran into trouble with the load we were trying to carry."

Morgan nodded in agreement as they continued the climb up the trail to the top of the ridge. They were almost to the top when they heard movement. The sound of men and equipment was coming from above so they slowed their pace and reached a point where they could see a line of troops working their way along the top of the ridge. At one point, the troopers had to go single file around an outcropping. They counted twenty-two as they passed.

Morgan spoke to Porter in a low voice, "What do you think? Should we start shooting?"

Porter looking through his binoculars said, "We can sure reduce their numbers, and they're practically sitting ducks. I'll start at the front, and you start from the rear."

Without hesitation, Porter raised his rifle and fired. The two hundred yard range was nothing for him and the AK-47. He heard Morgan's rifle from behind him as the first two men in the line collapsed in their tracks. The third one went off the edge of the trail and tumbled out of sight down the side of the mountain. As in all fire fights, the plan pretty much goes in the can once the bullets start to fly. The remaining troopers had not spotted their exact location so they just fired in the direction of the sound of the rifles. Bullets were cutting through the trees over and around them. Porter and Morgan exhausted the magazines in their rifles and stopped long enough to swap them with fresh ones. From their concealed position, they could hear the remaining troopers shouting back and forth among themselves once the firing stopped. Those that were able had moved off the trail to concealed positions.

Morgan asked Porter, "How many did you get?"

"Three for sure, and two maybe's; I bet they'll all need a change of underwear. How about you?"

"I know I hit two; probably several more."

Porter didn't take his eyes off the trail.

"That leaves as many as seventeen. If they're any good, they'll have this trail located and will be chasing us down the mountain. I suggest we move off the trail into the underbrush, work our way to the top and get in front of them."

At that moment, at least a dozen guns opened up on their trail. The troopers were sweeping the woods with automatic fire. Morgan and Porter hunkered down. Although they were concealed, they had no real cover that would stop a bullet. Morgan grunted when a round struck his left forearm between the elbow and wrist.

"They broke my f'ing arm, Porter, and I'm bleeding bad."

Porter crawled on his belly over to Morgan's position.

"Clamp your hand on the wound and put some pressure on it."

Porter pulled out his knife and slit Morgan's coat and shirt sleeve exposing the wound.

"This isn't good. Hold pressure on it while I use your shirt sleeve to bind it. How bad does it hurt?"

Morgan, looking pale, grunted, "I'm not feeling much; I'm just sick at my stomach."

"Hang in there while I work on it."

Porter opened his backpack and retrieved a pair of his clean knee high socks. He tied one of the socks over the wound and pulled the slit shirt sleeve back over it all. He then took the duct tape and wrapped the wound making sure that the flow of blood was stemmed. He next took Morgan's rifle, removed the ACOG scope and punched out the pins holding the upper barrel assembly to the lower receiver. He dumped out the bolt carrier group and charging handle so that he just had the barrel and housing. He took the upper and laid Morgan's arm on it. While keeping the arm straight, he bound duct tape around everything. He chunked the lower receiver, bolt carrier group and the charge handle in Morgan's backpack. In the span of five minutes and in the midst of bursts of gunfire, he had the arm splinted. He took the slit coat sleeve and pulled it over the arm and gun barrel and secured everything with three zip ties. The gunfire stopped.

"They'll be heading this way soon; can you get to your pistol?"

Morgan nodded yes.

"I can reach it."

Porter took the sling off the remains of Morgan's rifle and fashioned a sling for the broken arm.

"Morgan, see if you can wiggle your fingers."

Morgan was able to move the fingers and forced a grin.

"At least it didn't hit the nerve."

Porter pointed at Morgan's hand.

"Keep an eye on your fingers; if they start to get numb or turn purple, let me know or cut some of the duct tape. The swelling could cut off the circulation. I wrapped it pretty tight, because you'll be moving through some rough terrain."

Morgan looked puzzled.

"What do you mean I'll be moving through rough terrain? What about you?"

Porter pointed back down the trail.

"You're going to sit here until you hear me start shooting. Then you're going to make your way back down the trail to the shelter."

Morgan shook his head.

"I don't think so. Without the weight of my ammo, I can move just fine. I can at least back you up. I haven't lost that much blood. Besides, I'm not going to feel like doing much of anything once the feeling comes back into this arm."

Porter turned his attention to the ridge where he saw some movement.

"They'll be heading down this trail, but they won't be expecting me to attack. You sit here and shoot at any head you see popping up, but shoot only after you hear me shooting. I'm not going to start firing until I can see at least four or five of them."

"Good luck, buddy. Thanks for patching me up."

Porter crawled on his belly through the snow, leaves and pine straw. Shortly, he was in a position to see up the trail leading to the top, but he couldn't see the trail on top of the mountain where they had ambushed the troopers. That also meant that they couldn't see him from up there either. He lay quietly. Patience was his friend, and he was soon rewarded. The first trooper ran forward and took a position behind a pine tree. The next moved past him several hundred feet and got into some rocks. A third moved past both of them and took up a position in the underbrush. They were peering down the path and not in Porter's direction. All were partially exposed which was what Porter needed. All he would have to do is put a bullet through an exposed portion of their body. He wouldn't have to take a kill shot to put them out of action. After awhile, six troopers were scatted out along the trail. The nearest trooper was only ten feet away. When the seventh one started moving forward, Porter aimed at the head of the one that was nearest. He tightened his finger on the trigger, and the gun bounced.

CHAPTER 27

Dix woke in his bed in Jonas' cabin. The evening before, Jonas, Dix, and Fox had elected to go back to the cabin to replenish their ammo and to rest. He glanced down at the illuminated dial on his watch: 4:05 am. *That lick on my head and the loss of blood have taken a toll on this old body.* He rose, put on his boots and checked his weapons. He walked up the hall to the kitchen where he found Jonas and Fox getting geared up. Jonas had dug out two more Colt M4 carbines, additional ammo and some magazines. Fox and Jonas were busy pushing cartridges from preloaded clips into the magazines. Jonas pointed to Dix's rifle.

"I imagine you are about out of bullets by now."

Fox pointed to a handful of 30-30 cartridges on the bar.

"I can only kill nine more including what's in my rifle."

Noticing that his bandoleer was empty, Dix reached into his pocket and pulled out a well-worn box of cartridges. The green Remington box had the edges worn and fuzzy from riding in his pockets. He opened the box and slipped out the foam liner that held the bullets so they wouldn't rattle. Of the twenty rounds originally in the box, only twelve were left. He returned the liner with the cartridges to the box and chunked it on the counter.

"I'm in the same boat. When the reinforcements arrive, it won't take long to use these up."

Jonas handed him a new Colt M4 with an ACOG scope.

"These are sighted in to hit two inches high at a hundred yards."

Dix stood the old Springfield in the corner along with the remaining box of bullets. He hefted the Colt to his shoulder and adjusted the collapsible stock. Next he adjusted the sling to fit his arm and shoulder.

After making sure it was ready, he turned to Jonas and asked, "Have we heard anything from Porter or Morgan?"

"I just got off the radio with Captain Jones. Porter and Morgan are on foot crossing the mountain from the other side. They knocked out a squad and their vehicles, and the road is now impassable."

Fox commented, "Those perverts didn't have a prayer. I almost feel sorry for them. I've seen Porter shoot. If he can see you and has a gun in his hand, you're in serious trouble."

Jonas asked, "What about Morgan?"

Dix answered, "Morgan is a thinker, and he's a whiz at building mechanical devices. He's a good shot, but his skill lies in building things like IED's, special vehicles, drones and the odd mechanical device. He's one of those people who understand how things work."

Fox chimed in, "The best thing he made was that alcohol still."

Dix agreed, "His distillery investment is one of his best projects."

Fox pulled out the radio that he had taken from the dead officer.

"Let's power this up and see if we can overhear anything."

Dix turned on the radio.

"The battery meter is showing that it's almost exhausted. I suggest that we use it in moderation until we can figure out how to charge it. We need to look and see if there is a charging cradle in one of their vehicles out in front of the bar."

Jonas walked over to the front window.

"Turn out the lights. I have black tarps over the windows in this room. I want to open the door and step out to see if I can see or hear anything. If the coast is clear, I want to get out of here. I don't have to tell you that we're sitting ducks in this cabin. We can expect their reinforcements to come rolling through here at any time. They weren't expecting us to hit them as hard and fast as we did; they'll expect strong resistance this time."

Jonas stepped out into the night and listened. The wind had died down, and the only sound was from coyotes howling in the distance. He stepped back in and closed the door.

"The only thing moving out there is a pack of coyotes."

Dix flipped the lights back on when he heard the door close.

"Let's get out of here. I want to get back up the valley where we can ambush them."

They geared up and headed down the road walking toward the bar.

Fox grumbled, "I remember the good old days when we rode around in vehicles."

Dix glanced over at Fox and explained, "I don't want to travel into battle inside a vehicle. You're a sitting duck in a vehicle; I know, because I've taken out more than a few. In fact, you're even a sitting duck inside a house. Most rifles can shoot right into a house and the bullets can go out the other side. Nothing short of a rock or masonry wall will stop most bullets."

The bright moon reflecting off the snow allowed them to walk safely.

Jonas pointed out, "Most of the time, it's not safe to travel around here at night; the only thing that is working in our favor is the bright moonlight. This much light makes it harder for them to see us with their night vision equipment, but that's not impossible. Once we get to the vehicles in front of the bar, we'll start monitoring the radio if there is a charging cradle on board. My guess is they'll be delayed by the trees dropped across the road. When the road is cleared, we'll have our hands full."

The sun was up by the time they reached the bar. They found that the trooper vehicles were still sitting disabled in the road. Jonas located a charging cradle in the lead vehicle and put the portable radio on charge. While the handheld unit was charging, they found permanently mounted radios in each of the other vehicles. Turning on one of those radios, they listened as Wilson and Nichols planned and discussed troop strengths.

Dix looked at Fox.

"I'm glad you found this radio. We now know they have about forty-eight troopers heading our way and that they are expecting to corner us up on the mountain."

Jonas pointed out, "Their strategy might work. We've got to get up on the mountain and get Chuck and the women back down."

Dix turned to Fox and commanded, "Get on the bar radio and see if you can raise Cartwright, Jack and Chuck."

Fox disappeared up the bar room steps and through the open doors. Dix followed at a slower pace since he was still favoring his leg wound. He turned around to Jonas.

"Bring that Pine Mountain radio up here. We're going to get these stitches out. I'm not trapesing all over this mountain with those things irritating me like this. I don't need any more distractions."

"Let's get them all pulled including the ones on your scalp. We can always re-stitch them if you manage to tear them open."

Dix and Jonas walked into the bar just as Fox fired up the radio. "This is Fox. Is anybody listening?"

Cartwright answered first, "I just got back from where we dropped the first tree. They are busy hacking away at it. I look for them to be moving our way in about thirty minutes. I'm taking my family up on the mountain."

Dix took the mic. "This is Major Jernigan, do not go up on the mountain; you'll be trapped. There's a group coming down the hiking trail. Bring your family here to the bar. How many trees did y'all drop?"

Cartwright keyed his mic. "We dropped two more trees last night; that should delay them and give us an hour or so more time."

Chuck who had been listening asked, "What do you want us to do?"

Jonas took the mic. "Chuck, get the ladies up and moving in this direction. Remember to turn off and collect the IED's. We can reset them elsewhere once the battle starts."

Chuck answered, "We're on our way. I'm hearing a lot of gunfire in the distance."

Jonas looked at Dix and keyed the mic. "Chuck, which direction and how loud?"

"It's north in the direction that the trail runs, and it sounds a long way off."

"Y'all get moving, and don't forget to deactivate the IED's. Do not delay! I want you guys moving in five minutes. Tell the ladies who aren't riding on the first trip to start walking. You can pick them up on the second trip back. We'll see you in a few."

Old Man Jack came on next. "Get everyone up here to the farm, I know a place for everyone to hide, but I'm not saying where on the radio."

Jonas nodded as he keyed the mic. "They'll be on their way shortly."

Dix walked out on the porch and cupped his ears. In the distance, he heard some of the gunfire. He turned and went back in.

"If that's Porter and Morgan, that troop hiking in just lost some of their team members."

At that moment the Pine Tree Mountain radio came to life, "Nichols, Wilson here. We've been hit. I have six dead and four wounded, including me. I think we have them pinned down, and I sent eight of my best down the trail to flush them out."

Nichols answered, "How bad are you hit?"

"Not bad just a new part in my scalp. Do you have any idea how many are in the attacking force?"

"I'm not sure how many, but they're very good. They don't seem to miss when they shoot."

After a pause Nichols reported, "We aren't up against a group of simple settlers. All of our dead were piled up in front of the tree we are trying to move. Do you want me to send help? We're blocked here for another thirty or forty-five minutes. We didn't bring chainsaws so the troops are using axes and machetes to clear the tree in the road. It can be pushed out of the way once they get some of the canopy removed."

"No, it may only be a couple of them down there shooting. The guys I sent should flush them out quickly.

"We'll let you know when we're moving. Nichols out."

Dix gave Fox and Jonas a worried look.

"I think the question has been answered; Porter and Morgan have arrived."

Fox asked, "Alright fellas, what's the plan?"

Dix started unbuttoning his pants.

"The first thing we're doing is yank these damned stitches. Then we're going to make sure that the girls and the Cartwrights are heading to Old Man Jack's place. We may get some help from the single boys."

Jonas quickly had the stitches out of Dix's leg and head.

"Dix, don't be doing any splits if you can avoid it. I have an idea. Why don't you let me head up the trail after the girls get here. I want to go help Porter. I bet there are at least a dozen or more troops who are gunning for them."

Dix, cinching up his pants and rubbing the new scar on his head, relented, "You know, that might not be a bad idea. If we can get them charging up the mountain after Jonas, Porter and Morgan, Fox and I could come in behind them and attack from the rear. It might catch them off guard. Take their radio. You'll need to know if Nichols' group comes charging up the mountain in your direction."

Fox stepped forward.

"Do you realize if Porter and Morgan don't survive or become injured, that will leave just the three of us fighting as many as thirty-six young healthy troopers? I

375

imagine that these are lot more skilled and confident than what we've seen so far."

Jonas rinsed off his knife blade with some moonshine from a bottle on the bar.

"I learned one thing from all my years in the military and black ops. The reason black ops expanded was because the U.S. military had deteriorated under our last communist president. We had some really good officers and men, but they were slowly weeded out and replaced by communist party hacks. Officers were placed and promoted based on political correctness rather than their skill and leadership ability. The good ones were drummed out, so many of them wound up in black ops. When the job had to get done, it went to the black ops and private contractors."

Dix agreed. "These troopers are well equipped and appear to be disciplined, but they have absolutely no combat experience. They only exist to guard Pine Tree Mountain, and they do that with lots of warm bodies and an abundance of ammo. I don't believe any of them fought during the collapse. All they've done is keep Pine Tree Mountain secure."

Fox pointed out, "I realize we're fighting a bunch of pansies, but thirty-six pansies spraying the woods with automatic gun fire can still accidently kill us. Do you remember that movie where the special forces squad starting shooting at the alien? They mowed down a pretty good swath of jungle with gun fire."

Dix turned to Fox and said, "I bet they've spent more time in Yoga class than in combat training. Get on the radio with Captain Jones and see how many and where our reinforcements are."

Fox changed the frequency and keyed the mic. "Cooney, are you up this morning?"

The radio crackled. "Jones here. What's up, Fox?"

Fox handed Dix the mic. "Cooney, this is Dix. Things are heating up pretty fast. What's the status on our reinforcements?"

"The best time frame is that you won't be seeing them for maybe four days."

"How many are being sent?"

"I think you're getting a hundred or more."

"Keep us posted on their progress, won't you?"

Fox looked concerned and quipped, "A hundred versus three thousand, what do y'all think?"

Dix shrugged.

"Each man only has to kill thirty. I don't see a problem. We've had much worse odds before. Don't forget our men are the meanest, bad asses that have ever lived."

"You're right; maybe we should send half of them back."

"We may not need them at all. I'm thinking we need to just go into The Mountain and get to work."

Fox stammered, "Did you say 'in The Mountain'? I'm not ready to commit suicide. If I get killed, Becky will never let me hear the end of it."

Jonas cracked his knuckles.

"They are just going to keep sending them out. Next time they'll send several hundred instead of these squads, especially after we send these running home."

At that moment they heard the sound of Cartwright's truck pulling up. Jonas went to the front deck and motioned for them to come up. Cartwright and his family quickly came in and gathered around the wood heater. Jonas looked at Cartwright.

"Kitty and the girls will be here shortly. I want you to lead them over to Old Man Jack's farm; he has a place you can hide."

Cartwright nodded his agreement.

"As soon as everyone is settled, I'll be back to help."

Dix patted him on the shoulder.

"We can use all the help we can get. Contact us by radio before you head back. The situation is fluid at this point. I wouldn't be surprised if they didn't start sending some scouts on foot in this direction."

Chuck arrived in the electric ATV with five of the seven women.

"I'll be back in a few minutes; I have two more to go back for."

Jonas clapped him on the shoulder.

"Good work, kid. I'm riding back with you. Let me get my gear; you'll be dropping me off."

Kitty, who overheard him, asked, "What are you planning on doing?"

"Porter and Morgan are in trouble; I'm going to help."

She stopped him.

"Wait."

She grabbed him and gave him a big kiss.

"Please come back to me."

He hugged her back.

"My plans are to do just that. You're going to take the girls and go to Old Man Jack's farm. He has a place for you to hide, and Hester's already there."

Nadine's ears perked up and asked, "You mean my Mama's alive?"

"She was beat up really bad, but she was alive when his boys carried her back to the farm."

Jonas grabbed his battle gear, a small back pack and hopped in the ATV.

"Chuck, you are really good at following orders. You are going to drop me off when we pick up the ladies. I'm going up the trail to where all the shooting is taking place. I want you to help get the ladies moved up to Old Man Jack's place. Major Jernigan and Fox will tell you what to do after that."

Chuck asked, "When can I get in the fight?"

"You're in the fight right now. I need you to help protect the civilians. You'll be right in the middle of the fighting soon enough. I have a feeling Major Jernigan is going to be heading into The Mountain shortly, and we're going to need you to help guide us."

Chuck looked determined.

"I just hope I can stuff The Pontiff's good book down his throat."

"I hope you do too, son. In fact, I would like to be the one holding him down while you do it."

They met the ladies about a mile up the trail. Jonas put a couple of the IED's in his pack and headed up the mountain toward the fighting. Chuck turned the ATV around and headed back toward the bar. Jonas double timed it up the trail and heard a massive volley of gunfire in the distance. He knew what they were doing; he had seen the tactic used before. They were trying to flush the men or overwhelm and kill them by the sheer weight of ordnance being directed at their location. He had been in the same situation several times around the world. He knew that to maintain one's composure and courage when the world is coming apart around him or her was difficult.

He soldiered on until he was sweating, and his side was hurting from the heavy breathing. The firing had stopped, and he knew that he was getting close to the action. He slowed to a walk, pausing often to look and listen. Up ahead he heard movement and soon spotted a half dozen men along the trail concentrating their attention down the side of the mountain. He knew he was close to the west trail that led off the mountain because, when he was a young man, he had spent the night several times in a hiker's shelter further down that trail.

The nearest of the six troopers to Jonas should have been watching the trail south, but his inexperience had him concentrating on the mountain below instead. Jonas took aim on the man and prepared his mind to rapidly shoot all of them as fast as he could squeeze off his shots. He could easily hit the first three; after that the others would begin to react. Some might keep their cool and return fire, or they could panic. Panic would be his guess *after all* he told himself *they're probably a bunch of pansies*. Just as he raised his gun to shoot, shots rang out from below.

CHAPTER 28

Morgan was on his knees with his pistol cocked in his hand. He heard Porter shoot and saw a pink fog from the hot spray of blood appear in the air over the trail. This was followed by eleven more shots about a half second apart. He waited for someone to show themselves. At the next moment, he heard similar gunfire from up on the ridge trail. Several troopers came into view sprinting back up the narrow trail toward the rock outcropping that could only be passed single file. He heard Porter shoot, and then he heard another shot come from on top of the ridge. Two of the troopers collapsed, rolled off the trail and down the side of the mountain. The sound of their bodies could be heard falling through the trees and brush. Porter came running up in a crouch.

"Sounds like we have some help up top. It must the Major or some of his men."

Morgan de-cocked his pistol and returned it to its holster.

"How many did they send down?"

"I'm not sure, but eight won't be going back."

"Let's head up. There can't be many left, and I imagine the ones who are left will be running in the other direction."

Porter cut Morgan a walking stick.

"Hold back until I make sure it's clear. I'll let you know when it's safe to move."

Porter viewed the trail and cautiously made his way to the top.

Just as he reached the intersection of the two trails, a deep voice from the woods spoke, "You must be Porter Jones."

Porter didn't panic because he knew that if he were in danger, he'd already be dead or in a gun fight.

"Yes, I'm Porter Jones, or what's left of him. Who are you?"

"I'm Jonas Hank, one of Major Jernigan's recent recruits. Is Morgan alright?"

"Morgan's back down the trail; he's been hit, but he can walk. If you'll stay here and cover me, I'll go get him."

"I'll be glad to."

Porter went back down the trail where he retrieved Morgan and led him back to the top of the trail. Jonas looked at the improvised splint and sling.

"That's quite a contraption you have there. That's some good improvising. Where's the rest of your gun?"

Morgan pointed. "It's in my backpack."

"How bad is the arm?"

"The bullet broke the bone, but I can still wiggle my fingers, and the bleeding has stopped."

Jonas felt of Morgan's hand and took the pulse in the arm at the wrist and above the elbow.

"You seem to have good blood flow, and the hand is warm. How bad was the bone shattered?"

"I'm not sure; I didn't see any bones sticking out, but the arm feels like it has a hinge about halfway between my wrist and elbow."

Jonas cut the zip ties and pulled back the coat sleeve.

"It looks like y'all have it good and straight, and it's well stabilized. That'll have to do until I can get you back to my place where we can fix it proper. In the meantime, we need to get you hid in a safe place."

He retrieved some new zip ties from Morgan's backpack and rebound the coat sleeve over the arm.

Porter who had been guarding the trail had been listening.

"What's the situation?"

"We are between two groups of troopers out of Pine Tree Mountain. The ones we just encountered here and a force of twenty or more in the valley below. We managed to get one of their radios and have been listening in on their plans. The ones below were planning to ambush us from behind, but their strategy will have to change with the loss of this group."

Morgan cradled his arm.

"We counted twenty-two who came around that narrow point up the trail from here. I'm not sure how many were holding back behind them, or how many we killed or hit. We lucked up and caught them where the trail turned into a ledge."

Jonas spoke up, "According to the radio conversation we overheard, you killed six and wounded four initially. How many did y'all get down on the trail?"

"Eight, and I saw two go down from you and Porter at the end."

Jonas commented, "There are three more on the ground just ahead. If I am doing the math right, only a handful of the original twenty-two you counted are left."

Porter pointed to Morgan's arm.

"If we have another twenty or more heading this way, we need to get Morgan hidden somewhere safe while we work. I wouldn't mind following those troops back up the trail."

"Before we do that, we need to get the Major on the radio and see if he's heard anything."

Jonas keyed the mic. "Major Jernigan, are you listening?"

Dix answered, "Did you find Porter and Morgan?"

"I found them; we've made contact with the squads up here and have prevailed. Morgan has a broken arm. It has been splinted, and he is stable for now. Porter patched him up before I got here."

Dix keyed the mic. "You better count his fingers and toes if Porter has been doctoring on him."

Porter and Morgan started laughing.

Porter shook his head and said, "Tell him I didn't perform any surgery yet."

Jonas keyed the mic. "Porter says that he hasn't performed any surgery yet."

"Praise the lord; hide his knife before it's too late."

"Have there been any chatter on their radio?"

"No, about ten minutes ago Nichols tried to radio Wilson but has not gotten an answer. Nichols also

387

contacted the personnel carriers who have verified that there is no sign of Wilson or the squad."

"Wilson may not be able to answer; we shot them up pretty bad. What's the status on the force coming down the valley? If I were them, I would send a small scouting party up here to find out what happened. Then I would proceed as far as Cartwrights' or the bar and secure the area until I could get more reinforcements. They are going to have to try and isolate us. They must also think there are more of us than there are."

Dix keyed the mic. "We have everyone moved to Jack's farm. Jack, his boy Larry and Cartwright are on their way back here to the bar. They are going to meet Fox, Chuck and me, and I'll decide our next move. I expect them back any minute. Fox is hidden where he can see the last tree barricading the road; he'll report as soon as he sees anything."

"Ok, then, we'll sit tight and wait on your orders. Jonas out."

Dix pulled off the wool stocking cap and rubbed the stubble of fresh hair growing around the new scar on his head. He took a deep drink from his canteen and sat on the picnic table under the bar. The charge controller from the solar array on top of the bar slowly flashed a green light indicating that all was well and that the battery bank was nearing capacity. The dilemma before him was quite simple. He was currently outnumbered on the ground and vastly outnumbered in this campaign. Even with the hundred or so Constitution forces that were currently on their way, the odds were heavily in favor of the Pine Mountain forces. *This was not unlike the middle ages when a castle came under siege.* Dix sat and pondered. He had prevailed by doing the opposite of what most sane individuals would do. He survived in spite of being reckless. He thought back to all the times he threw caution to the wind because he had nothing for which to live. Blind vengeance gave him strength before, and it was providing the strength for this battle as well. All the perversion, insanity and corruption that brought America to its knees still had a seed bed growing in Pine Tree Mountain. Dix put himself in the shoes of his enemy. The squads would have reported to The Mountain by now; he envisioned The Pontiff summoning his staff and officers. They obviously had no compunction about torturing and sacrificing their enemy. If he were in charge and had absolutely no

389

regard for human life, he would send out several hundred men and kill everything that moved within thirty miles. He had two options: hide and snipe from cover and wait for the reinforcements or go on the offensive and invade The Mountain with the men he had. He didn't know the ability of Jack, Larry, Cartwright or Chuck, but he knew the expertise of Morgan, Porter, Jonas and Fox. Morgan was probably out of the fight and could only be counted on as backup. He himself was hampered from the leg wound and the lick on his head. Porter, Fox and Jonas would have to do the heavy lifting.

As Dix sat pondering the situation, Fox keyed the mic on his radio. "Major, they finally cleared that last tree and are moving your way. I expect you will see them in about twenty minutes."

"Fox, let them pass. I want you behind them. Since our people are hidden, we're not going to engage them. Jonas, are you listening?"

Jonas keyed his mic. "I've been listening. What you are thinking?"

"If I were a betting man," Dix replied, "I would think they're going to secure the bar and wait for reinforcements. We're going to come up the mountain to meet you guys. Can Morgan move?"

Jonas looked around at Morgan who had been listening.

"You heard the question. How bad are you feeling?"

Morgan struggled to his feet.

"I'm not planning on laying around up here; I can feel bad moving or feel bad hiding."

Jonas keyed the mic. "Morgan says he can move. Just follow the trail until you run upon some dead troopers. Morgan will be waiting nearby. We're going to go ahead and see if we can clean up any we missed. We'll radio back, and let you know if we all get killed."

Dix replied, "We'll be heading that way in a minute. I see Jack and the boys coming on the ATV. Fox, are you listening?"

Fox answered, "I'm still here. Where do you want me?"

"I want you to stick around down here and tell me what they're up to. We're going up to join Jonas, Morgan and Porter. Don't get shot, and don't get captured."

"I'll keep you posted from down here. Fox out."

Dix climbed the stairs and gathered the radios from the bar. He greeted the four men as they arrived.

"The Pine Tree Mountain folks will be here any minute. We're heading up on the mountain. Is everyone ready?"

Cartwright spoke up, "Sure, hop on, we're all geared up."

The ATV silently crunched through the snow as it made its way toward the trail up the mountain. Chuck was sitting next to Dix.

"Why aren't we staying to fight?"

Dix looked over at him and cocked an eyebrow.

"Don't worry, you're going to see more action than you can imagine. We're heading into the belly of the beast."

CHAPTER 29

Nichols was still shaken from the sight of the body pile lying in the middle of the road. She gave up trying to call Wilson. She changed the frequency and keyed her mic. "This is Captain Nichols; get me Olsen."

Her small convoy drove around the dead and moved slowly because they were expecting an ambush at any moment. Her driver was still pale after seeing the pile of their dead comrades.

Olsen came on the radio. "Give me a SITREP."

Nichols nervously keyed the mic. "Wilson came under attack, and I've lost contact with him. The drivers and vehicles are still waiting where they dropped them off, but they haven't heard anything either. They blocked the road with our dead. We moved them to the side, and we also have had to move three trees in order to travel down the road. We haven't come under fire, but it could happen at any time."

Nichols continued giving Olsen the map coordinates where Wilson had left his personnel carriers and for the mountain ridge that he was on when the attack occurred.

Olsen swore under her breath.

"Proceed to that biker bar and hold it. As soon as I confer with The Pontiff, I'll send out enough men to wipe out everyone and everything within thirty miles."

Olsen called out to Crofton, "Get in here."

Crofton came in and closed the door behind him.

"Is it time to run, chief?"

"Soon, but first I need you to summon the officers for a meeting in three hours. After I meet with The Pontiff, I'll have the agenda."

Olsen walked past Crofton and out into the tunnel where her ATV awaited. Her plan was simple: if she convinced The Pontiff to make the attack, she was going to follow behind her troops in the Jeep with all her provisions. Instead of following them, she would turn away heading north and then turn west until she was at least a hundred miles away. She knew that they were encountering more than just the local settlers. Only seasoned combat veterans could take out as many men as she had sent. This was much more than armed resistance, and she knew that there were probably more on the way. Her command consisted of people who had little or no combat experience. The sniper crews were the only ones with a lot of training and had had actual combat experience. Most of their experience came from the fighting alongside their Chinese comrades. Her other officers and troops came from people who were aligned with her politically and socially. Hiding in a fortress behind locked doors was easy, but coming up against a skilled and determined force was entirely different.

She navigated the short drive down to The Pontiff's office.

Danforth's old boyfriend greeted her by saying, "Major Olsen, The Pontiff is waiting."

He opened the door so Olsen could go straight in.

The Pontiff was standing over his map table.

"I just heard that we lost another patrol. Gya isn't happy with your performance."

Olsen bit her tongue and listened.

The Pontiff strutted around the room. A wisp of smoke was rising from the bowl of his hookah.

"I want to know what you plan to do about this."

Olsen walked over and pointed to the map where the troops were hit.

"As you can see the only passable route toward Eureka Springs is closed below this mountain pass. Between the ice covered roads and the destroyed vehicles blocking the road, that route is impassable. Enemy forces hit our squad along this mountain ridge, and we lost the squad in the valley when it reached the old biker bar. I've ordered Nichols to take the bar and set up a base camp. She should be nearing its location now. So far, she has only been slowed by the roadway blocked with trees. I propose we deploy forty squads totaling four hundred and eighty men. We'll go into the valley and down the top of the mountain and basically kill everything that moves. Once we completely secure everything in that valley, we'll move down onto the blocked road from the mountain and do the same thing on the road and valley in the direction of Eureka Springs. I will reassign half of the snipers to this force since most of them have been in actual combat."

The Pontiff plopped down behind his desk and took a long draw on the stem of his hookah.

"Do I have to tell you what's going to happen to you if this fails?"

"I won't fail; this is what we should have done in the first place."

"How soon before you can make this happen?"

Olsen pondered a moment.

"We will need two days to mobilize and two days to get all the troops and equipment into position. I'll personally take to the field with them."

The Pontiff seemed quite pleased with the plan.

"Stay and join me for the sacrament. My favorite speaker will be performing the service. I have an extra prayer rug you can use."

The prayer session went a little longer since it included the sacrament. Danforth's old boyfriend came in with three glasses of the wine they would be drinking. Olsen's head was spinning with so many thoughts that she almost missed the cue to partake of the wine. As soon as she drank it, she immediately felt a rush of energy. Obviously, the wine was a grape flavored beverage spiked with a stimulant.

The Pontiff announced, "The wine is non-alcoholic, and I had the physicians add a little something to it to make the experience more profound."

Olsen thought *the faithful will think they are having a religious experience.*

The Pontiff rose after the prayer and returned to his desk.

"My studies are going well. I have located an obscure text that describes the calling of the dead. Our spirit cooking sessions are going to be exciting tonight as I attempt to invoke the spirits from our lost comrades."

Olsen bowed.

"I look forward to hearing the results."

The Pontiff gave her a knowing look.

"I want you and all your officers at the session tonight."

"I'll see to it that all are in attendance."

Olsen climbed aboard her ATV and returned to her office. Crofton looked up from his desk as Olsen walked through the door.

"The meeting is scheduled, and the rumor mill is running at full capacity. Everyone wants to know what is going on."

Olsen saw the empty wine glass on Crofton's desk.

"Did you drink the wine?"

"No, I poured it down the floor drain. Why, did you?"

"I got caught in The Pontiff's office and couldn't avoid it. They spiked it with something. I feel almost euphoric."

Olsen went to her desk and created the agenda for distribution. She printed maps and busied herself preparing for the meeting. While preparing the maps, she carefully planned her escape route. She slipped the Ruger .380 into her back pocket and mentally steeled herself to the chain of events that were starting to unfold.

Crofton walked into the office.

"Nichols just radioed that they have reached the bar, and the area is secure and abandoned. She didn't encounter any resistance."

"That seems strange. After the fierce resistance we received the first time, I can't believe they haven't been attacked. I'm amazed they didn't attack them when they had the roads blocked with trees."

Crofton gloated, "They probably used the trees to slow them down in order to evacuate. We have them on the run."

"Not hardly," Olson snarled, "They just wiped out Wilson's squad. I'm sure they could run over Nichols whenever they get ready."

Olsen was waiting when her officers filed in. After the prayers to Gya, she got to the agenda.

"Before you are the plans for our mobilization. We are going to eradicate the infidels. Our first objective is to clean out the valley. We'll be attacking on two fronts. I want half of our snipers assigned to the various commands. Only use the ones with actual combat experience. I don't know if we have anyone in our command that has ever come under fire."

The euphoria in the room was almost electrifying as Olsen fielded questions and assigned duties.

"We are limited in the number of personnel carriers so we will have to ferry smaller groups. I want the snipers dispersed along the route to act as scouts and to help guard the deployment. I want trucks and personnel heading out in force the day after tomorrow. I want two man sniper teams with each squad. They'll be spending the night at their nest in the field so outfit them accordingly. I want to have this operation in the field and ready to roll in four days. By day six, I want every human being, in our operation area, dead or captured. After you assign duties to your officers and non-comms, prepare to attend The Pontiff's spirit cooking ceremony."

A look of joy could be seen radiating from the faces of her officers corp.

One of the most devout spoke up, "Thank you, Major, I can't tell you how long I've dreamed of being able to attend one of The Pontiff's private ceremonies. I'll never forget it."

The meeting broke up with the chanting of "Gya is great, Gya is great, Gya is great."

Olsen and Crofton chanted with them as they marched from the conference room and out into the tunnel. Olsen glanced at Crofton.

"The poor bastards don't stand a chance or have a clue."

CHAPTER 30

Hunkered down in the bushes on the side of the mountain within sight of the bar, Fox watched Nichols as she climbed the stairs. She was barking orders for the troops to quickly set up a perimeter and ready their defenses. A couple of mechanics went to work on the disabled vehicles.

Fox put the earbud from the radio in his ear and keyed the mic and whispered, "Dix, they've set up house at the bar. I believe they are moving in for a while."

Dix had been listening for Fox.

"Great, that means they are expecting reinforcements. Do you think you can make it up here without being seen? I want you going in with us."

"I'll radio you once I make it back up to the trail. Fox out."

Fox turned and carefully angled his way toward the mountain and away from the bar. He soon found himself laboring under the weight of his weapons and gear. His thoughts returned to his home down south; he longed for the simple farm life back home. He was sick of being cold and fearful, but, like Dix, he knew that the people in The Mountain were no different than a cancerous tumor growing in a healthy body. A person can't reason with a tumor, so one must destroy it. In a couple of hours, he made it to the top of the ridge where he found the trail was nonexistent. There was only one way to go, and that was up. When he reached the ridge, he found the trail again, and after catching his breath, he proceeded to rendezvous with Dix and the rest of the men.

He keyed his radio. "Dix, I'm on the trail. You might want to send the medivac helicopter to get me."

"Your ride is on the way. I'm sending Chuck back in the ATV to get you."

Jonas and Porter had left Morgan hidden next to the trail to wait for Dix. They cautiously went down the trail and hurried over the ledge that had allowed them to ambush the Pine Tree Mountain squad. Once they were off the ledge, they found two trails of blood heading up the trail. They found a trooper with officers' insignia and the name Wilson on his coat pocket. The man had a hole through his neck and had bled out about twenty feet from the ledge. Jonas jumped as Porter threw his Kbar knife at a target on the side of the trail. Jonas looked into the shadows as a wounded man fell over after being hit high in the chest with the big blade. The man had been wounded and made the mistake of going for his pistol. Porter removed the knife and wiped if off on the dead man's coat. With caution, they continued to follow the remaining blood trail. They passed a discarded back pack, a rifle and finally a pistol belt. The man was on his hands and knees crawling up the trail when they found him. He collapsed just as they overtook him. Before they could do anything, he coughed up a lung full of blood and died.

Jonas keyed his radio. "Major Jernigan, I think they're all dead, but some uninjured ones could be retreating."

Dix quickly answered, "I'm sending Chuck back down the trail to pick up Fox with the ATV. As soon as they get back, we'll be heading your way."

Chuck arrived with Fox in tow. Dix looked at Fox. "Glad to see you old man."

Fox moaned, "Dix, I'm tired, and I'm ready to kick some ass. I want to be home for Christmas."

Dix turned to Chuck and ordered, "Park the ATV over in the sun so the solar panel can charge the batteries while we're gone. We'll be on foot from here."

They donned their packs and weapons, preceded up the trail and across the ledge. Morgan peered over the edge at the bodies lying at the bottom of the cliff. He commented as they crossed, "I proclaim this ledge, Dead Man's Ledge."

When they reached Wilson's body, Fox exclaimed, "Those boots look like my size." He held his boot with the toe shot out up to Wilson's boot.

Dix called out, "Wait up a second, men; Fox is trying on boots." They laughed as Fox tried on the new pair.

"They fit better than my other pair." Fox also relieved Wilson of his Rolex watch.

Dix called back to him, "Can we continue if you're through shopping?"

Fox snapped the watch on his left wrist and pulled his shirt and coat sleeve over it. "Let's go; he's out of inventory now. I'm in the market for a new pair of sun glasses if anybody sees any that aren't shot up."

Morgan grinned in spite of the pain from his broken arm.

They followed the trail as it snaked its way up the spine of the mountain. In areas the trail flattened out into meadows and in other areas it was hidden in old forest. They came to a rock outcropping where they could see the valley below and the large lake at the bottom. Jonas pointed out the location of his cabin and the position of Bill's Bar. Dix sat down on a rock. His leg wound was aching, and his head was tender.

Jonas checked Morgan's arm to make sure that the blood was still getting to his fingers and that he was able to move them.

He told Morgan, "If you can make it to Pine Tree Mountain, I have a couple of med kits with morphine stashed with some other things I haven't had time to carry out."

Morgan nodded toward his arm and exclaimed, "I am very self-aware at this point."

Jonas retorted, "I expect it will hurt a lot more before we get you medicated."

Dix dug around in his pack and came out with a bottle of ibuprofen.

"I almost forgot that I had these."

He shook four into Morgan's hand and took four himself.

"If I remember, it's ok to take a massive dose for a short period of time. I know your arm hurts worse than my leg, and my leg is sore as hell."

Chuck, who hadn't said much, spoke up, "The Mountain has several doctors and a full hospital."

Dix replied, "If we can avoid killing the doctors, they might come in handy. Jonas, have you given any thought on how we are going to keep from getting killed once we get inside?"

"I've been giving it a lot of thought. We are going to have to isolate them on level three. We can take the ones out on level four and all the snipers because we can get them from behind. If we get to the armory, we can get suppressors for the pistols and rifles. Located on level four is also a bunker with C4 explosives and one where we can get blasting caps and timers, portable Claymore mines and hand grenades. Since a tunnel on level five was being extended, there's a dynamite bunker at that location as well.

"Jonas, if you were to bring down the entire facility, how would you do it?"

"Quite simple. Do you remember how the World Trade Center came down? After that first floor collapsed, the weight of the floors above it slammed down onto the ones below. The momentum of the falling floors collapsed the floors underneath. I believe that we can collapse the entire facility if we blow out the columns several floors from the top."

Dix looked around at his motley crew. "I think the first thing we need to do is mine the columns so we can blow the whole thing if necessary." They all nodded in agreement.

Jonas pointed up the trail. "They will be sending a force down this trail. The sooner you old farts and cripples can move the better, and the sooner we can get to the highway will be even better."

Fox gave him a disgusted look and asked, "How far do we have to go to reach the road?"

"Fox, we should be within five miles of the road. From there, the back door of Pine Tree Mountain is another eight or ten miles. I don't have to tell you what kind of terrain we'll be crossing."

"You've got to quit painting us such a rosy picture, Jonas. You know how much we like hiking, climbing and repelling. I just hope my being gut shot doesn't spoil everyone's fun."

After a good laugh, they proceeded down the trail. Expecting the Pine Tree Mountain troops to arrive at any moment, they spread out and just barely kept each other in sight. Porter, Fox and Jonas took turns taking point.

Chuck caught up to Dix.

"I don't mind taking point. There's no need for Porter, Fox and Jonas to take all the risk."

"I'm letting them take point because they are in the best physical shape and have extensive combat experience. I'm half crippled, and Morgan is doing good to travel. The others don't have combat experience, but they are good men to have behind you in a battle. I need you alive and well because you know your way around the inside of The Mountain. Remember what I told you. Everyone has strengths and everyone has weaknesses. Just do what I say, when I say it, and I'll try and keep us all alive. You should know that the odds are not in our favor."

"Just remember, Major; they're a bunch of fanatics."

"All the more reason to get rid of them."

They continued walking until Jonas raised his hand with a clinched fist. He jogged back to where Dix was waiting.

"We're at the highway. There are two personnel carriers and a fuel trailer is parked in the pull-off with the two drivers sitting in the lead vehicle. The carriers are armored, and if we start shooting, all we are going to do is mess up the paint."

Dix thought for a second.

"If we can get them out of the vehicle, we'll have a ride. Let's get positioned on either side of the vehicles. They'll have to pee sooner or later. Whichever one opens a door first will give us an opportunity to kill them both."

Taking an hour or so, Porter and Fox crossed the road and worked their way around to the opposite side. Once in position, they radioed back.

"Porter here. We are in position. If they open the door on the driver's side, I can have a clear shot all the way through the vehicle."

Jonas answered, "We can do the same from the passenger side."

They all sat in the cold wind and waited. Feeling safe behind their armor and bullet proof glass, the drivers were drinking from bottles and eating snacks. Dix checked his watch. They had been in position forty-five minutes. Just as they expected, the drivers had to leave the vehicle to relieve themselves. The driver opened his door wide to climb out. Porter mentally drew a line that would pass through the driver and through the front seat passenger. Just as the driver pivoted his body to step out, Porter's gun bounced. The bullet passed through the driver's chest from the front and exited through his spine. It continued on and struck the passenger in his left arm before entering his chest cavity. The second and third bullets from Porter's gun also passed through both bodies. Dix and the men quickly stormed the vehicle and pulled out the corpses.

Dix told the men, "We'll take both vehicles. We can hide the extra one up on the mountain in case we need it. Jonas, you guide the way."

They had driven about a mile when the truck radio came on. "This is Nichols. Any sign of Wilson?"

Dix answered, "No, Mam."

Nichols responded, "Take both vehicles back to headquarters. I don't think Wilson is coming back. They're going to need them to start transporting more people to the field."

Dix replied, "Yes, Mam, we're on our way."

Jonas led them up the highway for six miles or so before he turned on to a forestry road. The road was slick with ice and snow in places, but the heavy vehicles burst through and found traction beneath in the crushed limestone of the road bed. The road had been a driveway leading up to an abandoned hunting lodge. They pulled the vehicles around behind it and out of sight. Jonas pointed at the sun that was trying to set behind the mountain. "It's going to be dark soon, and if you notice those clouds, I expect some more snow or rain. I hope it's just snow. If it rains, we'll be climbing down the mountain on ice."

Fox climbed out and pointed at the lodge.

"Is there any place to sleep and keep warm around here?"

Jonas headed for the backdoor.

"There are some bunks, a fireplace and a rain barrel for water, but you'll have to bust through the ice on top. I also have some grub stashed inside."

Limping, Dix followed them. "How far will we have to go in the morning?"

"We have about a mile to go, but we can't navigate it this late in the day. The darkness would catch us, and I don't want to get caught on the side of the mountain in this weather. The snow will cover our tracks where we left the highway, and I don't expect them to start a campaign until tomorrow."

Dix pointed to the firewood in the wood shed.

"Everyone, but Morgan, grab an armload so we'll have plenty for the fire tonight. Don't worry; the wind will carry the smoke away from the mountain."

Jonas led the way into the ancient structure. It had been built originally as a post and beam barn. In later years, some wealthy men had it converted to a lodge. A large fireplace dominated the room. Jonas pointed to the kitchen behind a large bar lined with stools.

"The stove doesn't work. The propane gas ran out last year, and I never got around to bringing in another bottle. I use this place as sort of a depot when I drag stuff out of the mountain. I have an extensive med kit stashed here under the bar."

He pulled out the kit and a couple of propane lanterns.

"Morgan, come over here where I can look at your arm."

Jonas opened the kit and came out with a morphine injector. He cut the zip ties and helped Morgan remove his coat and shirt. Old Man Jack had a fire going in the fireplace, and the room started to warm a bit. The huge rocks that were used to build the fireplace would soon be radiating heat as well. Jonas wiped off a spot on

Morgan's good arm and injected him with the morphine.

Morgan sighed, "It's feeling better already."

"Even with the morphine, it's going to hurt like hell until I can get some Novocaine injected. Let me know if it becomes unbearable, and I'll hit with you some more morphine."

"Don't worry; I'm not like Porter."

With Porter and Fox assisting, Jonas cut the duct tape and removed the splint. Morgan grew quite pale as Jonas exposed the arm. In short order, he had him injected with the Novocaine and proceeded to clean the arm with an alcohol covered cloth. Jonas looked up at Morgan who obviously was in agony. He pulled out another dose of morphine and administered it. Then looked over at Fox.

"Don't let him fall off the stool; he may get a little loopy from the morphine."

"I've got him; he ain't going nowhere."

Jonas gently probed the wound and removed some bone fragments. He had Jack boil some water to which they added salt. When the water cooled, Jonas flushed out the wound. He then packed the wound with antibiotic ointment before wrapping it with gauze. He tore open a package containing casting material and wet it. After making certain that the arm was straight and oriented, he wrapped it properly with the casting material which quickly hardened in place.

Jonas told Morgan, "Wiggle your fingers."

Morgan wiggled his fingers.

"Good, if we can keep it from getting infected, it will heal. It would heal quicker if it had a metal plate and some screws or a rod in it, but we can't do that here."

He told Porter, "Look in the kitchen. There's some of those plastic cutting boards on the counter. Take one over to the fire, get it hot enough to bend and shape it. I want to make a hard sling for him to cradle his arm in."

Porter took one of the cutting boards and soon had it hot enough to mold. After getting it in the proper shape he further customized it with his Kbar. They soon had Morgan's shirt on over the cast and his arm in the sling. They placed a bunk near the fire and put him to bed.

Everyone tried to be quiet until Jonas stated, "With the load of morphine I have in him we won't be disturbing him. He could probably sleep through a gun battle."

Dix asked, "Do you think we need to take him down the mountain with us tomorrow?"

"We'll just have to see how he feels in the morning. I'll start him on antibiotics when he wakes up. I have an assortment sitting in a backpack that I was planning on taking home on my next trip back."

Jonas pointed to the pantry behind the kitchen.

"Men you should be able to find plenty to eat. There are a dozen cases of MRE's under the shelves."

That night they took turns standing guard. Just as Jonas had predicted, the snow came.

CHAPTER 31

Crofton asked Olsen, "Are you sure we have to attend The Pontiff's spirit cooking ceremony? I don't want to drink that crap they are going to be serving up. Have you heard what's in it?"

"I know what's in it, but we don't have a choice. He's going to attempt to contact the dead."

Crofton rolled his eyes and retorted, "The way our luck is running; he'll probably succeed."

Olsen wasn't smiling when she mumbled, "I hope to God we don't catch something from the blood, milk and semen."

Crofton said, "You go ahead. I'll catch up; I need to run back by my apartment."

Crofton watched as Olson disappeared down the tunnel in the direction of The Pontiff's ceremonial room. He turned and walked down the corridor in an unhurried manner. The last thing he wanted to do was attract attention. He went to his apartment and picked up his briefcase with his personal items that he didn't want to abandon. He casually walked to the elevator and proceeded up to level five where he had his

417

weapons and backpack stashed. *Spirit cooking will not be on my social schedule, and I won't be drinking something concocted by a bunch of lunatics.*

Olsen drove down to The Pontiff's office and ceremonial area. Her stomach was already queasy at the thought of attending another spirit cooking ceremony. Her first and last ceremony had been two years ago. The smell and taste had lasted for months. Finally, she was able to forget the entire experience. She parked out front and steeled her resolve to go through the ceremony. Most of her officers were already in attendance and some were absolutely ecstatic. The joy in their faces and eyes said it all. Olsen forced a smile and mingled with her officers while they awaited The Pontiff's arrival. Upon his entering the room with his entourage of Apostles and Pastors, everyone started clapping. The Pontiff stood at the head of the table and asked everyone to take a seat. The hookahs were lit, and the guards brought in trays containing the small cups full of what appeared to be the sacrificial wine. After the cups were placed in front of the guests, The Pontiff had the candles lit, and the chamber lights turned off. Olsen looked past him into the room where the sacrifices were held. He opened his good book and proceeded to recite passages from the book as his faithful murmured to them, "Gya is great."

The names of ancient deities were invoked along with his interpretation of the ancient text. The Pontiff raised his cup and looked out over his faithful.

"Let us drink our sacrament to our lord Gya."

They all raised the cups to their lips and drank the juice. The hookahs were lifted by the Apostles and placed on the table where the faithful awaited permission from The Pontiff to proceed. Olsen felt the drugs in the wine starting to snake their way into her mind. The hypnotic words of The Pontiff seemed to echo as he started to invoke the spirit of the dead to come forward. He took a draw from his hookah and motioned for his followers to join him. Olsen took a deep draw on the pipe stem, and the next thing she saw were the images of the troopers she had murdered surrounding her at the table. She fought the urge to flee as she forced herself to realize that she was under the influence of a strong hallucinogen. Evidently, The Pontiff was letting them share in the same concoction that he personally used in his sacrificial ceremonies. In her delusion, she could feel the hands of the dead caressing her shoulders and arms. She looked around at the others at the table and realized that each person was experiencing similar hallucinations. One woman was crying while another one was greeting someone who wasn't there. All the while the murdered troopers whispered things she couldn't understand in her ears. The carafes containing the blood and body fluids were served next. Olsen was powerless to resist. She drank the salty concoction and was drawn farther into the delusions.

As The Pontiff's chants echoed in her ears, she gradually became aware that she was extremely cold, and she was looking up at the ceiling of the cave. Her arms and legs were secured by chains, and she suddenly realized that she was naked on the sacrificial table. She couldn't understand what they were saying as the chanting grew louder. The Apostles were writhing, and they were pouring the bloody mixture on her body and licking it off her flesh. A rack was uncovered with the various blades that would be used for the dismemberment. Olsen felt her heart beating so wildly that she thought it would burst from her chest. One of the Apostles who was obviously aroused climbed on the table and reached for her penis. In his hands was a dark gray knife. The razor knife blade glistened in the candle light. She screamed.

Olsen jerked awake and realized that she was lying on the floor under the conference room table. Her officers were in various states of consciousness. One was wandering around the room, several more were out cold and others were talking to non-existent people. Two of the other officers were copulating. The Pontiff was still reading from his good book, and the troops she had murdered were still sitting next to her. Olsen had watched the cremation of Naomi Carter, but here she was sitting next to her. Carter couldn't be any more real as she reached out and took Olsen's hand.

Olsen asked, "Are you really here, or are you just part of my delusion?"

"Does it really matter? I'm here; doesn't this make you question if everything you've seen or felt your entire life is real or just a delusion?"

Olsen closed her eyes. *You've got to get a grip; none of this is real. I have to ignore anything that I know is not true.*

She struggled to her feet with the help of Naomi Carter, and the three troopers who had been with her. She left the room and headed out to her ATV with

Carter and the three troopers hanging onto her arms to steady her. She climbed into the ATV and waited for her companions to climb aboard when she realized that she was alone. She drove back to her apartment and entered. Her head was clear as she went to her bathroom to clean up from the ceremony. She took a swig of mouthwash directly from the bottle and gargled to get the taste out of her mouth.

Naomi Carter called from the other room, "That taste won't go away anytime soon."

Olsen hesitated to open the bathroom door. *I wonder how long I will be haunted by this delusion? Am I back in my apartment or still participating in the spirit cooking ceremony?*

Olsen stripped and stepped into the shower. She stood under the scalding hot water while it cascaded down her body. She was hoping that the water would cleanse her. She even opened her mouth and let the water hit her tongue and teeth. The taste was still there; only time would make it go away. She dried off, took yet another swig from the bottle of mouthwash and went to bed. The night light dimly lit the room, and the bed felt good. She closed her eyes, and felt Naomi climb into the bed beside her.

"How long are you going to haunt me?"

"I'm not haunting you. The Pontiff called me from the grave to help you." Olsen turned over on her side facing away from Carter. "Goodnight, Carter, I hope you are gone when I wake up."

She dozed off and slept undisturbed until morning. When she woke, she looked over where Naomi Carter had been lying the night before. Carter was gone. There was no indention in the pillow where her head had lain. *Thank goodness, she's gone!* Olsen rose, dressed and headed to her office. She was surprised to find that Crofton wasn't on duty. The Morning Prayer came and went, and still no Crofton. She called Crofton's apartment, and all she got was the answering machine. She left a message, but she knew Crofton was attempting to escape. She would give him another hour's head start before alerting security. She pulled up her lap top and sent a message to all her staff officers for a pre-deployment meeting in one hour. She walked out of the office past Crofton's desk; his coffee cup was on the corner next to his pencil box, as though he had just left on break.

The hour of the meeting came, and she called the head of security, "This is Olsen. My assistant Crofton has not come to work this morning. I need you to check and see if he's in his apartment; I'm concerned."

The voice on the other side simply answered, "We'll check on him and let you know what we find."

Olsen walked into the meeting room as her officers filed in. They all looked as though they had been through hell.

"Good morning, officers. Does anyone want to talk about what happened last night?"

Officer Bancroft raised his hand and asked, "How long are the dead going to follow me around?"

Olsen asked, "Are they with you now?"

"Yes."

Olsen looked around the room and inquired, "Does anyone else still have companions this morning?"

Four others raised their hands.

"I'm not sure how long the hallucinations will continue. I haven't seen any since I got up this morning. Did anyone not have hallucinations last night?"

No hands went up.

"Did anyone see anything that wasn't a dead person you know?"

Officer Carr raised her hand and declared, "I was surrounded by my dead pets."

Olsen walked up to the wall board and drew a rough map of the valley and The Mountain.

"We've got to proceed with the deployment. We've experienced something profound, but we'll have to soldier on. Try and ignore your companions; hopefully, they will go away soon."

Bancroft looked over his shoulder, put his finger to his lips and said in a low voice, "Shush, Sammy. I'll talk to you about that later."

He turned back to the table and said, "Sorry, but I had to shut him up." Everyone in the room understood.

Olsen pointed to her map.

"I want the snipers to head out late this afternoon and be in place where they can assist the task force."

After the plans were studied and the details ironed out, Olsen dismissed the group to commence with their deployment. She returned to her office to finish the deployment preparations. If everything went as planned, she would be in her Jeep and crossing the mountains in less than twenty-four hours.

The phone rang. Danforth's boyfriend was calling from The Pontiff's office.

"Major Olsen, The Pontiff needs to see you."

"I'm on my way."

Olsen drove down the corridor to The Pontiff's office. She half expected to see Naomi Carter, but she didn't make an appearance. Olsen popped a stick of gum in her mouth as she exited the ATV. She was attempting to eradicate the vile taste from her mouth. As soon as she walked into the office, she was ushered immediately in to The Pontiff. When she walked through the door, she was startled to see Crofton tied to a chair and beaten black and blue.

The Pontiff looked up with a devilish scowl.

"Olsen, I'm so glad to see you. We've got a lot to talk about."

CHAPTER 32

The next morning, the mountain was covered with about three inches of snow. The snow on the ground and in the trees made the landscape appear to be a winter wonderland. If the circumstances had been different, the day would have been joyous one. Morgan was stirring about the cabin. Dix had decided that Morgan would remain at the lodge where he could stay in communication with the approaching New Constitution Army. Dix and Jonas set up a radio and strung a wire for the antenna.

Dix asked, "Can you raise our men to see how close they are?"

Jonas fired up the radio and Colonel Miller answered, "Morning men, what's the situation?"

Dix answered, "I didn't realize that you would be leading up this operation. We're on the verge of invading The Mountain."

"Are you crazy?" Miller bellowed, "Why don't you wait? We'll be there in the morning."

"I wish we could. There's nothing I would like to do more than turn this entire operation over to you and head home. The problem is they are getting ready to mount a major operation. This is the only chance we're going to have to slip in and confine all them to level three where their operations center and living quarters are located. I'll have Morgan radio you when to head in. We'll call when we get the front door open. It's going to take a small group to slip in undetected and confine them. I want you guys to wait at Gord Holmes' place. He'll show you where to go when you get the call. There's also a twenty-plus man squad of troupers at Bill's Bar. Gord can show you where that is as well."

Miller called back, "Good luck; don't get killed."

"If we do, Morgan can direct you into The Mountain and give you a complete report."

Dix turned to the group.

"Here are my plans. We go into The Mountain this morning through the cave. We enter the facility after five pm, kill the security guards on level four and put Cartwright at the desk. Jonas, Jack and Larry will mine the columns on level six. Chuck will lead Porter and Fox to the sniper's nests and take them out. We'll then set up Claymore mines on the vehicle ramps going up and down from level three. We will disable the elevators and take out the ladders in the access tubes.

I'll go down to level one and kill the entrance guards. If we are able to manage all this without getting killed, we'll radio Morgan and open the front door so our men can enter. I wish we had suppressors. When we start shooting, the whole Mountain is going to wake up."

Porter reached into his pack and pulled out the suppressor for his pistol. Jonas pulled up a floor board and pulled out a Colt M4 with a suppressor. Dix smiled.

"That should get us started."

Fox spoke up, "How long do you think we can keep them confined to level three?"

"All we have to do is keep them bottled up long enough for our men to get in place."

Jonas pointed out. "There will only be about a hundred of us, and there will still be three or four thousand lunatics with an armory. If they are determined, we will be overwhelmed."

"According to the plans, the armory is in a cavern about one hundred feet square on level three. Chuck, do you think you can sneak back into the armory with a backpack full of C4?"

"Yeah, I think I can get back in."

"Jonas, can you rig up an IED and some way of triggering it so that the armory can be destroyed?"

Jonas reached into his back pack and pulled out the two IEDs with the motion sensitive triggers. "All we have to do is set these on top of the backpack with the C4. Chuck knows how to arm them. He has fifteen seconds to get out before it arms itself. It has a ten second delay to turn it off before it detonates. A backpack full of C4 should pretty much destroy the entire room and its contents."

Chuck spoke up, "I'm going to need a uniform in case I run into anyone in the halls. The room is open, and the weapons are in a caged area. A counter runs down the front of the room so weapons and equipment can be issued out as needed. Since they are getting ready to deploy, they will be issuing the rifles and side arms."

Jonas nodded and interrupted, "I've got you covered. I have the uniform that I use when I sneak in. It's stashed in the cave."

Dix said, "We'll set up the IED in the armory after we have secured the rest of the facility. Does everyone know what to do?"

Fox raised his hand and spoke, "If we are dealing with lunatics, they may not surrender, and we aren't carrying enough ammo."

"We'll have to cross that bridge when we get to it. If we shut off the power and water, I imagine they'll run out of food pretty quick on level three. Once they are hungry, I expect they'll have a change of attitude."

Fox took a deep breath and muttered, "If we can just get past that getting killed part, I think we have them licked."

Jonas told everyone, "The shift change for the guards takes place at seven, three and eleven. So if we go in at 5:00 pm, that will give us six hours. Cartwright, you'll have to wing it if anyone calls in or if anyone shows up unexpected at the security office."

Dix looked around at the group and ordered, "This is it men. Let's head out."

The trip down the snow covered mountain trail was hazardous. Jonas led the way over the trail that zig-sagged down into the gorge. They followed a stream that rushed over and around the rocks. They crossed the stream at the bottom by stepping from stone to stone. Soon they were heading up the bank on other side to the entrance of the cave that would take them

431

into the facility. When they reached the tree marking the entrance, they went around it, and Jonas took the lead. Each of them had a light clipped to the visor of their caps. Dix stuffed his stocking cap into his pocket and winced as he put his ball cap over his still sore head.

Jonas warned, "Don't get ahead of me. I have some IED's that I'll have to disarm as we go through here."

The trail into The Mountain was not an easy one to follow. This was a natural cave so there was no path with hand rails and steps, and the floor, was littered with boulders. A yellow nylon rope was the only thing that kept them from getting lost. In steep areas, Jonas's uncle had installed old aluminum ladders that had to be carefully negotiated. They spent the better part of the morning just getting to the cavern with the door leading into the facility. Once in the cavern, they found a comfortable area that Jonas had outfitted with camping furniture. Fox took a seat in a camping recliner while Jonas fired up propane lanterns.

Jonas pointed to folding chairs and a resin box containing food and juice boxes.

"Help yourself, boys. We have a few hours to wait. I don't think they can hear us in here, but let's keep quiet just in case. I have a privy set up in that far corner if anyone needs to go."

Porter, who had not said much, sat and checked his weapons. He installed the suppressor on his pistol and thought back to the time he stalked and killed the Chinese at the Crosby ranch. The Beretta pistol would get another workout today. Porter saw that Chuck was watching him.

"Chuck, when you take us to the snipers' nests stay behind me. Fox will back me up. Don't get involved unless Fox and I go down. You are the only one here who knows their locations and the best way to approach them. If you get killed or incapacitated, the entire operation will be in jeopardy."

"Don't worry. Major Jernigan explained it all to me."

Dix stood up and told the group, "We have a plan, but, as you know, no operation will go exactly as we anticipate or want. There is always the possibility that we'll be discovered, and then it could very well be every man for himself. If we see that we have failed, it will be the job of Jonas, Jack or Larry to light the fuse that blows the columns on level six. Each team has a radio. I don't want any chatter unless you fail to accomplish your job. At that point, I will redirect you. The chain of command is as follows: Myself, Jonas, Fox and Porter. If we four go down, every man will be for himself. I've chosen that order because I know exactly how these guys can and will perform. If I thought any of you were not up to the task assigned, you would be sitting up in the lodge with Morgan. Any problems or questions?"

He looked around at his command. No one disagreed.

"Once you have completed your assignment, meet on level four at the security office where Jonas and Chuck will prepare the IED for the armory. After it's deployed, and Chuck is back on level four, we'll notify Morgan to call Colonel Miller on in. We'll have to hold them on level three until the Colonel gets here in the morning. At that point, we'll turn it over to Colonel Miller. Let's coordinate our watches to make sure we're on the same time."

They sat quietly for the next couple of hours. Time seemed to stand still as they sat contemplating entering the facility. While they waited, Chuck put on the uniform.

At five o'clock, Jonas opened the door to the room. They could hear the sound of the natural gas generators down the corridor. As he paused at the door leading from the chamber with the electrical panels into the corridor leading to the security office, Jonas motioned for Porter to follow him. Porter's gun was cocked and ready. They passed the break room with the coffee pot and approached the room where the guards were located. Jonas made a motion with his arm and hand indicating that this was the room. Porter nodded and simply walked in the door. One of the guards looked up in surprise at the lanky young man with a big grin on his face. Before he could say anything, Porter placed a bullet in the middle of his forehead. The other guard didn't have time to react. A bullet through her head put her on the floor alongside of her companion. Jonas went back into the electrical panel room.

"Cartwright, you're up; Jack and Larry follow me."

He swapped his suppressed rifle for the one Dix carried.

"I don't need to be quiet where we're heading."

Porter came back for Fox and Chuck.

"Ok, Chuck, lead on."

Dix joined Cartwright in the security office where he helped move the bodies to one side. They sat and looked at the monitors. Level three was bustling with people getting off work and heading out to the lounges and cafeteria. Couples were strolling arm in arm as they walked down the corridors and stopped in front of the shops.

Chuck led Porter and Fox down the roadway to the ATV's charging stations. He chose the nearest one, and they headed a mile down the underground roadway. They stopped at a door in the rock wall; it was unlocked. They went down a passage in the rocks where the road ended at an opening.

Chuck whispered to Porter and Fox, "The sniper and spotter are just outside and to the right of the opening."

Porter had his AK-47 suspended behind his back. Taking the point, he casually walked out to the sniper's and spotter's location. The sound of the wind blowing through the trees and rocks masked him as he walked in their direction. Their nest looked quite comfortable with a covered roof and a radiant gas heater shining down on them from behind. They were sitting at a table where large binoculars were mounted. The snipers were intently peering through the binoculars and were oblivious to his entry. He quickly dispatched them and left them where they lay.

Jonas, Jack and Larry loaded the C4 from the bunker. Jonas filled a separate backpack full of the explosive, and on his way out stopped and gave it to Dix and Cartwright.

"Chuck will need this when he heads to the armory."

Dix nodded.

"Great, I'll slip down and open the door on level one. Cartwright, keep an eye on the monitor. If you see me get killed, call Jonas, but stay here and monitor our progress. If someone calls in for a report, you're going to have to just play it by ear. You're a former car salesman so I'm sure you can think of something to say. If nothing else, just shoot the bull."

Cartwright agreed, "I'll think of something."

Dix followed Jonas to the access shaft next to the elevators. They opened the door, and Jonas pointed down into the darkness.

"You can go down two floors, get out and use the elevator from there. If you try using the elevator from up here, it may stop on the third level, and we would be discovered too soon. Good luck, Major."

"I'm going to get in position. I will kill the guards and open the door at 8:00 pm. That should give y'all plenty of time to set the charges and kill the snipers."

Jonas clapped him on the shoulder.

"Good hunting, Major."

Dix flipped on the light attached to the bill of his cap and looked down into the abyss. He was glad it was dark. Four stories was a long way down. He tried not to think of what would happen if he missed a step and fell. Since he didn't have a safety harness to arrest his fall, he carefully took his time and counted his steps down. He went down thirty steps before he arrived at the door to the third floor. Just as he was even with the door, someone opened it from the other side. The maintenance technician was startled for the half second it took Dix to grab him by his beard and jerk him into the shaft. The technician grabbed at Dix's legs as he fell and almost jerked him off the ladder. Dix hooked his arm over the ladder rung and kicked at the man with his free foot. Finally, a kick to his face silenced him and sent him falling to his death in the bowels of the shaft. Dix reached out and gently closed the door and started his descent again. His heart was still thumping wildly when he reached the door to level two. He opened the door and was relieved to find that the corridor was completely dark. He stepped into the darkness and paused while he regained his composure. He walked over to the elevator, pushed the button and, as the doors opened, the bright lights streamed out almost hurting his eyes. He hit the button for level one and checked his watch. It read 6:50 pm. Unless he located a vehicle or a bicycle near the elevator, he had about a two mile walk. The door opened to a dark corridor. He got out, quickly darted to the side and out of the light. A moment later, the doors closed and all was silent. Unfortunately, he didn't see a vehicle so he started walking in the direction of the entrance. He knew from studying the blueprints the direction to walk. He had walked for about forty-five minutes before he thought he could hear some men talking. He flipped off his light and kept his hand on the wall to guide himself. He counted one hundred steps and paused to listen. He heard the faint sound of men talking so he continued walking in their direction. As he grew closer, he flipped the safety off the rifle. From somewhere in the darkness behind him, he heard a vehicle approaching. The headlights were punching narrow beams of light through the darkness. The reflecting light allowed Dix to see one of the solid rock columns that supported the roof and floors above so he ducked behind it before the vehicle arrived. When a full size SUV came by, he could see a driver and a passenger. It passed him and stopped at the huge overhead door leading out of the facility. The driver got out and was speaking with the guard when Dix approached from behind. He didn't shoot immediately because he wanted to make sure that he could trap all the guards on duty as well as the driver and passenger. He walked around the driver's side in the darkness, and positioned himself where he could see everyone. An office door was located next to the overhead door. The guard opened it and shouted to someone outside. Another man came in wearing a parka and packing one of the MP5 sub machine guns. The guard inside was not as heavily dressed and only sported a sidearm. Dix opened fire shooting the passenger of the SUV and then stepped forward to shoot the driver and both guards. The guard with the MP5 opened up with the gun on full auto as he fell. The only thing that saved Dix was the fact that he was standing behind the engine and wheels. A ricochet bounced off the rock wall behind him and struck him in the back. He felt as if someone had hit him with a baseball bat. He collapsed forcibly on the ground, but struggled back to his feet. He shot them all again and hoped that no one heard the shooting. Somewhere up on top of The Mountain Porter, Chuck and Fox were killing snipers. Hopefully, none of the snipers would be alerted.

Dix could feel blood on his back because his shirt was trying to stick to him as he walked to the door and waved at the men in the guard shack on the road about a hundred yards away.

One called out, "What happened?"

Dix hollered back, "Got my glove caught on the trigger; we're ok. Just scared the shit of everyone."

The guard called back, "For Gya's sake be careful."

He responded, "Can you look at my weapon? I think something may be wrong with it."

"Sure, bring it on out."

Dix exchanged the magazine in his rifle for a fresh one and walked toward the shack. As he reached the door, the guard opened it to let him in. Dix riddled the two guards and the shack with the rifle on full auto. His back was on fire and hurt with every breath. He shook his head *I can't wait to get back home; I'm too old for this.*

After rummaging around in the first floor office, Dix found the elevator fireman's key that is used by the fire department in case of emergency. He walked back to the idling SUV. The passenger side tire was flat, and the engine was knocking a bit. He hit the button to open the overhead door and watched while it rattled and shook as it coiled into a large roll at the top. He opened the passenger door allowing the dead man to roll out on the ground. He slammed the door, walked around to the driver's side and slid in. When he twisted to get in, the pain in his back was almost unbearable, but since he still had feeling in all his extremities and there wasn't enough blood coming out to kill him, he soldiered on. He had more important things to do at this point. Once Colonel Miller and the troops arrived, he would have time to have his back patched up. He turned the SUV around and headed back to the elevators.

Jonas, Jack and Larry made short work of mining the columns. If the mines were set off, the entire center of The Mountain would collapse onto the floors below. Jonas set eight Claymore mines on the ramp leading up to level four. He had Jack control the switches so the mines could be detonated in the correct order. They were spaced in intervals so that the first mine would not damage or set off the one behind it. The Claymore mine is an antipersonnel mine; it will blast a wall of BB's out in front of it. In the confines of the ramp, no one would have a prayer if they were within its blast zone. After they finished, he and Larry carried eight mines down the ladder to set up on the level two ramp leading up to level three. As they emerged from the door to the shaft, the elevator doors opened, and Dix stepped out.

Dix looked at them. "The front door is open."

Jonas pointed to the sack of Claymore mines. "We'll have this ramp closed to traffic in a few minutes."

Dix waited and watched as they set the mines. In a short time, they had placed the devices and had run the wires so Larry could detonate them. As soon as Larry was established, Jonas walked back to Dix.

"Let's knock out the elevators and the ladders."

Dix held up the elevator key. "The elevators are dead, and all but this one is sitting on the first floor. This one is locked here on the second floor."

"That just leaves destroying the ladders and getting Chuck to plant the IED on the third floor. Let's climb back up and see about taking down the two ladders."

Dix pointed over his shoulder with his thumb.

"I can't make it up the ladder. I'm packing a bullet in my back. We'll take the elevator. This fireman's key gives me complete control; it won't stop on the third floor unless I want it to."

"How bad are you hit? Do you want me to take a look?"

Dix shook his head. "No, if it was real bad I wouldn't be moving, and I'd be bleeding more."

Jonas knew better than to argue with him so he turned back to the elevator.

"There's two ways that we can get rid of the ladders: blow them or unbolt them."

Dix said, "I say blow them; it'll be quicker and safer. A charge set where it is attached to the rock face should take out the third floor sections. Do you have what you need?"

"Yes, Sir, I have about a hundred yards of dent cord. I can wrap the ladder supports, rails and rungs, and the ladder will disappear. If you can feed the cord to me from the top, I can do both ladders in about thirty minutes."

Dix pointed to the elevator. "Let's do it."

They took the elevator up to the fourth level where they met Porter, Chuck and Fox. Fox had his arm wrapped, but blood was seeping through.

"What happened?"

Porter piped up, "It's my fault. I normally double tap everyone I shoot; however, I was trying to save my ammo. One of them wasn't killed good enough, and he stabbed Fox."

Dix told Jonas, "Let's get Chuck and his IED down to the armory. While he's placing the charges, you and Porter install the dent cord on the ladders. Fox and I are going to monitor the security office, and let Cartwright feed you guys the dent cord."

Fox noticed that Dix was hit.

"Don't tell me that you're hurt worse than me again; you are always having to one up me."

Fox and Dix relieved Cartwright and monitored the cameras. Level three was quiet. Some prisoners were in the cells, and no one had discovered that the front door was open. Everything appeared as though it was business as usual. Dix checked his watch; the time was 9:30 pm. Shift change would happen at 11:00, so Chuck had to have his IED in place, and the dent cord on the elevators would have to be installed. The timing would be close, but they could do it. He just hoped that Chuck could accomplish his task without getting caught or blowing himself up.

Chuck clung to the rungs of the ladder with the backpack strapped to his back. Jonas followed him down with the dent cord and proceeded to attach it to the ladder. When they reached the level three door, Chuck stepped over to it and eased it open a crack. The hall was clear so he stepped out closing the door behind him. He took off the pack and slung it over just one shoulder to make it look more casual. He wanted to appear as though he was just heading out for a short walk. The armory was about a half a mile down the tunnel. When he passed the jail, he scratched his face and adjusted his hat in order to conceal himself from the guards who could recognize him. His pistol was tucked inside his waist band under his shirt. The armory had people working inside. He had hoped it would be empty, but they were getting ready for deployment. He walked in with the backpack. The motion detector IED was zip tied to the front, but at a glance it looked like the G.I. canteen in which it was constructed. He set it on the counter, clicked the button and heard the beep indicating that it was activated. The guy behind the counter looked up at him.

Chuck slapped his forehead. "Darn, I forgot something. I'll be right back."

The guy behind the counter returned to his chore. Chuck walked at a fast pace back to the elevator shaft door. As soon as the guy behind the counter made a move, the device would detonate. He had no more than ten seconds to put as much distance between himself and the armory as he could. He opened the door, quickly stepped in and closed it just as the device went off. The shock wave raced down the tunnel and shook the door that his hand still gripped.

A beam of light from above shot down onto him as Jonas called out, "Get up here! Our secret is out, and we've got to blow the ladders. Porter and Cartwright are down on level two with Larry."

Chuck climbed up the ladder and stepped out into the corridor. He was shaking from the adrenaline rush.

Jonas shouted, "Get away from the door! I'm going to blow the ladders, so hold your ears."

The two ends of the dent cord were hanging out of the doors leading to the ladder shafts. Jonas took out his pistol and shot the first one. A tremendously loud explosion disintegrated the ladder. He repeated it for the next ladder. The Pine Tree Mountain forces were now trapped on the third level.

Dix called to Chuck, "Lead me to open air where I can radio Morgan."

Chuck took him out to the first sniper's nest. Dix keyed the mic on the handheld radio. "Morgan, are you awake?"

"Yes, Sir, are you ready for me to send in the Calvary?"

"Call Colonel Miller and tell him that the front door is open, and the Pine Tree Mountain forces are trapped on the third level."

"Will do."

Morgan called back a few minutes later. "He is on his way. They anticipate arriving after daylight."

"We're going to be pretty busy for a while. Wish us luck."

Just as Dix and Chuck re-entered the building, they heard the first Claymore mine detonate.

CHAPTER 33

The explosion knocked Olsen off the bunk in her jail cell. Crofton was slammed up against the bars. Howling in pain, he looked at Olsen who was now up and looking at the collapsed wall of her cell. The guards quickly trained their guns on the two of them. While the room was filling with smoke, she could hear cursing, moaning and sobbing from the hallway outside. A number of the imbecilic believers were chanting, "Gya is great" over and over again. At least the ventilation system was still working so the smoke never reached high enough levels to kill anyone. The guards handcuffed Olsen and Crofton to the cell doors while emergency crews looked for survivors. Those people that were within thirty feet of the blast had been torn to shreds. Everyone within three hundred feet of the shockwave would experience permanent hearing loss, and many would have internal injuries as well.

Captain Noah Rivers, who was promoted to the rank of General to replace Major Olsen, ordered all the senior officers to report immediately. His chief of staff, Captain Mabel Hinson, hastily convened the meeting.

Rivers ordered fire control teams to respond as well as emergency medical personnel. The hospital and medical staff were quickly overwhelmed. He tried sending teams up and down the vehicle ramps, but all were pushed back by gun fire and Claymores. His frantic calls to The Pontiff went unanswered.

He finally told Captain Hinson, "Get in an ATV, go down to The Pontiff's headquarters and find out what's going on. I want an immediate report." Hinson disappeared through the office door.

Rivers grabbed his phone and called the security office on the fourth floor.

It rang several times before Dix answered, "Hello. Who am I speaking to?"

"This is General Rivers. Who the hell are you to ask me who I am? I give the orders around here."

Dix stewed a moment. "No, you aren't calling the shots around here anymore. I am calling the shots. If you want to be alive this time tomorrow, you will do exactly what I say."

"You can't tell me what to do!"

"Shut up and listen, General. We will kill anyone who tries to leave level three. The only thing keeping all of you alive right now is my kind and gentle nature. So

450

are you going to stand down, or do I set off some more devices?"

Rivers was silent as he pondered his predicament. "To whom am I speaking?"

"This is Major Dix Jernigan of the New Constitution Army. I need you to confer with your man/god, Elliot Planter, and call me back to discuss your surrender."

"Surrender! Why I'd rather die."

"I have no problem granting that wish, but first get with Planter and get back to me. I'm giving you until your second Morning Prayer to give me an answer."

Rivers hung up the phone and looked at his officers who were gathering around.

"I am waiting word from The Pontiff on how he would like to proceed."

Captain Hinson called from The Pontiff's office.

"The Pontiff can't be disturbed. He's been in meditation since the explosion. His assistant told me that The Pontiff is communicating with our lord Gya, and we would soon have a solution."

Rivers turned to his officers, "I have good news. The Pontiff is in contact with our lord Gya, and we will soon have guidance."

Most of the officers grinned with a sigh of relief. Several others were coming to the conclusion that The Pontiff might be a lunatic. General Rivers said an extra long prayer and waited.

The Pontiff sat on his throne in the sacrificial room, looked down upon the sacrificial table and saw that it was good. He drew deep on the smoke from his hookah, and he summoned his personal physician.

"I have conferred with Gya, and we are going to have to take this battle against our enemy to the spiritual level. We will take the sacrament at the First Prayer in the morning. I want you to mix up the solution we have so long considered."

"I already have the sacrament prepared and in the mixing vat. All I have to do is add one ingredient, and it is done."

"Gya has done me a great service in sending me such a wonderful physician. You will have a special place in the throne room beside us one day."

The Pontiff sipped the elixir provided, puffed on his hookah and was immediately in the company of the dead. He chatted and laughed with the specters from his mind as the physician left the room. The physician was a true believer. He had gone to college with The

Pontiff, and when they first started experimenting with Native American concoctions, they had explored many aspects of the spiritual world together. He went to the vat with a small bottle of clear liquid, activated the mixer and poured in the liquid.

Olsen and Crofton spent the night chained to their cell doors. Olsen listened when the guards received a call.

The guard answered, "Yes, Sir, we'll have them there in a few minutes.

The guard called for assistance and awaited their arrival. He had done this many times before.

When the head of the guards arrived, he pointed to Olsen.

"Seize her."

The guards bound her feet and hands with zip ties and tossed her in the bed of the ATV. Shortly, they had her chained naked to the large sacrificial slab.

The Pontiff turned to the guards.

"Go get Crofton as well. This will be a double sacrifice, and Gya will be so pleased. Our enemies don't have a prayer. I can't wait to see their naked bodies here on Gya's banquet table."

The guards quickly retrieved Crofton and had him lying naked alongside Olsen on the table as well.

Crofton cried out, "Please don't. I was only following orders."

The Pontiff didn't respond, but nodded to his guards.

"Bring in my Apostles and Pastors."

They all filed in and surrounded the huge slab of granite with Olsen and Crofton helplessly chained to it. The Morning Prayer commenced. All the Apostles and Pastors rolled out their rugs and were soon prostrate and praying. The sacrament was dispersed to the entire command. The prayer was said, and at the end the sacrament was drunk. The Pontiff didn't take the sacrament that was given to his people. With the exception of a handful of non-believers, the remaining prisoners, The Pontiff, Crofton and Olsen, everyone on level three died on their prayer rugs. The Pontiff grinned as he looked around the room. Then he turned his attention to the table where Olsen and Crofton lay in fear.

He took a draw from his hookah and drank from his carafe with his special elixir.

"Can you see the thousands of souls surrounding us and preparing to do battle with our enemies? All that is needed is the sacrifice."

Olsen looked over at Crofton.

"I can't believe it's come to this. He's a raving lunatic; look at him."

Crofton screamed when The Pontiff's knife laid open his abdomen.

The phone in the security office rang and Dix answered, "Are you ready to surrender?"

The voice was not General Rivers so Dix asked, "Who is this?"

"I'm private Jonathan Brooks. Everyone is dead! The sacramental wine had something in it. Everyone is dead!"

"Dead? What do you mean?"

"I mean that everyone who took the sacrament this morning is dead. The Pontiff is conducting a sacrifice, and everyone is dead!"

Dix started flipping through the various video feeds. Unmoving bodies were everywhere.

"I'm coming down. If this is a trick, I won't hesitate to blow up the entire facility."

"It's no trick."

"Let's go, men. I think they've all committed suicide.

"Chuck, lead me to The Pontiff's sacrificial room."

He grabbed his hand held radio and called to Larry and Jack.

"Stay put at the Claymores while we see what's going on. I think these lunatics have all committed suicide."

Dix, Chuck and Jonas went into level three with their guns at the ready. A few dazed people were wandering around in bewilderment.

"Chuck, take me to The Pontiff. I want to get my hands on him."

Chuck pointed to the door leading into his chambers. Jonas kicked the door open, and they went through the inner office and on into the room where The Pontiff was carving up Crofton who was no longer able to scream.

The Pontiff looked up, waved to the non-existent people in the room and yelled, "Take them. We will sacrifice them next."

Chuck looked over at Dix. "Major, can I have the pleasure?"

"Certainly, son."

Chuck flipped the safety off his M4 and emptied the thirty round magazine into The Pontiff who instantly collapsed. Advancing across the room, Chuck reached the good book's pedestal, where he ripped out a handful of the book's pages. Leaning over The Pontiff's riddled body, he forced open his mouth and stuffed the pages down his throat. They then turned their attention to Olsen who was still tied to the table, but very much alive. Olsen looked up and recognized Chuck.

"Chucky, thank God you're here. I thought it was over for me."

Chuck looked over at Dix.

"Major, I want you to meet Major Charles; I mean Candice Olsen. He or she is or was the commanding officer here. He also rapes the tea boys after he drugs them first."

Dix walked around the table and looked down at Olson lying in Crofton's blood.

Olsen looked up at him.

"Well, aren't you going to let me up?"

"No, I'm going to let you lie right here, and unless Colonel Miller overrides my orders, you're going to lay here forever. Archeologists are going to find your bones lying on this table exactly where you are right now."

They heard a shot, and then they heard another from down the hall. They walked out see Porter re-slinging his rifle.

"I told him to drop his gun. I guess he just wanted to die."

Dix shrugged.

"How many are left alive?"

Fox spoke up, "There are four prisoners and eight troopers. I locked them in an office down the corridor."

Dix looked at Chuck.

"Chuck, go check on the prisoners. See if they are your friends and if they are safe to let out. Leave the troopers locked up until we figure out what to do with them.

Dix called Larry and Jack on the radio. "Deactivate the Claymores and secure them."

"Jonas, remove the explosives up on level six. I don't want to accidently blow the place up."

Fox asked, "What are we going to do with all these bodies? We have a mess on our hands. Let's go up and call Morgan so he can tell the Colonel what's taken place."

They climbed out into the fresh air and climbed in the sniper's nest.

Dix raised Morgan on the radio. "Call the Colonel and tell him not to hurry. We have taken The Mountain. All we have left are the twenty some odd troops occupying Bill's Bar. I will try to talk them into surrendering. Jernigan out."

Dix should have felt joy at being able to defeat the forces in the facility. However, he was simply repulsed by the thought of a society like this. He had difficulty in comprehending the depths of perversion and insanity that had taken root here.

He got on the facility's radio and called Captain Nichols at Bill's Bar.

"Captain Nichols, this is Major Dix Jernigan with the New Constitution Army. Can you hear me?"

She answered, "Yes, what are you doing on our radio?"

"I'm calling from inside The Mountain. The Pontiff is dead along with virtually everyone else here. They were all poisoned or committed suicide when they took the sacrament this morning."

Nichols paused a moment and replied, "That's impossible; all those people wouldn't commit suicide. I don't believe you."

"Nichols, I don't really care if you believe me or not. I don't want any of my men getting hurt tracking y'all down and killing you. What can I say to you that will convince you? I can't put The Pontiff on the radio; he's full of holes. Olsen is chained to a big granite table in a pool of somebody else's blood."

She asked, "What do you see at the front of the granite slab?"

"I see what appears to be a man with a goat's head with golden horns overlooking a big throne-like chair. A hookah is next to it with some god awful concoction burning in its bowl."

Nichols answered, "We surrender. My troops and I don't believe in that crap. We went along with it to stay alive. What do you want us to do?"

"I suggest you pile up all your weapons inside the bar over by the pool table. Then come on back here. Stop about three hundred yards from the guard shack at the entrance and walk in single file with your hands on your heads. Any deviation from that will get you all killed on the spot. Plan on arriving at 2:00 pm. Any questions?"

"I understand; we'll be there at 2:00 pm unarmed."

Dix looked around at Jonas who had just returned from deactivating the explosives on level six.

"I need you to locate some Novocaine. I'm packing a bullet in my back, and Fox has a stab wound."

Dix called to Porter, "Here's the fireman's key for the elevators. Go turn them all back on. You'll find the other elevators on the first floor where I turned them off. Take Chuck and greet Colonel Miller when they arrive at the front gate. Fox and I will be in the clinic while Jonas patches us up."

Porter nodded.

"Will do. Let's go, Chuck."

Jonas went to work on Fox first. He promptly had Fox's wound cleaned and stitched up. Because Dix's back was getting stiff, he needed help pulling off his jacket and shirt. The bullet was exposed where it had lodged in the muscle that ran along side of the spine on his left side. Jonas injected the area with the Novocaine and, a few minutes later, plucked the bullet out with forceps. He dropped it with a ping into a metal tray, and pulled the wound closed with dissolvable stitches.

"You have one hell of bruise; you've come very close to being paralyzed. If it had penetrated another quarter of an inch, you would have been in trouble."

461

Fox said, "He's just showing off. I've never seen anybody go to such pains to almost get killed every few days. For God sakes, don't ever make the mistake of showing him a scar. For every one you have, he'll show you four."

They all burst out laughing and looked up as Colonel Miller was escorted in by Porter.

Dix held out his hand to shake Miller's, but Miller stood back and gave him a salute instead.

"Good job, Major. I know you don't go in for all this military protocol, but you all deserve a salute."

"Thanks, Colonel, but all I did was almost get me and everyone else here killed. These lunatics ended up doing all the work for us. They appear to have committed suicide or were tricked into committing suicide. At 2:00 pm their only remaining officer, Captain Nichols, will be arriving at the front gate to surrender with her twenty or so troops. I recommend that you put Jonas in charge of the facility. It's full of stuff everyone can use and has a fully functional hospital. After I introduce you to Major Olsen, I'm going to bed somewhere. It's been a long two days."

As they walked down the hall to The Pontiff's chambers, Dix pointed to Chuck.

"I'm promoting Private Chuck Ward to Sergeant. Sergeant Ward, I want you to tell Colonel Miller all about Major Olsen. Don't spare any details."

He turned and looked at Jonas.

"Go get Morgan and take some help to retrieve those personnel carriers. I'm going to find a couch in a room with no dead people and take a nap, but, first, I want the Colonel to meet Major Olsen."

CHAPTER 34

Dix drained his mug of beer at the bar and looked around at Kitty and her girls. Kitty and Jonas had had a beautiful wedding. They made a great couple. Chuck and Nadine were holding hands at a table, and he imagined that they would be next.

Fox came to the door sporting a new pair of sunglasses. For the wedding, he had slicked back his hair with gel.

"Morgan and Porter have the Duk fired up and ready to go. That diesel Jeep you found in The Mountain has been checked out and is ready to roll. All we have to do is pick it and the personnel carrier with the fuel trailer up at The Mountain and roll. Colonel Miller is going to send you four box trailers with everything on our list next week. All our gear we had stashed, including Jake's rifle, was right where we left it. Everything is stowed in your new Jeep."

Dix nodded.

"Thanks, Fox, I couldn't leave without Jake's rifle and my old Springfield."

With help, Dix and Morgan made it up into the Duk for the trip back to The Mountain. Once in the Duk, Dix turned, walked to the door and looked back.

Jonas came up the ladder and shook his hand one last time. "I'm glad you didn't get killed."

"Me, too, my friend."

Jonas hopped down, and Dix shut the door. Fox gave the Duk some gas and it rolled back up the valley toward the mountain.

Morgan looked over at Dix who was stretched out on the bunk. "As soon as I get my arm healed, I'll make that monument for your family in Gulfport. I'm pretty sure we can patch up your old catamaran for one more trip down there and back."

Dix lay back in the bunk and dozed off. Fox looked over at Morgan and Porter and whispered, "When I talked to my wife this morning she told me that Dix has been elected governor as a write in candidate. Do you think we should tell him?"

They all shook their heads no.

Morgan whispered back, "Hell, no. We'll never hear the end of it the entire trip."

Read on for an exciting sneak peek of:

TRAILS SOUTH

He stood at the railing of the ferry boat adjusting the straps of the life vest to his body. The wind across the open water was biting cold as the temperature hovered in the forty's. From where he stood, he could see Salt Spring Island behind him and the town of Crofton on Vancouver Island before him. He watched as the shoreline slowly drifted by. The tide was carrying the floundering ferry northward. His rental car parked in the line of cars waiting for the ferry to dock and unload was useless now.

The crew had scrambled to get all the passengers in life vests when the engines on the ferry went dead. He overheard one of them say that the radios were out, and no one had a cell signal. His phone didn't have a signal either because it was dead, and so were the phones of everyone around him.

Just north of the ferry boat landing in Crofton sat a paper mill. A huge flotilla of cedar logs was anchored at the edge of the bay waiting to be taken into the plant for their conversion into paper. On its current path the ferry would float into the massive raft of logs. The question was: *would the flotilla arrest the ferry's momentum or would the ferry rip the flotilla from its anchorage?*

If the ferry sank, the life expectancy of anyone caught in the cold black waters of the passageway would be measured in minutes. The temperature of the water around Vancouver Island hovered near fifty degrees which would give someone caught in it only thirty minutes before they succumbed to hypothermia.

Staring into the deep, cold water he wondered *would the Aurora from last night make an appearance tonight. Will I be alive to see it?*

Proof

Made in the USA
Columbia, SC
02 November 2017